A KILLING ON
CHURCH GROUNDS

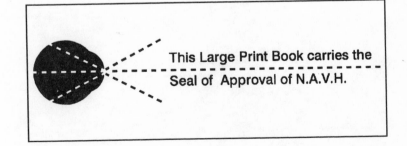

This Large Print Book carries the
Seal of Approval of N.A.V.H.

A KILLING ON CHURCH GROUNDS

BARBARA CUMMINGS

WHEELER PUBLISHING
An imprint of Thomson Gale, a part of The Thomson Corporation

Detroit • New York • San Francisco • New Haven, Conn. • Waterville, Maine • London

THOMSON

GALE

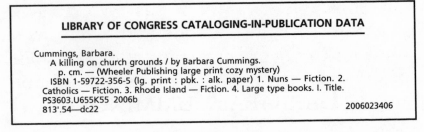

LIBRARY OF CONGRESS CATALOGING-IN-PUBLICATION DATA

Cummings, Barbara.
    A killing on church grounds / by Barbara Cummings.
        p. cm. — (Wheeler Publishing large print cozy mystery)
    ISBN 1-59722-356-5 (lg. print : pbk. : alk. paper) 1. Nuns — Fiction. 2.
Catholics — Fiction. 3. Rhode Island — Fiction. 4. Large type books. I. Title.
PS3603.U655K55 2006b
813'.54—dc22   2006023406

U.S. Hardcover
ISBN 13: 978-1-59722-356-0
ISBN 10: 1-59722-356-5

Published in 2006 by arrangement with Tekno Books and Ed Gorman.

Printed in the United States of America on permanent paper
10 9 8 7 6 5 4 3 2 1

To the real Sister Agnes, my wonderful great-aunt Mayetta, at one time a devout and devoted member of the Sisters of Mercy in Providence, Rhode Island. You took me into your mysterious and delightful world when I was very young and started the wheels turning. I foolishly thought I would have plenty of time to tell you how much you enriched my life. I was wrong. The cruelty of Alzheimer's took away your keen mind and magnificent spirit, but left your bright smile to vex and haunt us. I hope you're pleased with my efforts to bring you back to us.

To all the Sister Winifreds, women who might have joined the convent for the wrong reasons, but stayed for the right ones.

To my children and grandchildren, who make me proud just being who they are.

Most of all, forever and always — to my husband Bill. There's nowhere else I'd rather be than with you.

CHAPTER ONE

"May Etta? You okay? Hey, Sister Agnes!?"

"What?" My head bobbed up from the pile of potato scrapings it had plopped into, and my starched wimple began to tilt. I straightened it as I sent up a simple plea: *Please God, don't let that be Reverend Mother.* She had caught me dozing in chapel yesterday and this night kitchen duty was the result. But that was silly. Her voice was more alto, less basso. Father Lawton? Oh, dear Lord! If it was, I'd be transferred to St. Finbar's, where the school had only three rooms with four grades to each room — and the convent did NOT have central heating. *I'll say an extra rosary, Lord. Just don't let it be him — or her. Yes, I know I owe You twelve rosaries already, but I'll catch up this week, promise. One of each, starting with the Sorrowful Mysteries. Please?*

The steam radiator sizzled and popped, and shimmering light from the gas jets on the wall tinted everything a pale yellow. I peeled one eye open. Should have been peeling potatoes, and here I was staring at bushy-browed grey eyes, a pudgy slightly-smudged nose, and a pursed mouth topped by a scruffy blond mustache. I hate mustaches. Even this one. It belonged to my schoolyard nemesis, someone who had actually dunked my braids into a full inkwell in third grade and in sixth grade dunked me into the dirty surf off Buttonwoods Beach! The Beast, my brother Dave had dubbed him when we were kids, eighteen years ago. "Thank God, it's you."

Richard DelVecchio, a driver for one of Rhode Island's reputed crime lords, grinned. "Your veil's crooked, Mayetta."

I sighed and pinned the darn thing tighter, but the straight pins that held the cowl onto the wimple dug into my scalp and I winced. "It's a cowl and not a veil. And don't call me Mayetta. It's Sister Agnes, now."

"You'll always be Mayetta Morgan to me."

Stubborn, that's what he was. "Try Agnes."

"How about Aggie?"

"How about Sister?"

"How about you learn to stay awake in chapel, Aggie?"

How did he do that? He always seemed to

know what happened here, sometimes before the rest of the convent did. Wait. Convent. Him. Here. Inside. "You can't be here!"

"Already am."

"How did you get in?" He shook his head and rolled his eyes. "Okay, don't tell me. But you have to leave! What if Mother Frances comes down? Or Father Lawton makes a surprise inspection?" I groaned. "Do you want me to get transferred to St. Finbar's in the wilds of Exeter? It's below zero there in the winter!"

Richard tut-tutted as he removed his overcoat. "Now, Aggie, don't you worry. They won't transfer you. At least, not for this. And not yet."

"And you can guarantee that?"

"Yeah. Well, not exactly me, but somebody we both know."

He touched the side of his nose and winked, and I groaned inside, but my voice came out a few decibels lower than a wailing cat. "He cannot order the Bishop-designate to keep me here. Even *he* can't do that. Can he?"

"Shhh. Look, I don't know what he can or can't do. I only know what he does. And he's looking out for you."

"Why?"

"Because, Aggie, you treated his only son just like every other kid. Made him feel normal, and right after the poor mite's mother died and all. Which means you're not like those other penguins. All uptight and pious."

"Oh, thanks. Just what a nun wants to hear, that she's nothing like a nun."

"Oh, you're a nun, okay. You wear that awful black tent, you teach some pretty bratty kids and seem to like it, you pray, you live with eleven other penguins without going batty, you pray, you sing slightly off-key but with gusto, like the hymns are supposed to be sung, you pray some more . . ." He grinned. "And you try to stay awake in chapel. But outside of all that, like the man says, you're a really great tamata . . . uh . . . *la bella femina*. Everybody knows that. Even the old bat, her ladyship, the Rev-rend Moth-ah."

From years of experience cringing at Richard's way with words, I was certain he'd wanted to tack on a particularly nasty description to that last phrase, and was extremely grateful that he'd held himself in check. He picked up one of the potato peels from the pile I'd been sleeping on and held it aloft. It should have been paper-thin. It wasn't.

"Oh, for Christ's sake, Sister Agnes . . . even an eight-year-old can do better than this."

"Don't take the Lord's name in vain!" I grabbed for the peel and smashed it back into the pile. I had never been good in the kitchen. Before taking my vows when I was seventeen — ten years ago, now — I had almost burned the house down while I was making a batch of muffins. I'd put too much wood into my ma's wood-burning stove. All that smoke and, yes, flames, had been so unnerving that from that day to this I've hated everything that has to do with cooking. Which, of course, was tailor-made for the Reverend Mother, who thought the punishment should fit the perpetrator, not the crime. "I'm learning my way around the kitchen." I'm just not liking it, God forgive me. "And night kitchen duty's good for my soul."

"Sure. But what the man sent to you is good for more than your soul, Aggie."

When he hefted a huge burlap sack onto the table, I stared at it. "That had better not be . . . uh . . . contraband."

"You mean stolen."

"All right, yes. And it had better not be for me."

"It isn't stolen. Comes directly from his

farm. And it's not for you. It's for today's soup and bread line."

"But you could have brought that to the front door anytime."

"And you could guarantee that it would actually go into the soup, huh?"

I hesitated. "Well . . ."

"Have to tell the truth, Aggie. Right?"

Things did have a habit — no pun intended — of disappearing lately. The larder was short several haunches of venison and twenty pounds of homemade venison sausage that one wealthy parishioner had donated from his last hunting trip. And the hundred pounds of carrots that I'd helped carry into the cold cellar two days ago were almost gone. The convent opened the soup and bread line at seven a.m., every other day. How could eighty pounds of carrots be used up so quickly? Answer, they couldn't. Which meant that Richard was right. Again. That was maddening. What was more maddening, and more worrisome, was: what was happening to the food meant for the poor souls who had no income because of Hoover's bloody — *Sorry, Lord* — Depression?

Richard finished emptying the sack. I figured a good bit of early spring cabbages, spinach, kale, lettuce. My taste buds were already singing. But after he opened up packets of oil-cloth-wrapped lumps and when I saw what those lumps were, I nearly sobbed. "Saints and angels!" Beef. Huge slabs, liberally marbled with creamy white fat. In these lean days, our parishioners were lucky to get pork scrapings — if they got meat at all. Beef was absolutely a luxury. This much was more than what most families had in a whole year. "If we want to be sure this gets to the hungry, I should make the soup tonight. Myself."

"Not soup this time, Aggie. This beef warrants stew."

I nodded, and my heart felt even more leaden. "Stew. I have to make stew. Now." I gripped the edge of the large blue-and-white enameled worktable and sighed. "What am I going to do? I try, but I'm not . . . well, I'm not a very good cook."

Richard did not bother to stifle a laugh. "I've choked down your food. You're a terrible cook." From the sack, he removed a square box tied with green-and-white striped twine and opened it up. He flipped out a clean white apron and tied it around his middle. Then he reached inside for one of two shiny, lethal-looking knives. "So the man sent me here to help. And you know I'm one hell of a cook."

"Don't swear." He *was* one hell of a cook. *What a loud voice You have, Lord. Yes, I'm sorry. For that slip and all others I make today, I'll tack on another decade of the rosary to the ones I already owe You.* "And thanks for helping."

"Ah, don't worry. It's nothing. Besides, I owe you for that pigtail trick."

"You owe me for more than that. But this will make up for some of it."

We smiled at each other, remembering the good times, the wild times, the old times, before the Church had called me, before his boss had called him. Then Richard got to work wielding one of those sharp knives and I had visions that made me shiver.

I did not want to know what those knives had cut up recently. Although we had grade school memories between us, I did not want Richard DelVecchio to be here in this kitchen. I did not want to be caught doing something which was, yes, outrageous. I did not want more kitchen duty as punishment.

I did not want the beef to end up in some thief's belly.

So I said a quick "Hail Mary" and picked up the other knife. It slid into the meat so easily, I wanted to cry. Our knives were at least fifty years old, sharpened so often that they didn't hold an edge longer than a blink.

We worked companionably for a while, cutting meat, peeling onions, paring carrots, dicing celery and parsnips and rutabagas, until there were several mounds of them covering the large central worktable and the side countertops — a lot of vegetables, but not enough, I knew, especially when the word went out that the convent sisters had put real beef in their stew. For some of St. Catherine's parishioners, it would be the only meal they got that day, or maybe even two days, so stew was a luxury, one they would shout from the rooftops. Which meant the sisters would be swamped that morning. School might even be later than usual, since all of the convent's residents worked the line until every hungry soul had been fed or there wasn't any soup left.

As Richard dropped some of the potatoes into a coldwater bath in the large soapstone sink, he must have read my thoughts, because he said, "Need help if we're going to get this finished before the cock crows and the real sisters come down. Where's your sidekick tonight, Aggie? That long, tall drink of water."

"Sister Winifred stayed awake in chapel. She gets to sleep in tonight."

"Why don't you roust her? We could use her help."

"I can't go up to the cells now. Sister Justina is on guard tonight and she feels it is her solemn duty to report any infractions of the rules to Mother Frances. I'll be on night kitchen duty for a year if she catches me roaming the halls."

"And what will she do if she knows you have a man in your kitchen and you're all alone?"

I felt the blood drain from my face — and then the rest of my body. How I was still standing, I didn't know. It was a cardinal rule in the Order of the Merciful Sisters of Mary. I think it was number eleven. *When in the presence of persons of the opposite sex, each Sister must be accompanied by an experienced Sister, or supervised by an appropriate and approved parishioner.* Richard DelVecchio did not qualify as either Sister or appropriate. I wasn't even sure he could be classified as a parishioner, since he rarely came to Mass. "I could be cloistered."

"Time for a tall one . . ."

I bolted for the back stairs and hiked up my skirts to take them two at a time. But I realized my shoes would be noisy on the wooden steps, and took a moment to untie the high brogans and slip them off before I ventured up the stairs. At the top I slowed and darted from one darkened area between the gas jets to another, keeping an eye out for Justina's tiny form. By the time I reached Winnie's cell, I realized I could have tromped down the hall. Justina was positioned beneath a huge print of the Sacred Heart of Jesus, sitting bolt upright on the hard wooden chair she preferred, snoring like a Model T Ford.

Before I had even crossed the threshold of Winnie's room, she sat up in bed. It was dark as pitch in there, but she sniffed, "This had better be good, Aggie."

"Richard is in the kitchen. He's helping me make stew. With real beef."

She bolted from her cot and threw her habit over her head. Like the rest of us, she slept in her undershirt, chemise, bloomers, knee-high cotton stockings, and skullcap, so dressing in the morning was a snap. All she had to do was pin on her wimple — no small task in the dark, because of the straight pins — slip her bodice over her head, pull on her skirt and tie it, cover it all with a loose habit that she belted with cording, tuck in her rosary and crucifix, position the heavy ankle-length cowl on top of her wimple, and pick up her brogans. Then a quick flip of the bedding, and three minutes later we were both slipping through the shadows to the back stairs, where we put on our shoes before entering the kitchen.

When we arrived, delicious aromas wafted in the dim saffron-tinted light of the kitchen as Richard browned the chunks of beef in three massive fry pans. Vegetables bathed in water in several large blue-and-white enamel bowls. Stew pots sat on the floor, waiting their turn to be filled up. Had he brought bowls and pots with him, too? They looked brand new.

"Richard, how good of you," Winnie said icily.

"Sister, make yourself useful."

"I'll make the base," I offered, not wanting to get in on Winnie and Richard's years-long war of talking between clenched teeth. They grunted at each other because they were both my friends, but that was about the extent of their civility. If they would only give each other a chance, maybe . . .

I sighed. Winnie was protective. Richard was, too, in his own way. But Winnie's sense of honor was affronted by Richard's association with what she called Rhode Island's worst element. They could work together, like now, but I wondered if they would ever actually like each other.

Winnie helped ladle the finished pieces of

beef into several large bowls. I mixed up a couple of gallons of warm water with Worcestershire sauce, a few spoonfuls of bouillon powder, and Sister Phillippe's homemade catsup. When he caught a glimpse of what I was doing, Richard's eyebrows raised to the roots of his hair.

"That's what you use for a stew base?" he asked.

"My Gran always used this."

"Now I know where you learned to cook. God help us." He opened one cupboard after another. "Where's the herbs and spices?" I yanked open a deep drawer filled with Mason jars of last year's bounty from the herb garden. He selected seven and started adding bits of this and bobs of that to my mixture. Other than parsley, bay leaf, and thyme, I had no idea what he used, or why. But when he finished, I tried the doctored base and it was delicious.

"Now for the roux," he said.

"The what?"

"Flour and fat, to you. Where's the flour and butter?"

"Butter? For that much stew? We can't afford that."

"Okay, oil. Got any oil?" He whipped around and caught me before I could get away. "Not the kind you put in the lanterns.

Cooking oil, Aggie. Olive or corn oil, maybe?"

"I don't know what it is, but it's yellow."

He sniffed and tasted it and nodded. "Okay."

He added it to the stew pots after Winnie had taken out all the beef. Succulent little squares, all browned and dripping with — was that butter? I sneaked a taste. It *was* butter. And there was none left in the ceramic tub that always sat on the counter. Mother Frances would kill me. Richard added oil to the pots, then a good helping of onions, which quickly gave off delicious aromas that made my stomach rumble. After a couple of minutes, he added huge handfuls of flour and had Winnie and me stir it until it browned. Then he added some of the stew base to each pot and ordered us to keep stirring. Things bubbled and thickened and my nose hairs curled, along with the sounds of my stomach crying for just a tiny bite.

"I'm making it a little thin. It will have to cook for at least an hour, maybe more, on the lowest gas flame." He stared at me, then turned to Winnie. "Please don't let her handle the stove. When we were kids . . ."

"I've heard that one," Winnie said. "I'll handle the stove."

When the sauce was the way Richard wanted it, he added the meat back into the pot, then some of each of the vegetables. I've never smelled anything so wonderful. Beef. Real beef. And we might actually get some for ourselves at supper. If we didn't run out this morning, that is.

"Gotta go, ladies. It's almost four o'clock."

"Oh, my gosh, they'll be down any minute," I wailed. "How will I — we — explain all this?"

"Just tell the Reverend Mother that it was delivered." He pulled out a large envelope. "Give this to her. It's just a little note from you-know-who." He gathered up the burlap sack and all the vegetable parings. "These will be good for Hamlet, Othello, and Desdemona."

"Never mind your rabbits," Winnie ground out. "We have some, too."

"But you eat yours," Richard said with a shiver.

Winnie merely glared. "Leave some."

"Okay, but you better hide it from her ladyship." He was almost to the door when he snapped his fingers. "Almost forgot. He's having a truckload of Italian bread delivered in about an hour to go with the stew. And some biscotti and other breakfast goodies for you sisters."

"But your pots! And the knives?"

I prayed what the answer would be, so I wasn't surprised when he said, "What pots and knives?" He winked, raised his hand in the air in sort of a wave, and whistled his way down the path to the side gate.

"That man," Winnie declared, "will be the death of you yet."

CHAPTER TWO

At precisely four-twelve a.m., Sister Mary Phillippe, whose daily chore it was to prepare breakfast for the convent, tottered into the kitchen, missing Richard by a mere four minutes. She took one look at the bubbling pots and sniffed. Her mouth dropped, and she turned quicker than I'd ever seen her move and clumped down the hall.

I counted out loud, "Nine, eight, seven, six, five . . ."

At four, Mother Frances swished through the kitchen door and took up a stance not unlike my cousin Pete, the Marine. And like Pete, she was authoritative, and quelling. Before I could say anything, she held up her hand, sniffed the redolent air, walked to the stove, and counted the huge pots — there were four more than usual. She pulled off one of the covers, picked up a wooden spoon, stuck it into Richard's masterpiece, and took a taste just at the tip of her tongue, so she was not technically breaking her fast, and she could still take the sacrament.

Behind her came persistent murmurs from the other seven sisters, who were jostling each other at the kitchen door, each trying to get a good view of Sister Mary Agnes being thrown to the wolves.

Nothing happened. Nothing they could see, that is. But what I could feel was loud and clear.

She knew.

Although Reverend Mother Mary Frances was the best at hiding her feelings (a trait which must surely have come with every Reverend Mother's umbilical cord), there was for one moment a telltale twitch of her right eyelid. But she quickly schooled her features, laid down the spoon, covered the pot, adjusted the flame to almost nothing, and stepped back. She gave Winnie and me a thirty-second perusal. I know it was that long, because I was counting the boom-booms in my chest.

"We'll have to dilute this . . ."

I think I gasped. Winnie pulled at the back of my cowl, so I must have gasped. But Reverend Mother went on, ". . . with a little milk for our breakfast. We want to be certain there is sufficient for the poor souls who count on us. And milk is nutritious enough for those of us who get three meals a day." She turned to Winnie — to Winnie! "Will six vats do for this morning, do you think, once the parishioners hear about this?"

Winnie sidled a glance at me, then bobbed her head.

"And if that isn't enough," I ventured boldly, "there are two more huge casserole pans in the oven, both full."

"Thank you, Sister Agnes."

Her tone was cold, cutting. Darn my socks! Why can't I learn to keep my mouth closed? Why can't I learn to be humble, self-effacing, patient? After all, this wasn't really my doing. It was Richard's. And if I didn't shut up, I'd be in real trouble. Three hundred sixty-five nights of kitchen duty. *Make like a clam, Aggie!*

I expected a long interrogation, but she didn't ask one word. Not one. It was eerie. First there was Richard sneaking in and out of a convent, knowing all kinds of things about our goings-on, and now the Reverend Mother just plain knowing.

A giant shudder shook my frame from the inside out. I did not want to know where her second sight came from. I was plenty happy with the way things — and I — were. Well, satisfied, at least. All right, I didn't want to "rock the boat," as my sixth-form

25

pupils called it. By the grace of the saints and angels, it looked like I wouldn't receive more disciplinary action. Why would I want to call attention to the obvious fact that someone had helped me in the kitchen, especially that someone?

I had an acute sense of self-preservation, as Father Lawton called it. My Da called it plain old horse sense. Whatever it was, it had served me well. So had Holy Mother, the Church. Served me so well, that she had educated me above the rest of my family. She just hadn't seen fit to teach me to cook. I was female. That should have come with the frilly petticoats I'd long ago set aside. That it had not was a cross the Reverend Mother had to bear each and every day. She was bearing it very well — for her.

Until I gave her the note from Richard and she glanced at the handwriting on the front of the envelope.

Then she faltered. It was hardly perceptible, but if you added it to that eye twitch, you could say that this was turning into an interesting morning. Oh, good grief and gravy! Interesting? That was the understatement of the decade, and the 1930s so far were not the most interesting of times. Damnable. Demanding. Demoralizing. But not interesting. *These are the times that try men's souls.* Too bad Thomas Paine hadn't put something about nuns in there.

Mother Frances tucked the envelope into the folds of her loose habit and turned away from us to answer a knock on the kitchen door. Richard's bread order had arrived. This time without faltering, she directed the white-coated men to the larder, to store most of the order until it was needed as the morning wore on. The rest was quickly cut into thick slices by our three novices. Some went into the dining room, the rest into large baskets, ready at the back door for that morning's bread line.

As usual, we all trooped over to the church, to participate in the six o'clock early Mass and receive communion. Back at the convent, everyone fell into the tasks that they performed each morning: starting water boiling for tea and coffee, setting the table in the dining room, scooping up a large dollop of butter from the crock in the icebox, cutting up fruit and the pastries Richard's boss had sent — the happy duties of satisfied, hard-working sisters.

At precisely six-forty-five, breakfast was served. While Sister Justina read the offices of the day — this Wednesday, the first three rules of our Order and one of St. Paul's Epistles to the Romans — the rest of us lapped up our milk-thinned stew. Even thinned down, it was still surprisingly good. And the well-buttered, crusty Italian bread added even more nourishment. As usual, Winnie and I pocketed our fruit ration, to save for the neediest of our students. We weren't the only ones. At least three of the other sisters whisked theirs into their laps. Reverend Mother pretended not to notice.

By the time we struggled outside, two-by-two, with the huge pots of stew, the line of hungry people was already snaking its way around the block. Over the past year we'd found it easier to serve our soup from the pots. We set them on a row of bricks on the ground behind the stone wall that surrounded the convent property. Long ladles did quick work of filling tin bowls. Each person in line took a bowl, a spoon, and a small napkin made from misprinted scraps donated by Cranston Print Works. Everyone ate standing up, chatting in small groups in the gutter, on the cinder path that led around back to our storerooms, or in the vacant lot across the street. As they were emptied, Sister Mary Angelica, one of the new novices, collected the bowls and carted them back to the kitchen, where they were washed, hastily dried, then reused.

We soon ran out of the sliced bread and

Mother Frances sent me to get another basket from the larder. I decided to slice it outside, as it was needed, and picked up one of the new knives that Richard had brought and a good, old cutting board. But when I set up the bread-slicing station, Reverend Mother gave that task to Sister Mary Paul, another novice, and I returned to help Winnie serve up the stew.

The line had slowed down, and Mother Frances had to prod Sisters Angelica and Claire to get them going again. It was a hard job, and them so new at it. But not harder than the life these poor souls had had.

I noticed several people I had never seen before. A man and a woman, with four youngsters under the age of eight, reminded me of my sister Fanny's family. After them came a large woman, tall and stout, with a worn-out cloth coat that I'd seen in that week's rummage sale. She shuffled along with her eyes on the ground. She carried no purse but wore a large black cloche hat and shoes that were bursting at the sides. Bunions, probably, and not cared for at that, because she limped as she shuffled. Six boys — what Father Lawton would call louts — jostled each other and joked about the tin bowls looking like dog dishes. But each seemed to be trying too hard, perhaps in a manner reminiscent of some gangsters they had seen at a recent moving picture show at the Strand. What future did they have? Were they still in school? They weren't any of mine, nor Winnie's. Perhaps they came from a vocational school or Central High, or nowhere in particular. That was the worst, the nowhere to go, nothing to do.

There were a couple of dozen mothers, most carrying babes in their arms, with small children under school age. Three of them broke off from the other group and went up the cinder path, heading toward a small copse of trees between our back yard and Carmichael's Cleansers behind us. They looked tired, ravaged with overwork and too little nourishment. Several single men came and went quickly, with their eyes to the ground. Wary, they were, unwilling to look folks straight in the eye, or give them the time of day. Shame did that, made good, strong men timid. I wondered how many of them had left their wives, how many of the young mothers just in front of them had been left by men such as these.

Leaving a family wasn't all that unusual. People lost their jobs every day. Men lost their spirit. Women lost their hope. Which was why we had set up this morning ritual — to give hope to the hopeless, soup to the spiritless. Our bread and soup line had started when a few parishioners had come begging at the convent side door one morning. We fed them, and the next day there were twice as many. Now, we served over fifty. But that morning I was certain there were at least a hundred and fifty. Too many people without jobs. Too many people without hope.

I sighed and helped Winnie pick up the last pot, still half-filled with stew.

"For the old folks at Mary McBride's?" she asked me, mentioning a parishioner who had taken in several elderly women last year, and all of them unable to get out because of various ailments. We at the convent did what we could for them, but they needed more than we could give.

"I should think so," I said. "Let's put it in a smaller container and we can run over with it."

Mother Frances clucked and shook her head. "Because of the stew and all, we took much longer than usual this morning, and school starts in only thirty minutes. I can't spare you both. Sister Mary Paul," she called. "You will go to Mary McBride's this morning. You, Sister Agnes, and Sister Winifred, will help in the kitchen and later in the schoolyard. And you'd all best hurry."

We were to the back door when she added to Mary Paul, "And bring them some bread, Sister. They don't get good bread there."

What she meant was they got stale bread — from us and from Powell's Bakery. But I wondered if they'd be able to eat this, with its hard crust and all.

"Tell Mary McBride to have them dip the bread into the stew, to soften it," she directed Mary Paul.

"Yes, Mother," the pretty little novice said.

How did she do that? How did Reverend Mother read my thoughts before I thought them? The Sidhe? Those unseen Irish beings that brought blessings or curses, depending upon the hidden secrets of your heart?

I helped Winnie and Mary Paul make up a large bundle of stew and bread, and we even sneaked in three bananas and two pears.

"Sister Agnes," Mother's stern voice commanded, after Winnie left, "check the stores before you go over to the school. You must have used up most of our vegetables, and I'll need to order more today for the rest of the month. Send a note back to me by one of your stewards."

"Yes, Mother."

"And refresh yourself before you go, Sister."

Chilly though it was this morning, I had developed a fine sheen of sweat under all my layers, and I hadn't had a chance to repair the night's ravages. "Yes, Mother."

I fairly flew up the kitchen stairs to my cell, relishing a little private time to myself. That was one of the luxuries of being a nun — having my own room. A cell, yes, it was, with barely enough space for the cot, a small washstand, a three-drawer dresser, and a coat rack. But it was mine, a space I didn't have to share with four God-given sisters or a big bear of a husband.

I lit the candle in front of the picture of Jesus' Sacred Heart and began the prayers I reserved for the morning. One "Our Father" was all I needed to peel off my cowl and let down my bodice. Two "Hail Marys" accompanied my hasty wash in the cold water in the small bowl on the table next to my cot. One "Glory Be to the Father" helped me powder my upper body with cornstarch, over my chemise and all. I didn't forget my arms, making certain the pits were dry and dusted with starch before I replaced the bodice, ran a comb through my close-cropped hair, and positioned my cowl over my wimple. All that without benefit of mirror, for mirrors were vanity, and God forbid that any of us would be vain. The only thing I regretted was the mirror. Those danged straight pins bit into my scalp if I wasn't careful, and I didn't have the time to be careful. Ah, well, Winnie could help me later.

I gave a shake to my skirts, thinking I didn't have time to change, but a fine dusting of flour puffed out of them and I realized the sides were more grey than black. So I took another "Glory Be" to untie them and drop them onto a hook on the coat rack, fully intending to put a brush to them later in the day. I was bending down to step into the clean skirt in front of my small window when I saw movement out of the corner of my eye. Someone in the herb garden? Richard? No, couldn't be. But it certainly looked like him.

Well, if it was him, it wouldn't surprise me. Nothing could, after this night and morning.

I pulled up my skirt and threw everything else into place. I was tying my corded belt and tucking in my rosary and crucifix as I raced down the stairs. I wanted to have a moment to thank Richard for everything, but when I got to the garden there was no one there.

Oh, what a morning, after such a night!

The door to the cold cellar was sunk into the ground, down three steps from the garden path. It was open a crack, and I wondered if one of the other nuns had come to get something and forgotten to lock it up. Then I saw the broken lock on the ground.

"Oh, no!" Well, that explained the missing carrots, sausage, and venison.

I sighed, and said a simple prayer for the soul who thought she — or he — had to steal rather than take charity. *And what is charity, Lord, if it isn't an outward manifestation of Your divine love? Could You have a word with whoever is doing this, please? We sisters don't have much in our food cellar, but we share anything we have. Tell him he doesn't need to break into the food stores. Tell him that we'll give him what he needs. Of course, You'll have to whisper a few good thoughts into the ears of Reverend Mother. But You are the Miracle Maker Extraordinaire.*

And what if the culprit won't listen, I argued with myself. After all, he knew we fed the hungry, yet he thought he had to break in to steal food. Break, indeed. And what did he use to break that lock? I didn't see anything that might do so much damage to a sturdy new lock.

Ah, well. We'd just have to order more carrots and potatoes, and hope someone else donated some more meat.

And a new lock.

I hefted up the cellar door and peered down into the dark. There was a nice, clean, earthy smell that always pleased me when I had to come here, a combination of dirt and vegetable odors that reminded me of Aunt Flossie's farm. I reached for the lantern that always hung at the right inside the door, took it up, lit it with the wooden matches we kept right beside it, and began to descend the cement steps.

Something niggled at the corners of my consciousness. Something not quite right.

"Humph! And what's been quite right about this night or morning, if you please?" I asked the stillness of the dark. "First Richard, then the stew, then Mother Frances' reaction. So, what now, Sister? Some dog down here, or cat, or varmint? You faced last night. You faced Mother Frances this morning. You came out unscathed. Put your faith in the saints and angels. Shoulders back! Chin up! Well, maybe not. Maybe, chin down, or you'll fall flat on your face. And that would not please Mother Frances."

I tucked a hand into one of the wide

pockets in my skirt and pulled out the little notebook all of us sisters kept there. Pencil followed, and I jotted as I scanned our stores.

Potatoes to the right, nearly depleted. We'd best order another hundred pounds. Cabbages on the shelves above. They looked down about a dozen heads, but nothing that we needed to worry about unless — ah, St. Paddy's Day coming up. It would be a little bit of corned beef and plenty of cabbage that day, served at noon. Best get another two crates full. And another of the turnips which sat beside them. And probably double that order of potatoes. Onions, though, were plentiful. We had six fifty-pound bags, one with about twenty pounds gone. Enough for another month, even with the Irish appetite for onions and vinegar.

That only left the carrots, tucked into the coldest corner. I wondered how many we'd need . . .

"Holy Mary, Mother of God!"

A girl. Young, probably no more than eighteen. Sprawled half-on, half-off the small hillock that was our carrot cache. Blood covered the torn bodice of a very old St. Catherine's School blouse, and seeped into the waistband of a long black skirt. A small trail of blood dribbled over her right hip and pooled near her bent elbow.

And in the middle of her chest, one of the new knives that Richard had given us.

CHAPTER THREE

It was amazing how quickly the police could turn the well-run security of the convent into a madhouse, what with a half-dozen policemen poking and prying into rooms that gentlemen had not entered in years, not since they built the three-level structure. Their activity was welcomed — by me — because, try though I might, I couldn't get the image of that poor dead girl out of my head. There was something familiar about her, but I hadn't the time to cipher it out. I was hounded by her death, by the police, and by Reverend Mother.

So far, the good mother had exploded only five times, and — even a new novice could have predicted it — four of those times had been directed at me.

Was it my fault that I discovered the body? To hear Reverend Mother tell it, *yes*. My fault that there was a body there in the first place? *Yes*. My fault that one of our knives had been the murder weapon? *Yes.* My fault that — because she was wearing one of "our" school blouses — she had possibly been one of our students? *Yes, indeed.*

"The horror of it," she said, as she paced behind her office desk. "You, seeing something you should never have seen."

Was she perturbed at the reality that there had been something to see? Or was she most vexed that it had been me to see it? Probably the latter; hence the emphasis on the *you*. I was not her ideal nun, and this latest trial was more proof to the pudding.

"And with class just minutes from starting, you took your time to . . . how could you have done that? Why did you?"

Would she have been happier if I had fainted, or run screaming from the bowels of the earth, or pitched a fit after what I had seen? Probably, but that wouldn't have been me. Not me at all.

Or was her obvious distress due to the fact that I had sent a student to fetch a policeman before I'd told Reverend Mother what I had found? Did she think I had overstepped myself, that it should have been she who notified the police? If that were the case, I hadn't meant to shame-face her. Not then. Not now.

I was trying to be reverent, and trying

desperately to be patient, because this was a Reverend Mother the likes of which I had never seen. "You sent me to check the stores," I said, as gently as I knew how. But perhaps, as she had, I put too much emphasis on that *you.* She glared right through me, and I wondered if the ice-cold heat of that glare had burned a hole right through my habit. I dared not look down, but I did check out my chest, pretending I had gotten lint on my bodice. Upper torso still intact, but with her this flummoxed, I wondered for how long?

"And instead of checking our stores, you find . . ." She took a shuddering breath in. "You find . . ."

My own mind was in turmoil. Every time I blinked, that image flashed, etched forever on my retina. *Blink.* The poor girl was all red, like her — gulp — blood. *Blink.* And there it was again on the back of my retina, this time bottle green, like the flies that had begun to gather. Oh, dear Lord. *Blink.* And a flash to the yellowness of her skin in the dim light of my gas lantern. *Blink.* This was the worst of all — a bright awful white, like fireworks exploding in my brain.

I yearned for normalcy, for a Reverend Mother who railed and ranted, but was steady and stiff. Then maybe I could settle my own mind.

But first, I had to get Reverend Mother's mind off the trauma of that poor girl's death, back to something familiar, friendly. I did not want the Reverend Mother to crack like Humpty Dumpty. We did not have any King's horses or King's men. Unless you counted the new Bishop-elect as King. No, of course not. In the Church, he would be a Prince.

Oh, Aggie! Get a grip! Someone has to hold herself together, here!

"But I did check the stores, Reverend Mother. I have the list right here."

She snatched it away from me, then dropped it, and watched as it fluttered to her pristine desktop. Her gaze shifted from it to the small statue of the Blessed Virgin on the right-hand corner of the mahogany desktop, then to the ornate gas lamp to her left, and finally to the carved black-framed portrait of His Holiness, Pope Pius the Eleventh, that hung directly opposite, between heavily draped windows.

"There will be an inquiry, you know," she said, and sat with a grimace in her wooden desk chair.

"There is an inquiry. The police are at it now."

"Not their inquiry. There will be one by

the new Bishop or his administrator. He will come here —"

"Oh, surely not! Bishops never visit us."

"No, of course not. Monsignor Delaney, the chief financial officer. He will come. And examine every inch, ledger, nook, and cranny of my convent."

"I thought it was the Bishop's convent."

"Sister Mary Agnes, you will be still!"

I hadn't dared move since she'd dragged me into her inner sanctum. I'd never been this still. And I wasn't sure I could keep on being still. It wasn't in me, regardless of the ten years I'd been schooled by the Church to be the perfect nun. In order to wipe away the pain and sorrow of that morning's discovery, I needed to *do!* In any crisis — and in ordinary times — I had always needed to *do.* It gave me comfort. It brought me a modicum of peace. *And, Lord, You know I desperately need that peace.*

But right now, I needed to help Mother Frances get back some of her equilibrium. "Yes, Reverend Mother. If there's anything you think I might do to help . . ."

"Get to your classroom."

Because of the discovery and the influx of police and community onlookers, school had been delayed, but not for long. Since the Depression had struck our parish, some

43

of the mothers had gone out to work to help support their families. I knew personally the children whose mothers were combers at the cotton mills, shop workers at Shepherd's downtown, waitresses in small sandwich shops, teachers at the public schools, nurses at Rhode Island Hospital or Lying-in, or assembly line workers in the jewelry factories. We had a responsibility to these poor, overworked women more than anyone else. So, when classes started, Winnie had taken charge of my class and hers. Thank goodness they were right next door to each other. Winnie could open the connecting doors and supervise all fifty-nine students. If I knew Winnie, she was probably giving them a vocabulary test. She knew they hated that, but it would at least keep them quiet.

"But the police told me to stay here because they wanted to speak to me again."

"Well, the police don't always get what they want." She pointed an imperious finger at the door. "To your classroom."

"Yes, Mother."

"And shut the door behind you!"

I exited the office quickly and quietly, a first for me. As I took two steps away, I heard the unmistakable sound of the lock clicking into place. Poor Mother Frances. It would be a long time before she recovered from this morning.

I blinked away the kaleidoscopic images that I knew would haunt me the rest of my life and brushed a tear off my right cheek. It would be a long time before any of us recovered.

Questions were right now being asked of all the nuns. Other questions were sure to arise. I was already tallying some of them in my head, some that niggled, pushing, pushing for answers.

Foremost — who was the poor girl in the cold cellar? And what had happened to her, besides the obvious stabbing, that is. Pinpricks raced up and down my arms. Oh, that had been awful, seeing that! So harrowing. So pitiful. No one should have to die like that. Was she poor? Was she friendless?

I didn't know. All I knew was that she had died. Alone.

Well, not really alone. There had been the murderer. *Lord, please, no matter what I think I saw in the back garden, please don't let Richard have anything to do with this. He might work for a shady man, but I know him. He's not bad at heart. Truly, he's not. He's been my friend for almost twenty years. I can't believe he'd do anything like that.*

And certainly he would never leave any of

his boss's dirty work in our back yard. Not Richard. Not my friend.

Would he?

My heart was pounding as I contemplated the awful notion that Richard might be involved, one way or another, and I might never know how. I didn't think I could live with that, because right next door to doing something, I also had to *know*. Not knowing would be awful.

The murdered girl, her murder, and the unraveling of it — that was what I needed to know about. It all started with her, of course. She had come to our convent for something. Perhaps she had found it. Perhaps not. Certainly, she didn't expect to find what she did.

But, how had she gotten there? Was she the one who had broken the lock, had been stealing the food? Had she been one of our students? She had on a St. Catherine's blouse — that, I knew, by a shadow of pulled-out embroidered initials on the collar — but it was a few years old, and the style had changed. It might have come from the rummage sale. It might have come from her bureau drawer.

"Darn my socks! She could be anyone. But could she be one of ours? And what about the knife? How had that gotten there, to be used like that?"

"Still talking to yourself, hey?"

I turned quickly, recognizing that deep timbre. "Josiah." My cousin. Well, second cousin. Or maybe third? Great-aunt Flossie's grandson. He had always wanted to be a police officer for the City of Providence. Well, he had gotten there, and it hadn't been easy, not with Big Jim, his noodle-brained father, who wanted his sons to work in the brewery because they got free beer with their lunch! God save the man. He had one of the best of sons in Josiah, yet treated him like a leper. But Josiah had kicked the traces, and they had been hard, stubborn, Irish-proud traces. I was glad to see he'd triumphed, and now he looked professional in his new blue uniform with the big brass buttons down the front and a shiny badge on the left breast pocket.

"I didn't know you were finished with police school."

He smiled the famous Morgan grin, the one that made dozens of creases in his freckled face, the one that drew the fairer sex to every Morgan man and the pig-headed, noodle-brained sex to every Morgan woman.

"They call it an academy, May."

"Sister Agnes, Josiah, remember? Especially here, in this house."

"Gotcha, cousin. The walls have ears, huh?"

And voices. Loud voices. Especially loud voices when I was disobedient. "I have to get to my classroom, Josiah."

"But I need to double-check a few things."

"You can walk me there. We can talk as we go."

"Okay. Let's see — why don't you start by answering those questions you were asking yourself?"

"Oh, bother! You heard."

"Righto. Start with the girl. Is she one of yours?"

"I really don't know. I don't think I've ever seen her before."

"But you're not certain."

"No, I can't be certain. I teach the middle classes — last year, fifth grade; this year, fourth. She's obviously — was obviously older than that. Remember, each nun usually only serves two or three years in a convent and then she's transferred. So, she could have been a student here years ago, before I came."

"Is there any way you could find out? This is my first big case, and it would help me a lot to discover who the girl is."

"Of course, I'll try. But not just for you.

It's an outrage, killing someone like that, and on Church grounds. And she was young, so very young. No one deserves to die like that. Why do people do that? Our Father said, 'Thou shalt not kill,' but people keep on killing." I shuddered, pure pity washing over me, so that I all but whispered. "I never realized how awful that kind of death is. Her eyes were still open, Josiah. And the look in them! Oh, it was dreadful! She must have been terrified, because, of course, she knew what was happening. He stabbed her from the front, after all. An outrage. A devilish outrage. He must be caught. Soon."

"So, you'll help."

And Reverend Mother would have a cow. *But, Lord, it's the right thing to do. You must know that. And I'm in the right place, at the right time. So, if You'll bear with me, and help where I need it, I'll be forever grateful. You will? Gee, thanks.*

"Yes, of course I'll help," I said.

"Good. You were always the best of the Morgan mob, Aggie. Got more brains than the whole lot of us put together. And we never appreciated that in you. Why do you suppose that was?"

"You all thought it was laughable that a girl could be smart."

"Smart-mouthed, you mean," he said, grinning.

"That, too. But I had to protect myself somehow from you ruffians."

"So, about that knife . . ."

Uh-oh. I'd been around police often enough to recognize this technique. He was trying to catch me off-guard, the way policemen do. But this was my cousin, and I had always been able to handle him in the past and thought I could do so now.

Handling him, however, wasn't enough. Now I had a real problem. I shouldn't lie. But if I told the truth, then he'd know about Richard. But, of course, he would find out about Richard anyway. One of the other sisters would tell him. Richard had been at the convent. I couldn't deny it. But at least I didn't have to tell him everything . . .

Lord, I'll do penance until I'm sixty, but I can't tell him that I thought I saw Richard in the garden. It's not a lie, just an evasion. All right, I hear You! It's technically a lie. But it's technically the truth, too.

I didn't know that it was Richard. I had only caught a small glimpse of the man. It looked like him, but it looked like any number of other men, too. Darn my socks! Why were things so complicated?

"Aggie? What's wrong? You have this look

you always had when we were kids."

"What look?"

"Your just-about-to-lie look. Aggie, take my advice — don't lie. Just answer every direct question about this case that any police officer asks you. And answer it truthfully. There could be a lot of trouble if you don't. For you, and for the convent."

"I wouldn't do anything else. I've taken vows, and one of them was to be honest in all things, Josiah."

"Good. So how about that knife?"

"That's not a direct question, Josiah."

"Aggie, sometimes you are a pain in the __"

"Josiah! You are in a convent."

"Technically, I am in the alley leading to the school."

I looked around and realized he was right. I'd been so caught up in fear for Richard that I hadn't realized we had walked through the convent, then through the garden and down the cinder path that connected the convent to the church grounds. We were now almost at the side door to the school. "Technically, you're right."

"So, Aggie, can you tell me whose knife that was and where you got it?"

Oh, boy, Josiah was good. Almost as good as I was. He might even have learned it from me — or someone like me — because I had done it at least once a week, as all sisters do when they thought they weren't getting all the answers they needed from a student. He was testing me. Or testing someone he'd already spoken to. Maybe more than one person he'd spoken to.

"You already know the answer to that, don't you?" I asked.

When he just stared at me, I sighed and related the events of the morning, leaving out the quick glimpse of the man in the garden. As I thought longer about it, I convinced myself that it couldn't be Richard. I hadn't seen his long black roadster — what he called a Cord — only the figure of a man that resembled him. So until I could confirm whether it actually was Richard or not, I'd keep that bit of information to myself unless directly asked about it. Since that wasn't likely to happen, I couldn't be accused of lying. Technically, *But, Lord, if You can't shave hairs here, then I'll do a decade of the rosary every night for a week. Or month. Or whatever You decide. Yes, I know sometimes I don't have the time, but I always try. Just one more decade? Okay, that I can do.*

Josiah was plainly jubilant. "Richard DelVecchio. Here, in the wee hours of the

52

morning, in plain view of two nuns. And it was his knife." He grinned, and I didn't like the look of triumph in his eyes. "The force has been trying to get something on that guy for years, and he's always slipped through our fingers. Now, if I can tie him together with the girl, I think I might be able to solve this case and put him away for good."

"He wasn't with her! He had already left hours before I found her. And since she was still . . ." I gulped. "Still bleeding . . ." And shivered. "He must have been miles away when she was stabbed."

"Not so, Aggie. I did some checking after someone told me he was here. And don't look at me like that. It's not important who squealed. You were there. He was there. What's the big deal? But knowing what he did last night and this morning sent me around the neighborhood, asking questions. When you thought he'd left, he didn't go far, him and his cocky Cord. Only around the block. Looks like he was parked in front of Carmichael's Cleansers for almost four hours, then got out of the car around eight-thirty and cut through the alley. The last anyone saw him, he was walking up this very cinder path towards the convent."

He ticked off his findings by bringing one

finger up at a time.

Index finger — "Right guy, because he's a wrong guy."

Middle finger — "Right time."

Ring finger — "Right place."

Pinkie finger — "His weapon."

He got to his thumb and waggled it in the air. "Only one more piece of evidence to fill in and I've got my murderer."

CHAPTER FOUR

"You won't find that piece, Josiah. It won't exist."

"Don't be so sure, Aggie. We cops can find one needle in a dozen haystacks. If there's a connection to the girl, I'll find it." He hesitated a moment, then placed his hand on my shoulder. "I know he's your friend, always has been. Heck, he was my friend for a dozen years, before we all gave up knickers. But he's gotten himself into the wrong crowd, and our old friend is changed."

"Not so," I said, wanting to bat Josiah's hand off, but knowing it would only make matters worse. "I know Richard better than you. He's generous and kind."

"Yeah, to those rabbits of his. But to people? He's already been arrested twice for assault."

"But never convicted. And he'd never hurt a woman, Josiah." I couldn't keep the gasp in, nor stop the shivers from eclipsing me again. "Richard would never . . . could never do that." I swallowed down the bile and stared him straight in the eye. "Do you hear me, Josiah? Never could he do . . . that."

He gave me an awkward pat, and shook his head as he gazed at me. "Aw, Aggie, you're just remembering the way things were. I have to deal with the way things are." He then put his finger to his cap as if to tip it to me and smiled — not happily — then shrugged. "I have to do my job. You know that. But I promise you that I'll give DelVecchio a chance to explain. For you, and for old times' sake."

"Not for me. And not for old times' sake, Josiah. Because he's innocent until proven guilty."

"So they say."

But he knew that I knew that what "they" said wasn't always what "they" did. These days, witnesses could come out of the woodwork to lie, just for the small pittance the city offered for information to solve a crime. Three dollars meant food on the table for a week, maybe a month for a small family. For people who were hungry, lying wasn't a very big sin, regardless of what poor soul they hurt.

As Josiah walked away, it was patently

obvious from the determined stride to his step and the slight swagger of his shoulders that Richard was in trouble, perhaps more trouble than he'd ever been in before. And so might Josiah be, if he let this opportunity color his judgment.

My fingers worried over the large rosary draped over my belt. Just the feel of each bead usually gave me peace and courage and strength. *Glory be to the Father* — "There has to be some way to help him." *And to the Son* — "And stay out of the Reverend Mother's way." *And to the Holy Spirit* — "And not get tossed out of the con . . . Yipes!"

A strong hand had come from nowhere — all right, from the darkness of the side vestibule leading to the classrooms — and yanked me right off my feet. The darkness swallowed me whole. If there were the possibility of salt water around here, I'd count myself as Jonah. Jonah, being lifted high and carried into the maw of death. All right, not death. But it was bloody dark! My brogans flailed and found something solid. So, not blubber.

"Enough! No more kicking, Aggie."

"Oh, for heaven's sake, Richard, put me down. You are no knight in shining armor."

"And you're no lady fair." He shoved on a

door and we all but tumbled in. One quick nudge with his shoulder and my hip, and the door closed, leaving us in near-total blackness.

"Now what?" I wailed. "Don't you ever plan these things?"

"About as much as you do." He eased me away from him. "Aggie, you should have stuck to Reverend Mother's milk-thinned stew and left the bread for the others. Oooh, my aching back."

"Richard, the police . . ."

"Yup. I'll get to them later. Right now, I just want to be sure you're okay."

"I'm fine." I pushed away from him and batted the air in front of me, looking for a shelf before I slammed into it. My eyes finally adjusted and I could see the barest outlines of what I had suspected from the smell when the door closed. Chalk. And other supplies. Pens, pencils, paper, books. One pile of books looked sturdy enough and I plopped down on them. "Every time I'm with you, I'm in trouble."

"Ditto."

"Why in the world did you come here? You should be on your way to Boston, or New York, or . . . or . . . the moon! If you don't leave soon, they'll catch you."

"They won't have to. I'm going to give

myself up."

"You can't! You didn't do anything wrong."

He chuckled. At a time like this! "Aggie, you tacked on a question mark there." He hunkered down in front of me. "Don't worry, o-friend-o-mine. I'll get myself out of this mess. Promise."

He hadn't answered that tacked-on question mark. For one moment . . . No! The image of Richard in the garden. In the cold cellar. With a knife. Stabbing. No! No. No, surely not.

"When we found out, I talked it over with Vincent, and we decided that I should fight it out."

"Saints and angels. You've got rocks in your head. The both of you."

"Oh for crying out loud, Aggie, you know me better than that. I'm not taking on Providence's finest on my own. Vincent decided that I could fight it out with the cops with the help of his lawyers."

"So you aren't as noodle-brained as my lot. They would fight it out on their own."

"The fightin' Irish, heh?"

"Yes." *And I'm one of them, Richard. I'm going to fight, too. If the good Lord is listening, and willing. I'm just not going to tell you.*

"Vincent sent me here first because he just

wanted to be sure that Dan is going to be okay without me." He took out a package and handed it to me. "From me and Vincent. For you. He will be forever grateful for your help with the boy."

As he got to his feet, he was one dark motion of strength, and only the click of the door signaled that I was alone again. As I stashed Richard's contraband gift into my inner pocket, I looked up, my avenue to God's ears. "No goodbye. But, then, I guess good friends didn't need goodbyes. They always have lots of hellos." I slowly got to my feet. I could hardly lift myself, I was that weary, that discombobulated. But not too weary to forego my ongoing daily conversation with *The Ear of the World,* as my sister Fanny called Him. "And let those hellos continue for a good long time, Father, please. Richard's friendship is one of Your best gifts. But don't tell him I said that."

"I won't," a small voice said.

Would this day's surprises never end?

"Dan, is that you?"

"Yes, Sister."

"What are you doing in here?"

"It's my secret place."

He waved his little hand and by squinting in the gloom I saw the hidey-hole that he'd made for himself. Clever little boy, from a cleverly devilish family. But he was only nine years old, without a mother, with nightmares that didn't end, with only his father's driver for a friend. So a small mound of books and a stepladder set right under a tiny and only window became a fortress, with battlements and lookout holes. A small slate and chalk. Some well-worn and well-read books. Broken pieces of bricks. A small pile of stones. A tattered piece of blanket. Lead soldiers. A bank, probably full of the nickels his father gave him for milk, which he hated. I know he sneaked over to Adler's variety store to get pickles from the wooden barrel in front of the meat counter. Big, juicy dill pickles. A boy after my own heart.

"Quite a place you have here."

"Only you know." He peered up at me. "Sometimes I need to get away from all the kids whispering behind my back. You know what I mean?"

I nodded. He had a difficult time, because his childhood was no childhood. Losing his mother in an accident that many thought was no accident was bad enough. Add to that the fact that his father was one of the most feared men in Rhode Island, and the kid didn't have much of a chance to fit in anywhere. Dan — short for Dante — Ricci had fit up his own place, and right under the Reverend Mother's nosy nose. Good for him.

"I promise to keep your secret, Sister Agnes, if you promise to keep mine."

Winnie had a wing-ding of a lecture on bad bargains, but this one would buy me a little time, and give Dan some much-needed privacy. "You got a deal." I pulled Dan's shirt collar closed, straightened his school tie, and handed him his jacket. "But now we both have to get to class."

"Rats. I figured with all the cops running around, school would be cancelled."

"No such luck."

I was surprised when he took my hand. His was so small, but hard and strong, and he held on tight as we walked up to the second-floor corridor. There was hardly a sound in the building and our steps echoed sharply on the worn wooden floor.

We were two doors away from my classroom when he pulled his hand out of mine and looked up at me. "Will he be okay?" he asked, the words barely breathed, with a catch as if he were holding back tears. "The police — they won't hurt him, will they?"

I could pretend I didn't know what he was talking about, but Dante Ricci knew better. And he knew the answer to his question as well as I did.

"Richard will be okay, Dan. He knows what he's walking into. And your father will make sure he has the best lawyers to help him get through this."

"Yeah, I guess. But I want him to come home real soon. I'm going to miss him."

"We will all miss him. And before we know it, he'll be back driving you and pestering me." I suddenly had an idea that might help this young boy get through the worst of this mess. "Have you thought about helping Richard out while he's away?"

"Me? What can I do?"

"Take care of Hamlet, Othello, and Desdemona."

He grinned, then. "He'd like that."

"I'll get you some scraps from our kitchen vegetable leavings to feed them, and we'll ask your father this afternoon."

His father. I held back the shiver that was there just below the surface. I didn't know the Man, only what I'd heard and read about him, and that was plenty — and too much. War lord. Crime boss. Gangster. The papers changed his description with each thing he was accused of. Yet he had never been convicted of a crime. And he was something close to a loving father. Had to be. Dan was the proof of that. So which man was I going to talk to that afternoon? And how would I be received?

If You're not too busy, could You put in a good word for me, Lord? I'll try not to ask for more favors. But You know that's probably impossible, especially now, don't You?

Winnie was keeping sentry duty between the two rooms. She scowled and glared at Dan, tapped her shoe, then pointed to the empty seat in the fourth row of her classroom. He didn't cower as others would, which showed great good sense and some courage. Winnie's glare could make grown men shiver. She was steel and sharp tongue on the outside, but I knew her better, and she was nothing like her façade. She put that on because she had a role to play, discipline to keep, and an image to uphold. On the inside, she was mush. Mostly. Oh, all right, sometimes. But, then, if truth must be told, only with me.

As Dan slipped into his seat, she tugged me into the corridor. "Where did you find him?"

Well, here was a conundrum. My promise to Dan versus my best friend and confidante. If I hoped to help Richard, I'd first need her help. She could cover for me. She had a steel-trap brain that mirrored her

64

steely surface, and was razor-sharp, much sharper than most noodle-brained men we knew. And I had always been able to count on her in any situation. But. . .

"I made a promise to Dan not to tell anyone."

"It's that important?"

"Yes, I think it is."

"Okay. Just let me know if you need me."

"How about this afternoon?"

I filled her in on the background of what she didn't know about the morning's goings-on, but still didn't say anything about seeing Richard in the garden. I had to think about that on my own, try to figure out if I really had seen him. *Care to give me a little nudge, here, Lord?*

"Oh, Aggie! This is so dreadful for you. But have you ever stopped to think that Josiah might be right? Perhaps the simplest answer is the best answer."

"I don't know that blaming Richard is the simplest answer. It's the easiest one. But is it, truly, the best one?"

She looked at me with great, good affection. "I've always trusted your intuition, Aggie, and I will now."

"Thank you."

"Even though I don't like him, Richard is your friend; and we should always be loyal to our friends."

She straightened her shoulders and I realized that she was being exactly that — loyal to her friend. Me. How truly wonderful that was.

"So," Winnie asked, "what's this about this afternoon? What help do you need?"

"I have to talk to him."

"Him?"

"Dan's father."

"Saints and angels!"

"Can you take my afternoon chapel duty? I've been assigned to polish the altar."

"I'll get a novice to do it. I'm going with you. You'll need all the support you can get to face Vincent Gaetano Ricci."

CHAPTER FIVE

The car should have had a sign on it that read: *Stay Out of My Way.* It was a Cadillac and panther-like. Low. Black. Sleek. Stealthy. Where others rattled, this purred. But purred its power.

My steps faltered and I tugged on Winnie's skirt. "I don't think I can do this."

She whipped her skirt out of my hand. "You can do anything. Especially with your policeman cousin watching."

How I kept my head perfectly still was anyone's guess — or the Reverend Mother's teaching: *We do not show surprise.* The royal *we.* "Josiah is here? Where?"

Winnie gave an almost imperceptible nod towards a clunker of a car about a half block behind the panther. "Trying too hard to hide," she said. "Stands out like a rhino in a pride of lions."

Close enough to what I'd been thinking. Even so, I had missed them. Now that Winnie pointed them out, I realized there were three noodle-brains in the car. Josiah sat in the front, in the passenger's seat, a real step up in the police force, obviously. He glowered in our direction. But there was more satisfaction in that glower than I liked. He might be a good man at heart, but he was ambitious. Perhaps too ambitious. It meant he could be careless. And callous. And try too hard to please others at the expense of truth. That realization wasn't palatable. I wasn't perfect, the Lord knew, but I tried to find truth in everything. And right now the truth was that both Richard DelVecchio and Dante Ricci needed my help and I was being a coward, not wanting to face Dan's famous . . . um, infamous . . . father.

Shoulders back. Eyes forward. The Reverend Mother's voice in my ear: *Hands behind your apron bib so no one sees them tremble.*

"That-a-girl, Sister Agnes," Winnie said. "Into the jaws of death you go . . ."

"Winnie!"

"Sorry. Poor joke."

"Apology accepted. Wish me luck."

"You won't need it. I'm right behind you."

Behind, not beside; but close enough.

The back door opened as we approached, and I could see Dante bouncing up and down on the seat as his father got out. The resemblance was startling. The adult version of Dante was Vincent Gaetano Ricci. He had curly light brown hair and a square face. Only the dark stubble on his cheeks hardened him. That, and the turned-down brows over astonishing light hazel eyes. But where Dan's eyes were sparkling clear on the gloomiest day, these, I had a feeling, could be thunderous on the clearest day. Or perhaps I was wrong, because when he turned for a moment to look at his son, there was such deep affection that his gaze was that of a loving father.

"What has this mischief-maker gotten himself into now, Sister?" Vincent asked.

"Nothing." Oh, good grief! That was a croak! Me, a respected Roman Catholic nun, croaking like some new spring peeper. "I just thought that he could help Richard." And that was nearly a sob. *Get a grip, Aggie! You're not going to be much help to anyone like this.* And he was grinning at my discomfort. Grinning. Into the jaws of death, indeed.

"Shall we start again, Sister?"

"I think I shall." I extended my hand, and, surprise showing on his face, he took it. "I'm Sister Mary Agnes, Mr. Ricci. Richard DelVecchio's friend."

"It's Vincent, Sister. And ditto."

"Then will you swear to me that Richard is not involved in this morning's horror . . . or in anything illegal?"

"Ah, Sister, you of all people should know that it is not good to swear."

Well, he had me there. I noticed, however, that he hadn't answered the question. Not a good sign.

"But," he added, "I will tell you that I know he had nothing to do with this child's death. And that is all I'm going to tell you."

From the look of him — the no-nonsense set to his mouth, the stubborn gleam of warning in his eyes — that was all I was going to get. Surely, it was enough. But not for the police. They would need much, much more than Vincent Ricci's word. I, however, did not. And that made me much more at ease with this formidable man.

"Then perhaps we could talk in private about a simple matter?"

His brows rose perceptively. "With the cops looking on? Is anything that simple?"

"After this morning's tragedy, perhaps never again."

As Dan stared wide-eyed out the back window, I led his father down the sidewalk a bit, away from most of the bustle of parents and milling children, away from Josiah and his colleagues. With us came a couple of hard, large, strong-looking men, one walking in front of Vincent, one behind, each swiveling his gaze from side to side, taking in everything, and, I was certain, each offering his body to protect this man. *Lord, what have I gotten myself into? Stay close, too, okay?*

"I'd like to ask you if Dante could help Richard."

"Dante? How can he help? I'm doing everything I can to make sure Richard gets out on bail."

"I was certain of that. Your generosity to our parish and parishioners has always been appreciated."

"But not by everyone, right, Sister?"

Now why did Reverend Mother's face pop into my mind at that moment? And how did Vincent Ricci know this? Or was he merely fishing for information? I could have confirmed his supposition, but Mother Frances and I were cut from the same cloth — long black wool in the winter and long black multi-layered gauze in the summer. We might not see eye to eye, nor stand nose to nose, but I owed her the loyalty and respect of her office, if not herself.

"You of all people know the world, sir, and the different perceptions in it. Not all would agree with your methods or your intentions. But I must admit that your generosity here at the convent has helped dozens of people in these darkest days."

"Even if no one knows it."

"That is your intent, is it not?"

"Yes."

"Good. I've always thought that Saint Luke was a bit contradictory about hiding lights under baskets. After all, the Pharisees wanted the whole world to see what they did, and the Good Lord condemned them for that."

"Sister, that kind of thinking could get you into a lot of trouble."

Darn my socks! He was too right for comfort. "Sorry. I get carried away. We were talking about Dante and Richard."

"Shoot."

Oh, heavens! My whole body jerked at that expression and Vincent Ricci's expression changed to one of chagrin.

"Sorry, Sister Agnes. Just an expression."

I decided to ignore both his expression and the bulges under the bodyguards' coats. But a shivering had taken up permanent residence in my bones. One more reason to get the answers to the dilemma that had been dropped on our doorstep this morning. But first . . .

"Dante loves Richard," I said, "and misses

him. He feels helpless right now, and even at his young age he needs to feel as if he has some power. He would find that power if you would allow him to be a part of what you're doing."

Vincent tilted his head to the right and stared at me; then, as if he'd judged my intentions from my eyes — as I was doing with his — he nodded. "What did you have in mind?" he asked. When I told him about feeding Richard's rabbits, he grinned broadly. "Good plan, Sister. I've got plenty of new spring vegetables on the farm — the kind rabbits like — and we can get real pellets to feed those hairy beasts. I'll have Dan begin this afternoon."

This time, he took his hand out of his pocket and held it out to me. When I took it in farewell, he withdrew it and tipped his hat. My eyes widened, and he winked at me.

"One thing, Sister. Until this is cleared up, Dante will have his own bodyguard. Perhaps more. You will see one. You will not see the others, but they will be there. Their orders are to protect Dante, all the children, and the nuns. The priests will have to take care of themselves."

"Surely that's not necessary."

"We do what is prudent, and that is not always what is necessary. Good day to you."

It was when he was turning to go back to the car that I wondered if God was on vacation. Josiah and the other two hulks from the clunker car came at him from three directions. Ten years ago I'd have bopped Josiah on the nose, and my fingers still itched to do just that. But it was best that I fold them peacefully in prayer behind my apron bib. I did, however, take one step closer to my oncoming cousin.

"Officer Josiah Morgan, how nice to see you again," I said, but I deliberately put more half sour than whole sweetness in my tone. "Did you wish to ask me more questions?"

"Later, for sure, Aggie." My cocked brow and frown stopped him cold. "I mean, Sister Agnes. Right now, we've come for this lot."

Lord, give me strength!

"So you wish to speak with me, then," Vincent said.

"Yep. You can accompany me quietly, or we'll put you in handcuffs."

"You'll do no such thing!" I said, and gulped at my audacity. But I had to protect what I was bound to protect. "His son is watching."

"Not too soon to see what will happen if he chooses the wrong side, like his father has," Josiah spat.

"Nor too soon to see police strong-arm tactics."

Winnie put a gentle hand on my shoulder, then pinched to get my attention. "Sister Agnes, this is no time to draw a crowd."

Yet one was gathering and from the looks of things its mood was not on the side of the police. There had been a riot just a few weeks ago, and for much the same situation. Josiah stared at me; then his gaze darted from one face to another, from doors that were being flung open to cars that were stopping all along the block, and finally to heads being thrust out of windows. He was a new officer. Such quick action must have given him a moment's doubt that what he was doing was prudent, for he took one step back and shook his head at the officer who had taken out the handcuffs.

"Tell you what I'll do," Vincent said. "Just let me get my boy home and I'll follow you to the station house."

"You won't run?"

"Why should I? I have nothing to run from."

"Okay," Josiah said. "We'll follow close behind." He motioned to his cronies, turned quickly, and got into the clunker, waiting for Vincent.

"Sisters." Vincent addressed both myself

and Winnie. "I apologize for this ridiculous display of bravado. I hope we meet in better circumstances next time." He got into his own car, ruffled his son's hair, said a few words to him, and settled back as the car left, purring as it went. Josiah's car belched and bucked as it drew up behind, and anyone could see that if Vincent wanted to get away, there would be no match between his car and the police car.

Winnie slipped next to me and we watched as Richard's replacement driver slowed enough to keep Josiah and the others close behind him. Then we walked up the cinder path to the convent.

"What happened back there?" Winnie asked.

"I told him my plan. He agreed."

"Not that."

"He seems so normal."

"With two armed bodyguards and another as a driver? Are you insane?" She huffed up the path. "And don't evade the issue, Aggie. Not with me. I know there was something more."

The most observant eyes in the world, she had. "All right. But not here. The chapel, just before dinnertime."

She nodded and turned to go to the right and her own chores in the school, while I was headed for the parlor where I was slated to sweep the carpets and polish the brass.

After that, before I could meet Winnie, I had two things to do. First was to check out the contents of the package Richard had given me that morning. Second was to read the note that Vincent Gaetano Ricci had surreptitiously slipped into my palm.

CHAPTER SIX

Another of our novices, Sister Mary Angelica, pulled open the entry door before I had time to lay my hand on the knob. "This morning. So much commotion," she greeted. "So tense. Everyone."

I had gotten used to her habit of talking in pieces of sentences — as if she were always in a rush. Which, considering the work the novices had to do in the convent, more likely than not, she was. When Angelica first showed up at St. Catherine's, Winnie had opined that the poor mite probably once hoped to be a cloistered nun, had practiced silence too long, and now couldn't quite join phrases together.

Angelica leaned out into the crisp late-afternoon air, heartily snapped a cotton cloth a few times and dislodged a cloud of dust from it, then closed the door. "Tables, done. Bookshelves, next."

She followed on my heels down the corridor that led to the communal library, the offices, and beyond to the back stairs and the kitchen. Silence reigned, except for the *clack, clack, clack* of our heavy steel-tipped brogans on the wooden floor.

And one very deep voice coming from the Reverend Mother's office.

I stopped in mid-stride and Angelica slammed into me with a soft, "Ooof!" I pulled her around to my side, and jerked my head in the direction of the murmurings.

"Man," Sister Angelica whispered.

I rolled my eyes. But I wasn't stupid. I also whispered, "Good guess."

"No guess. He came."

"Who came?"

She threaded her fingers inside the neck edge of her bib and tugged it out. "Collar."

Good grief! Monsignor Delaney, or another emissary from the chancery? Already? It certainly wasn't one of our priests. Even the pretty but obtuse Sister Angelica would recognize one of them. All the more reason to hurry up to my room before implications could be made that I had drawn him in. Of course, I hadn't. I hadn't drawn Richard in, either, as I recall. Or that poor girl in the root cellar. But that hadn't stopped some sisters' gleeful or outraged glances, or

Reverend Mother's full-blown blow-up. And I'd hoped with time she would calm down. Not much hope of that now.

I looked to the ceiling and projected my thoughts to the realm beyond. *Too busy straightening out the rest of the world this afternoon? No time for our piddling problem? Oh, dear Lord, please keep me sane. Better yet, keep the Reverend Mother sane. We could all use a little vacation. You give us a little rest from our labors, here, and I promise — two more decades of the rosary. Make that four. Just tack them on to what I owe You.*

I was going to be on my knees until His Second Coming.

St. Catherine's students all say the Reverend Mother has bat ears. And a lioness's roar. Her office door was old and solid, but her less-than-lioness, treacle-sweet, "Sister Agnes!" carried loud and clear. I'm amending the students' description. Bat ears. Lioness's roar. Coyote eyes. She could see through oak. We were all doomed.

"Oh, dear," Sister Mary Angelica commiserated — or worried. It was pretty much the same thing. The young novice gave me a pitying glance — Or was that the beginning of a snicker? — then hurried down the corridor, where she slipped into the library, cotton battle gear in hand to rid the convent of dust. Out of the line of fire. Would that I had that privilege.

The inner sanctum door whooshed open, and there she stood, her back to the room behind her, glaring. Should I just drop to my knees and say, *I'm sorry,* and get it over with? Or would the penance be more severe than forgiveness?

"We require your presence."

The royal *we* again. First the worldwide Dust Bowl, now this. "Yes, Mother."

She indicated a chair. I slipped gratefully into it, and peeked at the cleric to my right. Man with collar? Angelica was a woman of few words, and fewer brains it seemed, but even she could not have missed the red beanie on the cleric's head and the red sash at his waist. A monsignor, but not Monsignor Delaney. Far more important than that. I'd only seen pictures of the gentleman seated in the chair facing the Reverend Mother's desk. Monsignor Robert Grace. A rising star in the Archdiocese of Providence, and one of the young administrators assigned to facilitate the changing of the guard after Bishop Hickey died last October. In the gloom of the fading afternoon sunlight, he looked tall. But, then, anyone would look tall compared to someone — me, perhaps? — who had the stature of a shoemaker's elf.

I crossed my ankles, properly. Tucked my hands behind my apron bib and folded them, properly. Waited at the edge of my seat — not at all to my liking — but properly. It was only my heart that wasn't acting properly. It was a wonder I could still breathe, it was beating that fast.

He extended his hand and I quickly kissed his ring, not daring to look him full in the face.

"Sister Mary Agnes," he said. "Bishop-designate Keough sends his greetings and commends you on your quick thinking this morning."

What?! Oh, I hoped that hadn't been heard. Or that my face hadn't registered my surprise. But what he'd said sounded suspiciously like a compliment, and I wasn't used to that, not at all. Mother Frances was surely swallowing bile.

"We are certain all of our sisters would have acted the same in a similar situation," she said.

Well, never let it be said that she wasn't quick to rise to the occasion.

He cocked his eyebrow. "Let us pray there are no other similar situations, Mother."

"Oh, no. Indeed not."

There, shot in my direction, was that glare again, quickly doused. Unmistakably clear.

If it did happen again, I could be certain of that transfer to St. Finbar's in Exeter with its icy winters.

As Mother Frances hurried to chase away the oncoming gloom by lighting the gas lamps on the wall and the one on her desk, Monsignor Grace watched her progress around the room. Then, when she was once again seated, he gracefully and concisely outlined the reason for his unexpected and out-of-character visit.

"The Bishop will be ordained on May twenty-second."

My birthday, but I didn't see any way to slip that into the conversation.

"He wishes this blot on the soul of the Church rectified, the miscreant caught, and justice done. And he wants all onus removed from this parish before the festivities."

Dear God, don't let me show my fear and surprise. How in the world did he expect that to happen, in — God, save us — only seven weeks? Unless, he and the Bishop, like the police, were ready to throw Richard to the wolves?

I hastily appealed, "The police have . . ."

"The police have their job to do to. They may have in mind the best interests of the people of Providence, but they do not protect and defend the best interests of the

Church. We must. Bishop Keough expects complete cooperation. From all of you at the convent and the rectory." He looked me straight in the eye, and I didn't flinch. *Good work, Aggie!* "We at the Chancery have had good reports about you, Sister Agnes. Your affinity for the people of this parish and the children in your school has not gone unnoticed. You seem to have good instincts. Use them. Find out what you can, Sister." He turned to include Mother Frances. "You sisters are the best information conduit the Church has. I ought to know. We have two Sisters of Mercy in my family." Once more, he looked directly at me. "If anyone can find out exactly what's what, you can. I have faith in you. So does our new Bishop."

He rose and picked up his fedora. Mother Frances rose, too, and followed him to the door. I trooped along behind her. I couldn't help but think of him as the Pied Piper and wondered if the notes from his pipe would lead to salvation or doom.

"And," he continued, "you have a vested interest in this, too, don't you, Sister Agnes? A personal interest. Not only because of one of your students, but also because of a lifelong friend?"

"Yes, your Eminence."

Now I knew why he was an up-and-coming cleric. His own information conduit must be formidable. Perhaps there was a modern-day version of Sherlock's Baker Street Irregulars here in the city of Providence — Grace's Broad Street Irregulars — and now I was a member.

He smiled and patted my shoulder. "Remember Holy Mother the Church. The truth will protect Her and all of Her innocent communicants." He took two steps towards the door, then turned. "Oh, yes. Whatever you find out, you must be certain that you deliver the information to me first."

I darned near choked. "Before the police?"

"Yes. We can't afford to be in the dark at this critical time in the Diocesan transition. We cannot tolerate the press badgering us the way they did today." He turned to Mother Frances. "Speaking of the dark — have you no electricity in this office?"

"No, your Eminence," she said.

"But the rest of the convent, surely."

"Not yet. Though the rest of the city has been wired for years, the Church has a long list and, because of the Depression, not much money. They completed wiring the church last month. The rectory is next. We sisters can wait our turn."

"Perhaps — if this is all cleared up quickly — you will not have to wait much longer."

I know nuns are supposed to be quiet and submissive, receiving with joy all that is given to them, and never questioning Church authority. But, holy cow, even Reverend Mother should have heard that there was more to that statement than a heartfelt wish. There was a bargain implied in those few words. Or was I reading something into them that wasn't there?

Well, in for a penny, in for a pound.

"Monsignor?"

If he were surprised that I had the temerity to speak up as he was leaving, he didn't show it.

"Yes, Sister Agnes?"

"This morning I had to send one of the students to fetch a policeman. That took a great deal of time. Perhaps we could better serve the Church and you if we had a telephone to contact you?" With emphasis on the *you*.

Mother Frances gasped. "Sister! Really, you cannot . . ."

He waved her quiet and contemplated my demeanor. Must have been just fine because his mouth pursed just a bit, as if he were trying to keep from smiling. He lost. Smile won. "Sister, that is a well-wrought plan. I will attend to it." He bowed slightly to Mother Frances. "Good day to you."

86

She gave a deep curtsy, almost a genuflection. And I braced myself for her next explosion of displeasure.

She glared at me and I had visions of Christ, just before he tipped over the first table in the temple. "Mary McBride's. You and Sister Winifred. Now."

Uh-oh. Reverend Mother had been around Sister Angelica too often. "But . . ."

She held up her hand in that age-old police gesture, and I shut my mouth, fast.

"You have said quite enough for one day. And you've been involved in far too much. A dead girl. The administrator coming here. And you aren't satisfied with that. No, you have to practically beg for a telephone. Rather, what you did could only be described as . . . as a bribe! You bribed a monsignor to have one installed. And to get wiring in this convent." She rounded her desk, opened the middle drawer, and pulled out a file folder. "I don't doubt you'll get both." She stood there for a moment with her head bowed, then her whole frame trembled. "I will never understand. I've never asked the Chancery for anything. But you . . ." She raised her head, took a deep breath, but did not meet my gaze. "Sister Agnes, you are not a good nun. You do not even come close to the minimum meekness of character a nun should have. Yet, he — a monsignor in the work of the Lord — seemed to like you."

There was so much sadness and perplexity in those words and her posture that I ached for her. I wished I could reassure her that I could someday, with a little more effort, become the nun she wished I were. But could I? Truly? Some things were best left unsaid. So, I merely stood there, waiting, and it wasn't long before she sighed and lowered herself into her hard, wooden chair.

"In the meantime," she said, "you have an assignment from Monsignor Grace and, apparently, the new Bishop. Attend to it." She held out the file. "The police sent over these photographs so I could show them to the other sisters or our parishioners. The new Bishop seems to want you to do that. So, you shall. They are rather gruesome, but the poor girl's face is clearly shown and recognizable. So are her clothes. If she was a member of this parish, Mary McBride and her boarders will know her, perhaps recognize her clothing, or know of someone else you should talk to."

"Sister Winifred and I will miss Vespers."

"I excuse you both. And I shall see to it that your meal is kept in the warming oven until you return."

"Yes, Mother. Thank you."

"Go."

I went. Directly to Winnie, who was helping set the dining room table for our supper. All the while, I held my hand against the side of my skirt. "Burning a hole in my pocket" had only been a phrase — until now. I was certain the darned secret thing that was in there rustled as I walked. But how was I to get to it or Richard's packet now? In private? For, although I trusted Winnie with my life — and my soul — I wasn't certain she was supposed to see what was contained in either of them.

CHAPTER SEVEN

Winnie and I walked from the convent down four blocks of triple-decker houses, several of them boarded up and abandoned. They were surrounded by small, sad piles of smashed personal belongings. The most pathetic of them were the toys, ground into the dirt, as if the kids who had owned them had given up their dreams of childhood and beaten it and their toys down into the earth with the same force that life had beaten down their parents. It was a hellish way to live. Some, however, were surviving, and I prayed those who had been forced out had found a means to keep body and soul alive.

Groups of young men, not too much older than the boys we taught, were gathered at the street corners and each called out in a friendly manner, *Good evening, Sisters,* as we passed. As I waved, nodded, and spoke to a few of them, I wondered if we sisters — and perhaps the priests in the parish —

could organize them to help clean up the mess that this Depression was making in our neighborhood. And maybe we could find some funds to pay them. *When pigs fly, Aggie.* Unless — now that was a thought. The first chance I got, I'd put my idea into action.

But I tucked those thoughts in the back of my head as I caught Winnie up on that afternoon's many twists and turns. Amazingly, she listened quietly to my description of the meeting with Monsignor Grace, only snorting once or twice. Okay, four times. But that was quiet, for her.

When I completed my description of Mother Frances' reaction to all that had happened, Winnie sneaked one small peek at me, then tucked her arm around my shoulders, gave an imperceptible squeeze, and withdrew it. Small comfort, but, as she well knew, very welcome.

"How long have we been here?" she asked.

"Nineteen months."

"Only five months short of two years."

I hadn't calculated it in a long time. But Winnie was right to do so now. I had to let the reality of the situation sink in for a minute. And the reality was that change was imminent. Our change. Darn my socks! Because nuns rarely stayed longer than three years in any convent, Mother Frances would have to find another place for both of us. So far, Winnie and I had served together most of our years since we left the novitiate. We'd been separated only three times, and each time we transferred, the Lord must have worked His ways to get us back together. But now . . . Oh, it was too bleak to think about.

"After what just happened," Winnie said, "I'll lay you dollars to donuts that Mother Frances is plotting her revenge."

"Winnie!"

"Well, what would you call it? She came very close to describing you as the worst nun in the world. That's a blot on her ability as a teacher and her reputation as an exemplar. She's going to want to hide you away somewhere. And for sure we aren't going to be companions again. It's her recommendation that the mother house relies on, after all."

"Exeter for me."

"That would be my guess."

"I shouldn't complain, I guess. After all, I'll still have a home."

"A cold one."

"But a home, nonetheless." I shuddered at what I had avoided by my decision to join the convent. "Look around you, Winnie. We have a home, and so many others don't even have that." We were both lost in our own thoughts for a few moments. But mine were dreadful, soul-searching ones. "Am I really all that bad?"

"Of course not. You've just had a string of bad luck."

"Right. Starting with all that wasted time I spent in my cradle."

"As long as it isn't cradle to grave."

Just then an unmistakably strong and deep, yet female, voice split the tension. "Well, 'tis nice to see you two, 'tis! I was expecting that wee mite, don't you know?" The small lilt to the cadence gave stark evidence of its origins in the Emerald Isle. Twice removed. It was Mary McBride's grandfather who had made the trek over the roiling waters. But each of his descendants kept a bit of the brogue, in respect and pride. It was so unlike my family, whose ancestors couldn't wait to shake the sod from their boots and become completely Americanized — if that were possible with the noodle-brained contingent we women had to put up with. They saluted the flag with one hand, and punched out the Americans with the other. God help them, for they didn't help themselves.

"And a good evening to you," Winnie said,

before plopping down beside Mary on the two-seater wooden swing someone long ago had fastened to the roof of Mary's porch. "And which mite might that be that you're expecting?"

"The little angel, o'course. She's been in and out of here all day, first bringing soup with that other novice, then later, the news of what went on over at the convent. Bad times. Bad, bad times. And I hear tell 'twas you in the middle of all that ruckus, Sister Agnes. Must have been dreadful, that."

"That and everything since," Winnie said.

"Oh, I don't doubt it, a'tall," Mary said. "I hear tell that the man himself paid you a visit in that great big touring car of his." She laughed a bit of a cackle. "I'll bet yev had your fill o' dreadful things."

I pulled up a small, white wicker rocker and lowered myself into it gently. The last time I'd been here, the chair I'd chosen decided to disintegrate under me, it was that old. Once I realized that this one wasn't going to turn into kindling wood, I relaxed — as much as I could. I thought to correct Mary about Vincent Ricci's visit, but decided mum's-the-word was the best policy in this situation, at this time.

I could, however, respond circumspectly. "Dreadful? Ah, but it would be more dreadful if we couldn't find out who the poor girl was. And it would be a sin if the miscreant isn't brought to justice. So, we all have to do our part to help."

"Which, I suppose, is why the monsignor was at the convent. And, perhaps, why you're here?" she asked.

When I first came to St. Catherine's, it astonished me how quickly news got around the neighborhood, because it was such a huge, diverse kind of place. It housed, among others, Italians, French Canadians, Portuguese, Eastern European Jews, and three Greek families — the kinds of groups you wouldn't think would communicate one with the other. But now I knew there was some kind of tribal drum system, and — credit where credit is due — the shaman beating the quickest and loudest was right here, all smiles and grey fluffy curls and deep blue eyes. I wondered how quickly the gist of our visit this evening would be passed from one porch to the other, from one ear to the next mouth. Yes, I had been right in keeping my opinion of Vincent Ricci to myself.

"Mother Frances sent us to see if you had any information that would help in the investigation," Winnie said.

"She wants to keep the police from invading the convent again," I explained. "They totally disrupted her efficient routine and caused the delay of classes. We can't have that happen again." *Now, You know that's not exactly a lie, Lord. Not exactly the truth, either, I know. But it's better than broadcasting the real reason, don't You think? Monsignor Grace would be none too pleased to have his mission from the Bishop as a topic for neighborhood gossip, after all. But if You think I should do penance for the half-truth, just give me a sign. What's that You say? On safe grounds? I thought so.*

"How can I help?" Mary asked.

"Not just you. Everyone in the house might be useful in identifying the young woman."

"Some are already asleep. But I'm certain the others wilt be greatly pleased ta take part in this investigation. 'Tis a real adventure for poor folks who don't have much excitement in their lives. And you could come back to talk to the others another day, perhaps?"

"To add a little more adventure to otherwise boring days?" I asked.

We all chuckled, and agreed that was just the ticket they needed to spark their energy. We made a date for late the next morning, a Saturday, when school would be out. Then we began the tedious task of trying to find out who the victim was.

The first two boarders were of a kind as Mary — between fifty and sixty-five years old, with porcelain complexions (and I really wanted to know how they did that, because mine was like a fuzzy peach), grey hair turning to white, and sparkling eyes: one set was grey, the other brown.

Kathleen Mallory took a quick look and then just as quickly averted her grey eyes. Such drama, for crying out loud! The woman had been a chicken plucker in her day. I had plucked a chicken for my Gran once — and once was more than enough. So, I knew what a bloody mess it could be. Surely this woman had seen her share of gore. And the crime scene photo didn't show all that much blood.

"I don't know the girl," Kathleen said, "but the blouse is one of ours."

"St. Catherine's?" I asked.

"Yes, and no. Yes, it's a St. Catherine's shirt. About five years ago they changed the collar and buttons. I picked out all the embroidery from forty-seven shirts you nuns had in the storage room. Learned patience whilst plucking those feathers for thirty years, I did, so I was the head picker under Mother Urvine. So it's probably one of the ones I picked."

Winnie was about as incredulous as a twelve-year-old whose parents still talked about Santa Claus and the Easter Bunny. "How can you tell? You didn't see the photo for more than a few seconds."

"Long enough to see there are no bits of thread in the pickings part. Leona Marsh left thread, and she was the only other one who worked with me."

"Then what's the *no* part? If it's a St. Catherine's shirt, it's a St. Catherine's shirt."

"Yes, it's a St. Catherine's shirt; and, yes, it's one of the ones I altered. But, *no,* it isn't just a St. Catherine's shirt. It might be one of the ones the parish gave me to take to my granddaughters as payment for my labors. My daughter-in-law Myra — who doesn't have the time or space for me, she says, when there's that great, sunlit room in the corner of the second floor that would be just perfect, but . . ."

"Now, Kathleen," Mary McBride interrupted, gently but firmly, "the good sisters don't have time for that."

"Well, somebody should. It's a crying shame! Nobody has time for the old anymore. Nobody except Mary, here."

She was right. I should spend more time

with her and the others. We all should. But Mother Frances had her schedules and very little time was allotted to the Kathleen Mallorys of this world. I wondered if this wasn't a perfect place to start spreading the Lord's work. I'd just have to speak to Mother Frances about that. Or, perhaps, Monsignor Grace? *Yes, I know, Lord, that's a devilish thought.* But a good one!

"You were saying about Myra?" I prodded.

"The last time she was here she mentioned that she had cleaned out the girls' closets and brought all the old things to the rumble sale you sisters had last November."

"Rumble sale?" What in the world was that, I wondered?

"You know," Kathleen insisted, "where they pile all those clothes in a rumble and sell 'em for practically nothing."

"Oh! A rummage sale."

"Rummage? Nope. We old ones always called it a rumble sale. Anyhow," Kathleen continued, "it might have been Myra's. But you'd have to ask her if her shirts were among the things she donated."

"Thank you, Mrs. Mallory," I said. "That's a big help."

But that was the last help we got. Not one of the elderly ladies who were awake had any idea who the girl was. Ruth Pelmet, however, had her own opinion, but it wasn't a kind one. "Probably one a them sidewalk gals," she said. "They allays end up with more than they bargained for."

Winnie rushed out of Mary's house as if her heels were on fire. "Sidewalk gals! I know we're supposed to use discernment in all things, including our association with others; but we're also supposed to love thy neighbor. There wasn't much love in that sentiment."

Winnie had such a big heart — except where Richard was concerned. But he was a man and could take care of himself. This young girl obviously couldn't. Hence, her outrage at one — all right, two — reactions to her. She'd walk it off in half a block. I hoped.

"With all that malice, you would think one of them could have dredged up some knowledge of that girl, even if it were only gossip," she said, fatigue and exasperation apparent in every syllable.

"We've only just begun to unravel the mystery of this child," I pointed out. "At least we have one lead."

"Yes. To a rumble sale. Some lead. Anybody could have taken that shirt."

"Maybe. But I have a good feeling that

we'll find out who and what we're looking for." I yawned, and at the same time my stomach growled displeasure. "It's been a long day."

"Yep. A dead body, police overrunning the convent, Dante's father. . ." She stopped suddenly in the middle of the sidewalk, two houses from Mary McBride's triple-decker. "In all the commotion, I forgot! What happened between you and that mobster?"

"Winnie, as you echoed the Lord, love thy neighbor."

"I try to love him. I just hate what he does."

"You don't know what he does. And that's beside the point. He's Dante's father."

"Right. And a mobster."

"A supposed mobster."

"They use the word *alleged* in the papers."

"Alleged, then. In any case, the police haven't yet convicted him of any crimes."

"*Yet* was the important word in that sentence. You know it's only a matter of time."

She tugged at my skirt, and the secrets in my pocket rustled. I cringed, but she didn't seem to notice me or the rustling.

"Cut the pigeon droppings," she said. "This is your old pal talking. What happened between the two of you this afternoon? When you shook hands, it looked as if he had thrust a hot poker through your heart."

Best friends since that first day in the novitiate, that's what Winnie and I were to each other. I loved her, but I also knew that she was more persistent than a bee looking for pollen. She'd be buzz, buzz, buzzing around me forever, so it was a waste of time to hide anything from her.

"Not through my heart. In my hand." I reached inside my pocket and brought out the crackling paper from Vincent Gaetano Ricci. "He slipped me this under the cover of his handshake."

"What's it say?"

"I have no idea."

"What!?" She took up her right field stance, leaned forward, and planted her hands on her hips. "Mayetta Morgan!" She always reverted to my birth name when she was truly exasperated. "You haven't opened it yet?"

"When have I had the time? He gave it to me a little before four-thirty. Monsignor Grace inserted himself into the next twenty minutes. Mother Frances dressed me down for ten minutes after that. I took four or five minutes to get you, another ten to help pack up the leftovers for the old folks. We've been at Mary McBride's for almost an hour. Now we're on our way back to the convent. In the cold and gloomy March dark, I might add. And without supper."

"There's a street light in the middle of the next block. Go. Now. Read the thing."

"You don't want to see what's in it?"

"Are you daft? A secret note from the Providence Don? Handed to you right under the twitching nose of your cousin, the cop? Of course I do. But he gave it to you, so I'll wait and you can tell me later. If there's anything to tell."

True to her word, she waited, but not patiently as she shuffled from one foot to the other, and glared at me from out of the gloom. I sighed and hurriedly turned over the paper. It wasn't really a paper, but a small envelope. The address only said, *Mister Ricci.* There was no stamp. But it had been opened. I lifted the flap carefully and slipped out the one sheet of paper. The faint light from the street lamp cast a yellowish glow, so it was difficult to read. I had to hold it up and cock my head to get a good look at it. Even then, it was difficult.

More than that, it was frightening! And what it contained had a great deal to do with us, God help us.

CHAPTER EIGHT

There goes that voice again. *The Lord helps those who help themselves.* I'll work at it — starting now.

Vincent Ricci's correspondent had good penmanship. The sloping letters and round style called to mind the years of teaching penmanship to girls and boys who would rather practice sacrifice bunting than Palmerian loops and ovals. Only one boy in all my years of teaching had mastered the style, and he had become a priest. None since. But this note was pure Palmer, and beautiful Palmer, at that.

Sir,
I know your son Dante and he's a great little boy. I left this in his lunch bucket because I thought I should tell you that there might be something terribly wrong at St. Catherine's. I'm trying to find out if I'm right in what I suspect. If I am, I

might need your help, but I don't want anyone to know that I'm snooping until I'm certain. I will contact you again.

"Well, look at that. It's not signed."

"It's not what?"

"Signed." I held up the note. "Come see."

Winnie hiked up her skirt, bolted to my side, and snatched the note out of my hand. As I had done, she squinted as she read it. "Huh! No self-respecting male would use the word *terribly* or all these wordy sentences! Obviously written by a female. And judging from the penmanship, a Catholic-educated one, at that."

"My thoughts, exactly."

"She wasn't in any hurry, either. No splotches of ink, the kind fountain pens make when scraped hurriedly across the page."

"Which means she wasn't a youngster."

"You think not?" Winnie asked.

"When was the last time you saw one of your students with a fountain pen? I've never seen anything but pencils."

"Our students aren't rich."

"Dante is, but even he uses a pencil. And notice the paper. It's low quality and even in this light it looks yellowish."

"That might be this light," Winnie pointed out.

"It might."

"By your skeptical tone, you don't think so." She studied my face, then her eyebrows shot up to the heavens. I never could school my features, especially from her. "You know who wrote this!"

"Not exactly. I think — and I know this is going way out on a limb — but it seems reasonable to me that this was written by that poor mite I found this morning."

"That's a big limb, Aggie. There are myriad permutations and combinations you would have to eliminate before you could get to that solution."

There she went with the math stuff again. She was a whiz at math. And science. I, however, stuck to the finer arts, and the kind of logical deduction that could be derived from classical literature. I could hear Mother Frances and her "nuns are never pompous." I wasn't. Just analytical. Oh, bother! Even that sounded pompous. Perhaps it was. Perhaps not. After all, Plato might have postulated shadows on the wall of a cave, but he also threw light into the gloom. And if I were right about the author of this note, we were heading into dawn's early light. Then, if the saints and angels were with us, hopefully we'd have this mystery deciphered by half-past noon — tomorrow, I hoped.

"I know the complexities, Winnie. But please put doubt aside and just think about it. Why would Vincent Ricci get this note, at this time? I believe the world abounds in coincidence. But this much? No, it must be related to the murder." No one could mistake her stubborn expression. "Throw away your mathematics, for goodness sake!"

"Are you crazy? It's math that makes the world go round."

"No, according to the Savior, what makes the world go round is love." When she squinted her eyes and pursed her mouth the way she always did when she was perturbed, I figured two could play that game. "Darn my socks! Just think logically. You can do that. I saw you do it four years ago, December twelfth." Winnie's lips curved upward, if reluctantly. Well, at least she didn't bite my head off, so I jumped in where angels — everyone in the country knew the rest. "We've got this note. We've got its contents. And we've got what I found this morning. Add them all together, and what do we have?"

"A math equation."

"Winnie!"

"All right! Put the two together, stir them up, and out pops a murder and a warning."

"No. And yes."

"No and yes? I'm beginning to side with Mother Frances. Sometimes you are the most exasperating human being on the face of the earth."

"I am not! I know you. You're just ornery because you're hungry. Forget about food for five minutes and think with your brain synapses, not your alimentary canal."

"I bet you never thought you'd put those two phrases together in one sentence."

"Winnie, pay attention!"

"Supper's starting to congeal."

I stabbed at the paper. "Look, you got some of the ingredients in this puzzle — the note, its contents, and the dead girl I found. And you stirred them up; but when you dumped them out of the pan, you got them the wrong way round."

Hey! Maybe I did know how to cook, after all. Just not with actual food.

After a few moments, Winnie's demeanor changed, then she grinned as Plato's light finally illuminated the cave of her mind. "Ah, I get it now! Your gangster friend got the warning first and then the girl was murdered."

Still in the dark, but getting brighter. And

I had always thought Winnie's intelligence outshone mine. Maybe they were just different. "You're leaving something out."

She gave me the note and pulled my arm. "Now's the kind of situation that makes me wish I could swear! Tell me the rest of it on our way to supper. My stomach's been growling for twenty minutes."

I folded the note hurriedly and put it back into its envelope, then tucked it into my pocket. Before I could begin explaining my wunderkind deductions, however, two of our novice nuns hailed us. Sister Angelica was loaded down with two bags. "Leftovers from the kitchen for Mary McBride?" I asked. "You already brought over a ton of food this morning."

"Old linens," Mary Paul piped in. "Mother Frances has had us cleaning up a storm since her visitor left. Justina said she's never seen the like of it. I wonder what happened in Mother's office?"

Angelica chuckled. "Sister Agnes happened."

"Oh."

Mary Paul took two steps back, and almost tripped over a rusty bike tire. Guess she thought I was contagious.

"Well, we all have our work to do for Mother Frances," I said, and hoped my tone was cheery, not lethal. "Hurry right back. Curfew is coming on quickly. And she will not like it if you get back to the convent after lights-out."

"Unlike some I could mention," Mary Paul said, "we always obey the order's rules."

I wonder who she meant by that?

Winnie gave me no time to get back to our discussion. She bolted the last half block and made a straight beeline to the kitchen and warming oven. Supper was warmed-up soup line fare, and it was still Richard delicious. It was also silent. Justina saw to that. I couldn't even ask Winnie to pass the salt without being shushed by the elderly nun.

"Mother Frances does not wish you to speak until you've spoken to her."

Those were her words, and she was sticking to them as if they were Gospel, all the way to Mother Frances' office door, where she knocked once, then retreated.

"Come!"

Reverend Mother kept us standing while she finished up some paperwork, then locked it in her drawer. When she indicated the chairs in front of her desk, she surprised me, but I gratefully sat.

"What did you find?" she asked.

Uh-oh. I hadn't told anyone but Winnie about the note. And I hadn't given a thought about how I could divulge it without bringing more anger from Mother Frances. A good nun simply does not hide things from her Reverend Mother. Especially when she's dealing with someone the police describe as a mob leader. She might not call Vincent that, but she would think it.

"No one identified the girl," I said, crossing my fingers and struggling to cross my toes. Not in these brogans! Leaving out the note was technically a big evasion, but it couldn't be helped. Now, if only Winnie didn't give anything away.

"But there was one woman who recognized the blouse," Winnie quickly added, which helped to soften Mother Frances' frown. "Or thought she did. She remembered hours of careful picking of the threads in the embroidered school emblem. So, at least we have one lead."

"Good."

"We actually have two," I added. "Well, not exactly a lead." Frown, again. "Not all the residents were awake, so we probably should go back to talk with them."

"Probably? I'd think that was a definitely. I'll see to it that we have something to bring them tomorrow morning. You shall deliver it, and talk with those you did not talk to this evening."

"We will also need leave to follow up on another lead." I explained about Kathleen Mallory's daughter-in-law and the rummage sale items.

"All right. You may have the entire day tomorrow. But you must attend the five o'clock morning Mass and receive communion. The rest of your Saturday, you shall spend in solving this crime."

We were at the stairs when Winnie whispered, "She doesn't expect miracles, does she?"

"Why not? This is a Church founded upon miracles."

"But not murder."

"What do you call the cross?"

"Not murder on church grounds."

"I could mention St. . . ."

"Never mind!"

"I notice you didn't bring up the you-know-what."

"Neither did you."

"I didn't want to worry Mother Frances." She snorted. "Since when?"

"Since all we have is supposition."

"Sensible supposition."

"Thank you."

"Credit where due."

"Plus, I really didn't want to involve Vincent Ricci."

"That is one of the biggest whoppers you've ever told. What you want is for Mother Frances to be in the dark about his visit and his request for help." She started to laugh, and had to clamp her hand on her mouth so it didn't escalate. "Saints and angels, what a day. You've got the police looking to you for answers. And a gangster. And the Bishop. And Mother Frances. I don't know which one to fear the most if you can't get any answers."

"I fear the jury at Richard's trial." The tears came quicker than I expected and I used my apron to brush them away. "He's a good man, Winnie. A good friend. And I know in my heart that he didn't do this. It doesn't matter who asks for my help. It's Richard I'm doing this for."

"I'll keep him in my prayers tonight."

Her loyalty stunned me. I staggered a bit and mumbled a quick, "Thank you."

She gave a little wave and a good night before she entered her cell and closed the door.

Exhaustion settled in as soon as I entered my own cell and saw my welcoming cot. I sat on the edge and slipped off my brogans, intending to curl up on the top without undressing. And that's when I saw it. The small drawer in my washstand was not quite closed. But I had a routine every morning. Every drawer, every door — securely closed.

Heart pounding, I made a quick survey of the room. The dresser looked okay at first, but my one brush and comb were slightly off the doily I kept them on. I opened each drawer and simply stared at the contents.

They were not as I left them.

Fear is most definitely cold. It gripped me as I sank onto my cot. What was I going to do?

Someone had been in my cell, had opened my drawers, had searched through my things.

CHAPTER NINE

There might be something terribly wrong at St. Catherine's. That's what the note had said. And that's why Vincent Ricci had ordered bodyguards for the school — not only because of the murder. And certainly not because of the few break-ins and missing vegetables and meat.

I apologize to every noodle-brained Irishman in the world — all seven million of you. I have joined your ranks!

I had combined the place where the murder had occurred with the reason I was there in the first place, and assumed that they were connected. I might have been right. After all, what did we have, really?

Something terribly wrong.

Murder.

Missing vegetables and meat.

Break-ins.

But now we had this search. And that didn't fit with a few carrots and potatoes

115

and venison sausage. I had made a complete stew of things, and I had been completely wrong.

Hadn't I?

Headaches did not run in my family. We Morgan women braved through pain of every kind. The men needed a good pick-me-up to suffer through, and I wished I had a good slug of communion wine to stifle the pounding in my head as I tried to decipher what was going on.

It seemed on the surface to be a little thing. Just a hurried search, for God knew what. But it was more than just a hurried search. And only a nun would understand how totally outrageous this was.

I wanted to pound on the floor and scream down the house. I wanted to storm into every cell and give them the third-degree, the way they did in the moving pictures.

What I did was gag and splash water on my face, trying to calm down.

Never had this happened before, not in the fifteen months I'd been here. Not in all the years I'd been a nun had I heard of anyone's cell being searched, not even by the meanest-spirited Mother Superior. We nuns might not have all the luxuries of the world, but we had privacy. Unless permission was given, no one ever intruded. No one ever borrowed anything. Ha! There wasn't anything to borrow. There wasn't — but in this case only because of happenstance — anything to find.

That, of course, was coincidence. Had I not been harried all the afternoon and evening, I would have taken Richard's parcel and Vincent's note up to my cell. Since there were no locks on anything and there were only three standard drawers and one small one in my cell — as in every other cell — it would have been easy for someone to slip in and . . .

No! That was impossible. Correction, improbable. Not impossible. It was, after all, a house with no men. No locks, except at night. No guards at the doors, except for one old nun, slightly deaf and perhaps a trifle batty. No valuables to tempt those in need — and far too many were in need these awful days.

Darn my socks! I had just eliminated anyone from outside. But I shouldn't do that, of course, because Richard had managed to get in. So, if anyone desperately wanted to, then anyone could.

Yet . . .

Who could have done it?

That was the big question, wasn't it? The question Josiah thought was easily answered by pointing a finger at the only "bad" guy in the area. But this time Richard was behind bars, unless he was out on bail and wanted to get his package back.

A package I hadn't yet looked at.

Where was my head? Aching, aching, aching.

I pulled the small parcel out of my pocket and looked at it. Mary, Mother of God, the darned package would not stay still. Backwards thinking! The package stayed still. I moved. Or rather, my hands did. They shook and my brain refused to send the message to my fingers: *Just untie the darned string!*

Yes, I know, Lord! Terrible language. Seven "Hail Marys" before lights-out tomorrow.

I ended up ripping the green-and-white striped string with my teeth, then tore at the paper. I stuffed them both into my pocket. If someone was searching, he or she would have to search me to find anything.

Inside was a small box with tape on it. *Richard, if you ever get out of jail, I'm going to kill you.* More stuff for my pocket. I was going to crackle as I walked.

It was a pretty box. Imitation alligator covering, gold embossed letters. *Gisenti. Milano et Roma.* Pretty name, Gisenti. And inside? Diamonds? Pearls? Or just Italian gold?

Saints and angels! It didn't shine, although it was silver. Well, not exactly silver. My fingers trembled as they slid over the surface, and instinctively jerked away from the round cylinder. A gun. Richard had given me a gun. A tiny gun, no bigger than my palm. With mother of pearl inlaid in the handle. A lady's gun.

I was doomed. If I told Mother Frances, no matter what the new bishop said, she'd force me out of the order or send me to the state hospital, the only crazy nun there. If I didn't tell her and anyone found out what noodle-brained Richard had done, I'd be behind bars, right next to him.

What had he done? Why had he done it? What in the world was he thinking?

What was I thinking? Sitting here, holding a gun in a box.

I closed the lid, eased quietly off the bed, tiptoed to the door, and opened it. I stuck my head out and peered right, then left. There was a soft thunk to my left, and then quiet. I left my door open and hurried two doors down the corridor to Winnie's room. I eased open her door and stuck my head in.

"You awake?" I whispered.

She sat up and rubbed her eyes. "You crazy? You should be in bed. Asleep."

"Shhhh." I pushed her over to the wall and sat on the edge of her cot. "I opened Richard's packet."

"There was a packet?"

"It's a long story."

"Not now. I'm getting up in only four and a half hours."

"It had something in it."

"Most packets do."

"It's — uh — see for yourself." I held it out, almost dropping it.

"Your hands are shaking like corn stalks in September."

"Just open it."

"Yipes!"

"Hush!"

"He couldn't have given you cold cream? We could use that!" We stared at each other for a few moments, then she sighed. "You know how to use it?"

"Shoot it?"

"That's the purpose for a gun, isn't it?"

I shuddered. "Yes. I know how to shoot it."

"And Richard would know that?"

I nodded. "He taught me one summer. At his grandfather's farm." I gulped. "The same place he keeps his bunnies." At the

120

horrified expression on her face, I hastily added, "Only at targets! Paper ones."

"Okay, so the gangster gave you a gun. Why?" She traced the mother-of-pearl the same way I had. "It's too small for a man's hand, so it probably isn't his, and he's not trying to hide it with you. It's made for a woman. For you." She closed the lid and gave it back to me. "I repeat. Why did he give it to you?"

I had been thinking about that, and there was only one answer. "Protection. He wanted me to have protection."

"Bull's eye. You think you're going to need it?"

"Dear God, I hope not. But after what I found when I went into my cell, I'm not sure."

"There's more to this story?"

"It's not a story. It's my life." I told her about the search and how I'd discovered it. "And if this situation is related to the murder . . ."

"Another *if.* Go to bed. We'll talk about it tomorrow." She pushed me off the cot. "And do something with that gift."

By the time I got back to my cell, I was more flustered than before. Another *if.* Another mystery.

If.

Who.

What.

A pox on those words! A pox on Richard and his gun! I made sure the gun was snug in the case, then closed and tucked it into my pocket, as safe now as it had been all day. Then I tried to think. I was tired, really tired; but I had to proceed logically, not jump to conclusions. Sighing, I realized this was not going to be easy. It was only logical that I tackled the last conundrum — that someone in this convent might have been the culprit who searched my meager belongings.

Assume and *might.* Two more words to add to the plague of poxes.

My eyes were getting heavy and my limbs felt like wet sandbags after a hurricane; but I had to reason this out, and prayed that I didn't fall asleep the way I did in chapel.

So, Aggie, look at this logically, a la Plato!

There were eleven nuns in the convent, counting Mother Frances. Sisters Justina, Phillippe, Paul, Angelica, Gabriel, Claire, Lawrence, Joseph, Winnie, Mother Frances, and me. Mother Frances, Justina, and Phillippe remained in the convent during the day. The rest of us taught in the school. Eight grades, eight teachers.

If it were one of the other nuns . . .

No, that was impossible. Wasn't it?

We all had our duties. Teaching at the school took up most of the daylight hours. Then there were the chores we had to perform each day, before and after classes started. If I needed to find a sister, I could find her in the same place at the same time each and every day. There was order, routine, safety in that kind of life. In all the years I had been in the convent, no one deviated from the schedule. Well, there was one exception.

Me.

The unpredictable nun.

And I was the only one living in this convent that I knew for certain hadn't searched my room.

No, that wasn't quite true. I knew for certain that Mother Frances hadn't done it. She might think me a nitwit nun, but she was one of the most trustworthy women I knew. She loved the Church. She loved the convent. She would never sully her habit, nor break a commandment, nor her vows — for any reason. She had reason enough for wanting me out of her convent. She didn't have to go searching for another one.

There was one other nun I could scratch off my suspect list. Winnie. I was certain she could not and did not do this. Besides, she hadn't been out of my sight all day. Except when I was with Mother Frances. Or talking to cousin Josiah. Or with Monsignor Grace.

That left a lot of time for her to search. But there was no reason for her to search.

There wasn't any reason for anyone to search! Not unless whoever had done it knew there might be something important to find in my room.

Or was it only my cell that had been searched? Perhaps Winnie's had, too. I hadn't thought to ask her, and I doubted that she had thought to look.

Oh, this was maddening. And frustrating. Logic didn't help when all it did was put me on a circuitous route, going nowhere. Finding nothing. I yawned. Finding no one. I lay flat on my back in the center of my bed to continue my ruminating. I hated sleeping this way, so it was uncomfortable enough to keep me awake.

After me, Mother Frances, and Winnie, there was Justina. She kept guard at the side door when one was needed. But she was so old and frail that her body wound down quickly and she often nodded at her post. Several times I'd found her snoring quietly, and tiptoed past her without her being at all aware that I'd come in. If she had been on guard duty today (and that was probable because of the murder), then it was also probable that she had nodded off as usual. Anyone, then, could have slipped right past her. Her gentle snores belied a deep sleep.

But someone would have had to know that.

Which meant . . .

There was something . . . something whirling through my mind. Something I had seen or heard. Something not quite right, perhaps out of place. A clue! Isn't that what every detective looked for? So, I was a detective, now, not a nun? But all detectives carried weapons. Oh, good grief! Mother Frances didn't have enough problems. Now she was saddled with a defective, detective nun — with a gun! I giggled, but then a little black mouse nudged me, hissing in my ear like a steam engine — *whish, whish.* I peeked over and discovered a huge black mouse pinching my elbow.

"Winnie! For crying out loud!"

"Shhhh! No more crying out loud. You have to get up."

"I am up. Go back to your cell. It's time to sleep."

"It's time for Mass and then our visit to Mary McBride."

"No, that's tomorrow."

"Aggie, this *is* tomorrow."

I bolted upright and our foreheads cracked against each other. "I solved the case!"

"You did?"

I nodded, and then giggled at the sight of Winnie standing like a saluting British sailor, her hand holding the bump that was starting to rise. I tugged my wimple into place and it covered most of my own bump.

"It was out of the ordinary, and then I knew."

"Tell me later. We're out of the ordinary. We should be at Mass, receiving communion."

I hopped off my cot and straightened my habit, brushing lint off the skirts and settling my cowl over my shoulders. I grabbed my missal and trotted after Winnie. We both slipped past a sleeping Justina and ran down the cinder path, into the church.

"Quiet as a tomb," Winnie whispered. "Father Bryant is saying the early Mass."

"Which means the pews will be empty." Father Bryant was eighty-eight years old and he often forgot the Latin he had learned as a youth. Altar boys ducked early services, just because they might have to cue him in Latin — which they didn't know well enough — or catch him if he stumbled —

which he did often.

Nine brave souls had opted for the fits and starts of Father Bryant's liturgy. We slipped into the first pew and Winnie leaned over to whisper, "What was the solution?"

"What solution?"

"You said you solved the case."

"I did?" Yes, I vaguely remembered saying that. But why? "I don't remember a thing."

"Nothing?"

"No."

"Must have been a dream, then."

Or another part of the nightmare.

The opening bells rang the entrance of Father Bryant and we set everything aside to concelebrate with the elderly priest. At communion, Winnie and I rose to kneel at our place at the altar rail. Father Bryant raised the host. And stopped.

The altar boy hissed the Latin phrase at him, but he paid no attention. His eyes narrowed as he stared over my left shoulder.

Dare I look? Mother Frances would kill me. I was mentally packing my touring bag with all the warm clothes I had to my name — not concentrating at all on Christ's sacrifice, and for that I tacked on another two decades of the rosary. I said a hasty, *Sorry, Lord,* and turned my head to see what had transfixed the good priest.

"Holy Mary, Mother of God!"

Father Bryant ended the prayer, "Pray for us sinners," and the altar boy gave him a sharp rap with the gold plate he should have been holding under Winnie's chin. The old priest faltered. "Where am I? Oh, yes!"

I turned back as he leaned forward and placed the host on Winnie's tongue, then fumbled in the ciborium to dig out one for me. I tried very hard to concentrate, to think only of Christ, to pray for the repose of the souls of those in Purgatory. But all I could think about was the shape slumped in the corner near the confessional. A large shape. A shape that looked suspiciously like a human being. A shape that wasn't moving.

Finally, as the host touched my tongue, I found my prayer.

Please, God, don't let there be a knife and blood.

CHAPTER TEN

The final bell rang the ending to the Mass, and Father Bryant strode down the aisle, making straight for the dark shape in the corner. A man's shape, I could see, now. I dragged Winnie right after him. No knife. Ours, Richard's, or anyone else's. No blood that I could see. Maybe underneath? Father nudged the shape with his foot, and none too gently. Arms and legs just sort of flopped at each tap of his black wing-tip.

"Up!" Father Bryant ordered. "Up, I say! If I've told you once, I've told you a million times — no sleeping in the church! There's a warm shelter two blocks north, and they have hot coffee with rolls. Now get . . ." Nudge. ". . . up." Kick.

Heavenly hosts! This nightmare would never end. Now we had a crazy priest to contend with.

"Um . . . Father, I don't think he's going to get up."

"Course he is. He always does. Silas Tate, you get up this instant."

Where was the closest telephone, so we could contact the police? I could send one of the altar boys, who were gawking at the three of us and poor Silas, but they'd no more know what to say than I did. The side door opened just then and Mother Frances entered, with Sister Mary Paul close behind, her arms loaded down with linens for the altar. She took one look at the wayward nun and the man in a heap on the floor, and slunk behind Mother Frances, peering over her shoulder, her eyes slitted and fearful, as if I would leap over Mother's shoulder to bite her.

Had she searched my room? This afraid-of-shadows girl, who had lots of growing up to do? It hardly seemed likely.

But, then, none of what had been happening lately seemed likely.

And it kept getting unlikelier and unlikelier — if that was a word — when Mother Frances dropped to one knee and shook Silas' shoulder. "Wake up. It's that time, Silas. There's coffee with real cream and sweet rolls at the convent. Just knock on the door and Sister Justina will serve you."

Heaven help us, when he didn't respond, she snapped a finger on his nose.

"Um . . . Reverend Mother Frances . . . uh, I think, you know, he's not going to wake up."

"Of course he's going to wake up," she said. "He's just a heavy sleeper."

"The sleep of the dead," I muttered, hoping she would realize . . .

He shot straight up. "Quit flickin' that finger, Sister! I'm a gettin'. I'm a gettin' good."

Did my heart stop? It felt stopped. I clutched my chest to be sure it was still beating, found a steady but very rapid pittering and pattering, and sucked in what seemed like my first breath of air in my whole life.

Later, on our way to Mary McBride's to talk to the women we hadn't seen last night, I was still shook up. "It was like Lazarus, rising; but it wasn't the Savior's intervention. It was the coffee and sweet rolls. With cream. It must have been the cream that did it."

"The man wasn't dead, Aggie."

"He was dead in my mind." We walked in silence for two blocks as I tried to take stock of how easily I had accepted the false notion of another dead body. "Winnie, I don't like the feeling I had back there. It washed over me so fast, and it hasn't abated in the least."

"You were scared. You have more than enough reasons to be scared."

"Yes, I suppose I'm a bit scared. But it's more than that. I was certain that man — Silas — was dead. God, help me, I was certain of it. In two days I've gone from a pretty complacent nun into someone who sees death, destruction, and evil everywhere."

"It is everywhere."

"Theoretically, I've always known that."

"There's a *but* at the end of that sentence."

"But now it's no theory. I have seen it, and it has left a horrible impression on my mind and in my soul."

"How many *buts* are there going to be in this conversation?"

"*But,* the worst thing it has done is make me anticipate still more of it. Take Silas, for example. I thought he was dead. I expected him to be dead." I gulped and the words got strangely strangled as they came out. "I expected him to be murdered!" What could Winnie say to that? What could I say to it? "I don't like me right now. I don't like what I've become — a cynical spectator of a dangerous, evil-filled world."

"Oh, Aggie! I'm so sorry."

"Me, too." We walked in silence for a few steps and thoughts bounced all over my brain. "You know, maybe we shouldn't be sorry. Maybe this is good. Maybe I needed to be shaken out of my too quiet, too easy, too safe world." A few minutes of ruminating and I sighed. "Maybe I needed my perceptions skewed away from that complacency. I . . . we . . . have all seen the Silases of this world. The men who sleep on street corners, in crates and boxes they call home. They hardly breathe. They lie still as a tree stump. The world has gone so mad that we've gotten used to them. And that's bad, Winnie. That's so wrong! So, one good thing has come out of this. After what I saw yesterday, I'm not as used to it as I was." Tears pooled in my eyes and I blinked rapidly to keep them from falling. "Yesterday morning, the sun still held dominion in the sky, all was right in the heavens, and the world revolved to the beat of Christ's love. This morning, none of that seems real. They are only shadows on the wall. The only things that seem real to me are death and destruction and hate. And I fear that hate! I am so angry, I could scream." I clutched my fingers and stopped dead on the sidewalk. "Winnie, I want to hit someone."

"Not me!"

"It's welling up inside — that urge to smack the person who's done this."

This time, she stopped dead on the sidewalk. I have to stop using that word — *dead*.

"Smack? You want to smack the person who's done this?" She started to laugh. "You've got a gun in a fancy box — and please don't tell me where you've got it — and all you want to do is smack someone?"

I stared at her, and there she was, laughing so hard that she doubled over. Why was she doing that? I couldn't for the life of me see what was so funny.

"Oh, my good Lord!" She gulped and hiccupped. "Mayetta Morgan, you are priceless." She grasped my hands and gave a sweet squeeze. "I'm so glad you're my friend." She shook her head. "Smack someone! Imagine the world if all anyone ever did when he got mad and scared was smack someone. Not pick up a gun or a knife or any other horrible weapon that kills." She linked her arm with mine and hugged me close. "The world may be a little askew for you right now, but rest assured that the convent has rubbed off on you. You are truly Sister Agnes."

"A confused and very angry Sister Agnes."

"Good. That will fuel your need, and now my need, to put a face to this evil and sweep it out of our community — like Christ and the money lenders — only we won't need a temple to do it in."

"No, just a convent and a church."

"Wherever there is evil, good people must act to stop it."

"Do you think we can?"

"I think we must."

CHAPTER ELEVEN

A crisp, but warm, March morning had Mary McBride's small porch filled to bursting. She waved to us and held up a large cup she had clutched in her hand. "Coffee or tea, Sisters?"

"Tea for me and Aggie," Winnie said. "Cream and sugar, if you have them."

"We do, indeed, Sister. Why else do you think the neighbor ladies show up at this ungodly hour of a Saturday?"

Three heads bobbed, and I recognized Josie Giusti, Janice McCain, and Dot Klein — the grand dames of the most populous ethnic groups represented in the neighborhood. Obviously, the word had been passed from one house to the other that we were coming. Why did the phrase "curiosity killed the cat" keep bouncing around in my brain instead of "Hail, Holy Queen"?

Josie made room next to her on the wooden swing and nodded to the folder in my hand. "That what you're doing here?" I handed her the folder and she studied it, then passed it to Dot. "Young, wasn't she? And such a little thing. What a pity."

Mary came onto the porch, balancing a tray holding delicate teacups with a gold and pink floral design. There were several slices of buttered toast with a small, heavily-etched glass pot of strawberry jam next to them, and a saucer of crisp fried bacon. Breakfast! And not a moment too soon or late.

"Help yourselves, Sisters. Already sugared the tea, you know. Thanks to Mother Frances, there's more, if you want it, there is."

Help yourselves? There were people actually starving, but my stomach had its limits and the smell of fresh tea, strawberries, and bacon had it roiling with need. One bite of strawberry-jammed toast wasn't enough, but I had Mother Frances and my Newport friend, Mrs. Henrietta Vandergelder, to thank for the ladylike manner I had of waiting my turn. That lasted three seconds before my Gran's daily warning to *dig in or there won't be any left!* took over, and I reached for a slice of bacon and ate it with my hands. *Well, Aggie, you haven't risen far from your boardinghouse reach.*

Winnie and I blew on the tea to cool it and took tiny sips so as not to burn our lips. "Perfect," Winnie said, then helped herself to the toast and jam, while I savored my own toast and watched the photo of the dead girl change hands. Although Dot's eyes had rounded before she hastily passed the photo along, I couldn't tell if there was any recognition in her or the others' gazes. I thought I'd give them all a bit of time before asking the questions I'd prepared — uppermost being: *Do you recognize this girl?* And then: *Have you seen her in this neighborhood lately — or ever?*

But before I had more than two sips of tea, a steady metallic purring sounded far off and got louder and louder. Dot leaned forward to catch a glimpse of what was coming.

"Well! Will ya look at that?"

The dark green sleekness of a Cord roadster seemed to take up the length of a whole front yard as it cruised slowly to the curb. The ladies held their collective breaths, except for Winnie, who muttered, "Gangsters. Can't go anywhere without them these days, especially when you're with Sister Agnes."

I knew who it was before the door opened, and when Richard's cocky grin chased the morning gloom away, I breathed a sigh of relief and sat back.

Winnie huffed. "He's out."

"He is, indeed," Mary said. "Wonder what the bail was?"

"Not enough," Winnie said.

I pinched her wrist as gently as I could. *Oh, all right, Lord, so I pinched hard, but she deserved it, and I do not intend to tack on any additional decades of the rosary. Not this time.* She took the hint and shut her mouth, but crossed her arms under her breasts. When would she give him a break? As my Gran always said, *When you see Lucifer walking down the street wearing mink underwear.* Really had to use a big dollop of imagination for that one — unless you were a nun, who wasn't supposed to have that kind of imagination. Ha!

Richard bent back into the car and came up with a huge brown box tied with his favorite green-and-white striped string — like the kind that had wrapped the beef. Such a short time ago. Such a simple, short time ago.

Richard mounted the steps and stopped in front of Mary. "I come bearing gifts."

"That's what they said before they assassinated Caesar," Winnie muttered.

"Wrong century and country, your ladyship. Try Greece and the Trojans."

"You drop a wooden horse onto me porch, Richard DelVecchio, an' I'll be callin' yer ma," Mary warned with a chuckle.

But we all knew that if Richard or anyone else violated her space, she'd do it. Ever since her husband died of a heart attack just after Black Thursday and left her with bankrupted holdings, her house, several huge mortgages, and no income, there hadn't been a day that went by that she wasn't on her telephone, passing along some piece of news, or registering some complaint. How lonely was her life?

"The only horses I've got are under that hood, and they're mechanical," Richard said. He winked at me, dropped the box into Mary's lap, and cut the string with a pocketknife. When he raised the lid, the most delectable scent drifted over the porch. I was sure each of the ladies was salivating. Had to be. I was.

"Oh, my stars!" Dot said.

Josie licked her lips. "Is that chocolate cake? I haven't had chocolate cake in almost a year. Please let it be chocolate cake."

"Made with cocoa powder," Richard said.

"That's chocolate in these lean days," Josie said. "Oh, good Lord, frosting!" She dipped her finger in and took a small scoop.

I think she said a prayer of thanksgiving, then tasted. "Oh, my stars! It's real butter, and as good as it gets."

Richard beamed. "I was going to make muffins, but thought this was a time to celebrate. I'm calling it my Get Out of Jail on Bail Million-Dollar Chocolate Cake." He took a deep breath of air. "Feels great, being out of that hellhole."

"Richard!"

"Got an acceptable word for it, Sister Agnes?"

Winnie didn't fear to tread anywhere! She'd have a hard time getting her wings and halo. "How did you get out on bail?" she asked. "Isn't murder a capital offense?"

Richard chuckled. "It takes plenty of capital. One million dollars, to be exact."

"And gangsters have one million dollars while others have nothing."

"Some do. And some are generous with what they have."

They were staring each other down, like my cousins at the annual family picnic. Bocci games, horseshoe pitching, softball, whatever — they forgot they were cousins and became instant enemies. Noodles for brains, the lot of them! This morning, that included Winnie and Richard.

"All right, that's enough. You're both my

friends. Why can't you get along?"

From Richard, "Because we are your friends."

And from Winnie, "Because we want what's best for you."

"Here's what's best," I said. "Cut it out! We've got more important problems than this infernal war."

" 'Tis only a pissin' contest, Sister," Mary said. At my gasp, she lowered her gaze and made the sign of the cross.

"Can't be that," Richard said. "The good sister isn't a guy — unless that penguin suit hides something it shouldn't."

"Richard DelVecchio," I said, "you are in big trouble."

At first he looked defiant, but then a sheepish expression slowly spread across his visage. "Sorry, Aggie. And sorry to you, too, Sister Winifred. Spent too many hours in that jail, listening to language that would curl your hair." He touched Winnie's shoulder. "Sister, honest, I am sorry. And don't you worry none. I will confess this morning's disrespect. Promise."

While Winnie had the right to feel aggrieved, they both had the good grace to look abashed — probably because for the first time their display of one-upmanship had been witnessed.

I looked from one to the other. Sternly. Like a teacher. "Can we just enjoy this wonderful cake and then get on with our task this morning?"

"Of course," Richard said. "Mary, if you have a knife and cake server and some plates, I'll portion this out to the ladies."

She shook her head and scooped the box into her arms. "The others above stairs will want some, too. Dot, I could use your help in the kitchen."

I wonder if anyone else has noticed that eating something delicious is always a silent affair. Who can stop to talk? It takes real concentration to savor every tiny morsel, including the bitty crumbs left on the plate. They taste best when picked up on the end of an index finger and brought ever so slowly to the tip of the tongue, to lie there on a taste bud and melt. Only Heaven could offer better than that.

It did offer one more thing. While Winnie, Mary, and I struck out with three of the residents, Clarisse Jessup — who was ninety-two years old and ailing — woke up long enough to squint at the photo, then closed her eyes and yawned. "Mildred Young's granddaughter from Fall River."

"You're sure?" Winnie asked.

"O'course. She was right here, just last week."

"I dinna see her," Mary said.

Clarisse stretched and turned over on her side. "You was at the store. Only visited but a minute, but it was her, all right. Bonnie." Gentle snores ended that conversation.

"She sleeps most o' the day, and is gettin' a touch a that old folks' dementia," Mary whispered. "Sometimes says things happened yesterday that really happened years ago."

We went into the hall. "Is Mildred awake?"

"Should be. Let's ask her if Clarisse saw what she said she did."

Mildred's room was the sunniest we'd seen so far, and the others were generally pleasant. Sheer curtains puffed out as a breeze blew in through a crack at the bottom of the window. Curly maple bureau and bedside table looked expensive and older than dirt, as did the ornate grooming aids on her bureau. They were silver, but probably plate. The only thing that wasn't an antique was the narrow iron bed in the corner — which looked like it had come with the room. It was painted white and covered with a brightly patterned quilt.

"Made that herself afore her eyes went bad," Mary said. "Wonder where she's taken herself off to?"

I touched the stitches. Tiny and even. Hard to do that in your youth. Mildred was seventy-six and had cataracts.

"I'll check the bathroom," I said, and rapped gently on the closed door across the hall. "Mildred? You in there? It's Sister Agnes and Sister Winifred. We'd like to talk to you about your granddaughter."

Betty Collins' head popped out of her room two doors down. "She's in there, all right, but you best knock loud. Must be losing her hearing along with her eyesight. Hasn't answered anyone, and she's been closeted inside for almost an hour. Get her to hurry. I don't like using the commode chair, and there's others who have been waiting, too."

"That sounds like Mildred," Mary said. "Starts soakin' her aches away and forgets the time. Her bath water always cools down by the time she's ready ta come out."

"She took a bath last night," Betty said. "Same as me. Never heard tell of her taking another bath in the morning. Not like we have men folks coming to visit every night. Oops. Sorry, Sisters."

I choked down my astonishment. It wasn't because of the sex part. I'd lived with brothers, after all. Let's face it — a nun might not have a relationship with the opposite sex, but that didn't mean we were ignorant of what went on between men and women. But for women this age? Good grief!

"Get the key to this door," Winnie said to Mary.

There was a slight tinge of fear in her voice, and it suddenly struck me that she might be right. There could be cause for alarm. An old woman who was locked in a bathroom for almost an hour, who couldn't see, was suffering from dementia and forgetting things?

No, dementia and forgetting things were Clarisse's problems.

Mary came back with a ring of keys and tried several before getting the right one. "The door seems to be stuck," she said. "I can't budge it."

I threw myself against it, nearly knocking Mary over, so when it opened, it flew into the room, and I was the first one to see the tub, filled to the brim with water. And — heaven help me — the first one to see the old woman lying still as stone in the bottom of it.

Mary found dead lady in bath room

CHAPTER TWELVE

A chorus of cries and weeping went up in the hall and bedrooms as Winnie and I plunged our hands into the warm water and struggled to get the body out of the tub. Mildred was slight, frail. Her body was slick and she kept slipping out of our grasp. I managed to get her head up, but she tilted, then rolled over, so that she was now face-down.

"Holy Mary, Mother of God, help us," I said.

"She's not comin' down to pluck Mildred outa this tub," Mary said. "We best get Richard."

"You will do no such thing," I said. "She's not dressed and deserves some dignity."

"An' how much is the poor soul goin' to get from the police or mortician?" Mary asked.

"Get a sheet," I said to her.

"To cover her up? Are ye daft?"

"No. To get her out."

"And how you goin' ta do that?"

"You'll see."

"It'll take me a minute to get one. They're on the line, drying."

"Thank you, Mary, for that and for all the work you do with these poor souls."

" 'Tis my pleasure, this."

Winnie closed the door behind Mary, then came to stand beside me as I searched the room carefully. "Could she have fallen, Aggie?"

"Are there bruises?"

Winnie walked to the foot of the tub and looked closely, but I could tell by her sour expression that she did not like seeing a body like this — or at all!

"I can't see any bruises."

"I don't see towels or a facecloth near the tub, either. And what about the soap? It's over there, beside the sink."

"But there seems to be a film of soap on her . . . form."

"Yes. And none of that adds up. Every woman I know — including us — hangs a towel on a hook right next to the tub or lays the towel on the commode. That way, it's right at hand when we get out, and we can wrap ourselves in it. Look. There are two hand towels, there by the side of the tub.

Old and well used. Yet, the only large towel in this room is on a hook behind the door, at least six feet away." I went over and touched it. "It's damp; but how could she have used it if she's still in the tub? So what are we supposed to believe, that Mildred fell in the tub and drowned, and then the soap and facecloth flew across the room, nice and neat and tidy? Well, it isn't tidy. It's messy."

"It doesn't make sense."

I looked carefully at the scene. "Let's go over this and see if we can figure out how it could have happened." As I spoke, I walked around the room, trying to picture it in my mind. "Mildred was in the tub."

"She could have been getting ready. Undressing."

"True. Then maybe there was a knock on the door."

"Would she have undressed in front of someone and then gotten into the tub herself?"

"I wouldn't."

Winnie shivered. "Nor I."

"Okay, then," I said, "she was already in the tub, and there was a knock on the door. Or maybe someone just came right in, because surely it wasn't locked. Safety above privacy, that's what my Gran always says."

"Maybe someone simply found her this way and then cleaned up the room."

Could it have happened that way? I tried to picture it, but the truth was, for that to happen a woman would have had to give up her sex and dive headfirst into the noodle-brained half of the world. Women were better than that. "Think again, Winnie. If you found a dead body, what would you do?"

"Scream."

"Right. So would anyone else."

"Unless she had something to hide," Winnie said.

"Yes. Like a dead body that she had . . ."

"Murdered." Winnie looked at me and I felt her sadness from across the room. "It couldn't have been an accident?"

"Maybe. Maybe she didn't really intend to murder Mildred, but only . . . what? Keep her quiet?"

Well, she was certainly quiet now. As a tomb! And then it came to me.

"That works," I said, "only if the two murders are connected! If that girl yesterday were, indeed, Mildred's granddaughter, and if she did come here, why did she come?"

"To see her grandmother."

"Yes. But *why?* And why did she come only a few days before someone stabbed her?"

"You know, don't you?"

"Not yet. But I think . . . yes, it makes sense if she came when she discovered something wrong, something she wanted to talk over with her grandmother."

"Oh, wait! I see where you're going with this. Whoever killed her didn't want anyone to know what she had talked to her grandmother about. And they also didn't want Mildred to tell anyone!"

"That's a real likelihood, isn't it?"

"Makes sense, when all this doesn't," Winnie said. "But what happened here, today?"

"Well, if you only had a few minutes to do this, and you didn't want to get caught, you wouldn't have much time to think about what you were doing." *Aggie, you would have done well in Hollywood City!* This was almost as complicated as the moving picture, *Monkey Business.* But our monkey business gradually began to make more sense.

"Look at her." I said. "She's old. Her skin is translucent — a sure sign of some debilitating illness like my Aunt Mame's. She looks as if a zephyr would blow her over. But she might have been stubborn, just like my Aunt Mame. Maybe the murderer asked her not to tell and she wouldn't agree. Now, he has a . . . No! Wait! It can't be a he."

"Aggie, I don't like what you're saying."

"But it's logical! If a man had come through this door, Mildred would have screamed down the house."

"Unless she expected him."

"No one expects a visitor in the bathroom!" I paced the small area in front of the claw foot tub, too much Mother Frances' habit lately. "So, she, the murderer, comes in, probably friendly, chatting a bit. But she hasn't really come to chat, because she has a real problem — we've come to ask questions that she doesn't want us to get answers to. She must shut Mildred up. And poor Mildred was there, in the tub, exposed, probably trying to shield her body from view."

"I would."

"So her hands would have been in the water. She wouldn't have been too alert to danger, just modest — especially if she knew her attacker. How difficult would it be for someone younger and stronger just to lean over, push her head under water, and hold it there until . . . until the end?"

Winnie gulped and averted her eyes. "Not very difficult, I guess."

"And what if you, the murderer, were scared, but determined. You did something horrific, and then you had to get away. But

152

what if it was all spur of the moment and you didn't really think this through very well? What if the habits of a lifetime kicked into gear as you left the room? Your hands, and maybe even your arms, are wet. So you need to dry them on the towel. You have it in your hand and are anxious to get out of here. I know what I do before I leave the bathroom. You do it, too."

"Do what?"

"You clean up the room. Put the towel where it can dry. Put the soap in its holder on the wall." Winnie looked from tub to sink to the door and I knew she was picturing doing just that. "Habits of a lifetime . . ."

"So," Winnie said, "that means we truly do have another murder."

"I think so, yes. And this one, right over our heads. While we were all on the porch having our tea."

"How do you know that?"

"The water is still warm."

Winnie crossed herself and her lips moved in prayer.

Mary tapped on the door and stuck her head in, holding out a sheet. I thanked her, rolled up my sleeves, and pinned them in place. "Help me, Winnie."

Between the two of us, and a great splashing of water, we managed to shimmy the sheet under Mildred's body, wrapping it around her. Mildred was so thin, there was plenty of sheet left to knot and hang over the side of the tub.

Richard would probably understand what I was going to do. We'd spent enough time on his and my grandfather's farms to know how to hoist a carcass into position. *Sorry, Mildred. Didn't mean to imply that you were in any way related to a member of the porcine family.*

"Help me pull," I said to Winnie.

"Let me give you a hand, an' all," Mary said.

Though Mildred was small, it wasn't an easy thing to get her out of the water. She was — literally — dead weight, and slick with soap, to boot. But with the three of us tugging hard on the ends of the sheet, we managed to get Mildred out of the tub and onto the small bath mat. I knew it was useless, but felt for a pulse anyway. When I found none, I took my first real look at Mildred Young and found her eyes open, staring straight at me.

I shuddered. It was déjà vu. It was yesterday. It was forever.

Mildred's stare mirrored that of her granddaughter.

If I'd had any doubts, I had none now.

The resemblance was unmistakable. There were at least fifty years between them, but the two women had the same head shape, same small nose, same eyes. And the same look in death.

It was eerie, seeing that frightened, yet knowing look. I couldn't explain it better than that. I just knew that at the moment of death both women knew. What they knew, I hadn't yet figured out. But my anger was multiplying by the minute, fueled by a deep, primal rage.

Oh, dear Lord! Mother Frances' deep, primal rage would know no bounds. To find a dead body once was nigh onto sacrilegious. Twice? I might not last until nightfall at St. Catherine's without an ally. Lucky for me, I had one, and I had to use him. I could not allow anyone to take me away from this. Not now. I was involved, like it or not. And I was mad as a wet mongoose. Whoever had done this had best not get within striking distance. I had never felt less like a nun than I did right then.

Not to worry, Lord. I'll be my own lackadaisical self before long. I can't help it. It's what I am. And don't worry about my anger right now. It isn't vengeance I want. It's justice. And I make to You a solemn promise. These two women will receive justice.

Even if it meant giving up all I had worked so hard to attain.

"I need to use your telephone," I told Mary.

"In the kitchen on the wall."

The hall was clear, although heads peeked out, then quickly withdrew. I would get to them later, perhaps tomorrow after the police left, and this time they had better be more forthcoming. I had accepted their quick denial that they knew the girl. Now, I was convinced they knew more than they were telling. Two murders in two days! And one of them was — I was betting — done by a woman. If they weren't willing to tell me what they knew, I was willing to bring the wrath of God down on their heads.

Richard was waiting for me at the top of the stairs. I'm sure my countenance showed the fury inside because his eyebrows shot to the heavens, but he had the sense to ignore my anger. Knowing him, however, that wouldn't last.

"I wanted to rush in there and help," he said, "but the good ladies wouldn't let me get any farther than this."

"And rightly so."

"What can I do now?"

"Contact my cousin. There has to be a telephone somewhere in this neighborhood. Josie's house is closest. Ask her."

"You want me to call the police?"

"Why not?"

"I'll be their first suspect."

"And you have six alibis that you didn't do it."

"But isn't there a phone here?"

"I need to use it." I pushed him. "Go. Go."

When I got to the kitchen, I realized I'd never used a telephone in my life. And I'd sent Richard away! *Like the murderer, I'm losing my equilibrium, Lord. Stay close, okay?*

Everyone in the moving picture shows knew how to use a telephone. Heck — *I'll do penance for that slip, promise* — even my noodle-headed relatives knew how. I'd watched them all, several times. Couldn't be that hard. *Just do what they do, Aggie. When you get there, pick up the handle, put it to your ear, listen through one of those round things, and . . .*

Wait! Mary said it was on the wall? But all I'd ever seen were those black ones that sat on a table.

The kitchen was not as pristine as the rest of the house, what with remnants of the cake-cutting littering the large oak table — knife and cake server needing to be cleaned, and lots of crumbs waiting for someone to eat! Happy to oblige, and dreading the confrontation with the telephone, I began putting the kitchen in order as I went. Take a few crumbs, clean the silvery knife. Take a few more crumbs, clean the table. Crumbs, put away the remaining china in the glass-fronted cabinet with the rest of the set. More crumbs, disassemble the box and put it in the closet, on a shelf next to the packing supplies, which included a large roll of green-and-white striped string. Did everyone use that, now? I finished the crumbs and cleaned up the sink.

Well, there wasn't anything else to do — and I *really* tried to find something.

Across the room, the oak contraption mocked me, offering working parts I had no idea how to use. There was no dial. No little holes to put my finger in. And no double earpiece. Just a box on the wall, a cone-shaped thing on a wire, some holes in the wall box, and a crank on the side of the box. Darn my socks! There should be instructions printed on the danged thing! The moving picture starring Paul Muni about Al Capone called *Scarface* and Mrs. Vandergelder's cottage in Newport flashed into my mind. Yes, I know — they couldn't be farther removed from each other. But there they were, my only recollections of how this thing on the wall could work.

So calm down, Aggie. You can figure this out.

When Winnie and I were having tea with Mrs. Vandergelder, she had used hers to call the servants. Maybe this worked the same way.

I plucked the cone thing from its holder and held it to my left ear, then turned the crank with my right. There was a crackling sound, and then a female voice said, "Operator."

What in the world was an operator? And how could she help? "This is Sister Mary Agnes from St. Catherine's parish."

"Yes, Sister. To whom do you wish me to connect you?"

"Monsignor Robert Grace."

"I need to know his telephone number."

"What's that?"

She sucked in her breath and I could swear I heard a chuckle. "Where would his telephone be, Sister?"

"At the Chancery office or at the Bishop's residence in Providence."

"Thank you, Sister. I'll connect you. You just stay on the line until he answers."

"Thank you."

Clicks and metallic rumbling sounds emanated from the cone-shaped thing at my ear. And then two tinny sounds, then a pause, then another two tinny sounds.

A man's voice said, "Diocese of Providence Chancery Office."

"Monsignor Robert Grace, please," the operator said. "A Sister Mary Agnes is calling."

"One moment, please, while I try to locate him."

Please and *thank you.* This was a very polite form of communication!

Richard returned before I could reach Monsignor Grace. He gave a thumbs-up sign and then lounged against the kitchen wall. Finally, after a few minutes, Monsignor Grace said, "Sister Agnes. How are you?"

I explained the situation and listened to him, then replaced the cone onto its holder.

"So we each have friends in high — Aggie!"

Without warning, the room spun. My eyes burned. My stomach rolled. My chest hurt. My legs buckled and I fell to my knees. "I can't. I can't."

Richard pushed my head down. "Easy, there. Take some deep breaths. Breathe in. Hold it. Breathe out. Again! In. Hold. Out."

I saw brogans and knew Winnie had come into the kitchen. Uh-oh!

She rushed to my side and tried to help me stand, but Richard's hand on my head held me in place.

She flailed at Richard. "What in the hell are you doing to her?"

"Winnie!" *In. Hold. Out.* "Swearing." *In. Hold. Out.* "Naughty." *In. Hold. Out.*

"Delayed reaction to everything that's happened," Richard said. "She'll be better soon. I hope."

"Winnie." *In. Hold. Out.* "Penance." *In. Hold. Out.* "Twenty." *In. Hold. Out.* " 'Hail Marys.' "

Richard patted my head.

"Stop that. I'm not a dog."

"She's back!"

So were the police, Josiah leading part of the pack.

Richard helped me up and within moments Mary's orderly world was turned upside down and inside out. The mortician came and pronounced Mildred dead. Officers went from room to room asking questions — probably not the ones I would ask.

Meanwhile, Josiah escorted Winnie, Richard, and me into the front parlor, and spent five minutes lecturing me about messing up a crime scene.

I huffed at him. "How could you expect me to leave that poor woman in the tub? It was obvious that she was dead. Drowned."

"Oh, you think so?"

"Don't you?"

"We won't know until there's a post-mortem. The coroner will determine the cause of death."

"But surely you have an opinion."

"It's not my opinion that counts. Only the facts count."

I sneered. "Your kind of facts had Richard behind bars. Your kind of facts are nothing but supposition and aren't worth the brain cells you're using up to store them."

"Aggie, I'm a good cop."

"You're an ambitious cop. You just might be wrong. But it just might be hard for you to admit it. That could prove to be dangerous — even for you."

"Aren't you describing yourself?"

"I'm a nun, Josiah. I have no ambitions. I follow the Savior's admonition in Matthew, to seek first the kingdom of God. In that kingdom there is truth and justice. I intend to see the first come to light, and the second fulfilled."

"The truth is that your friend Richard, here, was at the scene of both deaths."

"Murders," I mumbled, rankled by the nasty emphasis Josiah had put on the word *friend.* "They were murdered!"

"The other one, yes. But you know this one was, for a fact?"

"Yes." I didn't want to explain to him, didn't want to do his job for him. But if he went off on another Richard witch hunt, the truth might never come out. "Richard has an air-tight alibi for this murder." I glared when he snickered. "While it was happening, he was right here, on the porch, with me, Sister Winifred, Mary McBride, and her neighbors. Six good women will verify that he never left the porch." And then I told him about the soap and the towels.

And he laughed.

"You're betting on murder with that? There are a dozen explanations that spell . . ."

"If you say suicide, I'll punch your lights out."

"Accident. If it's not some kind of disease that gets them — and that old lady looked really sick — then accidents are what usually end up being the causes of death for old people."

I crossed my arms and stood there, tapping my foot, but he wasn't budging. "We are leaving," I said. "If you wish to talk to us about the true facts of this case, you know where to find us. And that includes Richard."

"Sure. Go on. The answer is going to be

simple and I won't need to talk to you at all."

I couldn't leave Mary's house fast enough; and I didn't have to drag Winnie away with me, either. She came, more than willingly. The front bucket seat of Richard's Cord was soft and comfy. But not comfy enough to cool me down. "He's an imbecile! A noodle-brain! I can't believe he's my cousin."

"Ah, the sweet sounds of a woman," Richard said over the back of the seat to Winnie. "But at least she's no longer gasping for air."

"I never gasp."

"Shame on you for that lie. You going to confess it in the box this afternoon?" he asked.

"This is no time for levity, Richard," I said. "There have been two murders. The author of that note was absolutely correct. There is something terribly wrong at our parish and people are getting killed to hide the secret. We have to find out what that secret is."

"That's it? Just find out what secret is worth two lives?"

"That's it."

"And all this mayhem is magically going to stop?"

"Oh, no. We're going to have to work hard

to stop all this. I don't think it's going to be easy to find out what the secret is. We will. I have no doubt of that. With God on our side, how can we fail? But once we do find out the secret, then we'll really have our work cut out for us."

From the back seat, Winnie groaned. "Don't tell me!"

"Then we have to catch the murderer."

CHAPTER THIRTEEN

"You still have that — uh — present I gave you?" Richard asked. "You may need it."

"Darn my socks! If I dropped it in the bathroom . . . or in the tub!" *Not the tub, Lord! If Josiah finds it, he'll lock me in the hoosegow! Or worse — Richard will go back inside!* I began patting down my skirts, to make sure it was still in my pocket. "No, it's okay. I have it."

Richard bumped over a protective dirt berm on the right side of the road, then swerved back. "What are you doing? Do you really have it with you? In your pocket? Nice going, Sister Agnes!"

I brought out the box, tugged the cover off, and checked that the dousing in the bathroom hadn't done it in. "Whew! A little wet on the outside, but okay inside. Just a bit damp, but I'll dry it off and oil it tonight. After confession. After chores. After Vespers. After supper. After Saturday bath time. Oh, nuts! Where is my head? I don't have any gun oil. Well, then, I'll just have to sneak some cooking oil from the kitchen."

Yes, I know, Lord, more decades of the rosary. What is it now? Two hundred four-teen?! How could it be that many? Well, of course I believe You. You told us yourself that You are the only one in existence who can't tell a lie. Assuming, of course, that You weren't lying when You said that. Whoops! Two hundred fifteen.

"Not cooking oil, Aggie!" Richard said. "You'll ruin the mechanism."

"Mayetta Morgan, you are going straight to hell," Winnie said. "No detours to Exeter needed at all." She reached over the seat and made a grab for the case. "Give me that box so I can put that thing back."

"Jesus, Mary, and Joseph!"

"Richard!"

"That was a prayer, Aggie." He shook his head. "I don't believe it. I do not believe it. You're carrying it in the case? What are you going to do if you need it? Tell the bad guy, 'Wait a minute, I have to open this first'?"

"There may not be a bad guy," Winnie said, snapping the cover shut. "Aggie thinks a woman killed Mildred."

"She joking, Ag?"

"Nope." I filled him in.

"Wow. A woman. I never thought about that. But it doesn't matter. You're still in danger, and someone could still get at you. So, you have to have that ready to use. Not in a case."

"No!" Winnie said. "She will never have to use this thing. Never. And you shouldn't have given it to her in the first place."

She leaned way over and pushed it onto the shelf in front of the steering wheel. I had to rescue it before it slipped into Richard's lap.

"Be careful with that," he said. "It's as old as I am, and I'm not sure, but jarring it just might make it go off."

Winnie made the sign of the cross. Twice. I do believe she whimpered. "Oh, dear God! You mean it's loaded?"

"How the hell else is it going to protect you? Of course it's loaded."

"Aggie could have shot her foot off. Or some other extremity. Or mine. Or anyone's! You are a menace, Richard DelVecchio."

"I can be mean, Sister, but I am NOT a menace."

"Lower your voice about six thousand decibels," I told Richard, and realized that for the first time in days I was having fun. Okay, it was at the expense of my friends. But their conversation — a damn the torpe-

168

does, full speed ahead variety — tickled my funny bone. I only hoped they couldn't see how much I was enjoying this. Heretofore, Richard's patience had been unbelievable. Winnie's was wearing thin. But at least they were talking to each other like — okay, not friends, not even close. More like Attila the Hun facing down a much taller Napoleon Bonaparte, but this time Winnie was Attila.

Richard gripped the wheel as if it were the only thing keeping him from wringing Winnie's neck. "Look, your ladyship. In words of one syllable — regardless of sex, there really is a bad guy out there. And before you say anything, let me assure you — it isn't me."

"There were two- and three-syllable words in there. And that's not much assurance."

"Will you never cut me some slack?"

"How can I, when you keep doing bad guy stuff, like giving a loaded gun to a nun! How normal is that?"

"In this kind of situation, when there have already been two murders, and when they're linked to St. Catherine's? And, when the nun can shoot better than I can —"

When Winnie glared at me, mouth agape, I shrugged sheepishly and gave sort of a half grin, and her eyebrows hit the edge of her wimple. She really had to stop doing that.

She looked like a circus clown.

"It would be criminal not to help protect Aggie," Richard said.

Wasn't that nice of him, Lord? He really is a good friend. Okay, maybe the gun was a tiny bit of a hop up, but his heart is in the right place — as You know. Perhaps You could whisper that bit of information to Winnie? Just forget what I said about that lying stuff, okay? You can't forget, but You can forgive? Well, something's better than nothing, thanks.

"And the gun's for your protection, too, Winnie. Until we figure out what's going on and who's doing it, you're in as much danger as she is. In fact the whole damned convent is in danger." He hit the steering wheel. "Damn it to hell!"

"You really should reserve a seat in the lower tier for him, Aggie," Winnie said. "Make it close to the molten core."

"Oh, I can get into hell, okay," Richard said. "I just can't get inside the convent to protect you. Can't get a bodyguard — can't get any man in there!"

"Well, now, that's not exactly true," I said. "There are some men who are always going in and out of the convent."

"Holy Toledo! And you walk round carrying your protection in a case. I'm going to have a heart attack before this is over." He pierced me with his *look,* then shifted it to sight the road ahead. "And if you're right and one of these murders was committed by a woman, then you're so vulnerable, it makes my hands sweat."

The anger in his voice was ominous — or would have been if it weren't also tinged with a dollop of fear. And I knew, because I knew Richard, that the fear was for me.

He hit the steering wheel again and I inspected it to see if it cracked. Must be a good steering wheel. But not such a good driver. The trusty Cord roadster swerved to the right yet again.

"It's okay, Richard," I said. "The only men who can get in the front door always stay on the first floor. And unless they're family or special visitors, women are only allowed in the parlor."

"Great security system. I sneaked into the convent once or twice. There are enough out-of-the-way places on the first floor and the parlor to hide a small army."

"I won't even ask why you sneaked into the convent."

"Oatmeal cookies. When I was just a kid." I dug my elbow into him. "Hey! They were good."

"That was because you didn't share." I crossed my arms against my torso. "At least

I can sleep well, knowing you're not still sneaking in."

"You forgetting the stew?"

"Oh, good grief! Well, at least there are no others sneaking in."

"You sure about that?"

"Well, at least there's no army. There are only the parish priests and the clergy they get to replace them on their days off. You're surely not suggesting that any of them are bad guys?"

"Can't rule anyone out."

Winnie trounced on that one. "Including yours truly, then?"

"Sister Winifred, I — did — not — do — this. Or the other murder. Got it?"

"Uh-huh. And I suppose murderers never lie about their guilt, right?"

He took his hands off the wheel and punched them into the plush ceiling. "I give up!"

I tried to stabilize the wheel and I will never figure out how just that small movement somehow twisted Richard's boat of a car to the left. We went just a tiny bit over the centerline — only about half the width of the car. So why were the other drivers shaking their fists and honking at us? I really did not want to know what they were shouting, but I was fairly certain that their mouths needed a good soaping out.

Richard batted my hands away and got us back in line. "What the hell did you do that for? Grabbing for the wheel like that! You don't even have a license! It's a good thing we're only half a block away from the convent." His gaze sidled my way. "Where'd you put the — uh —"

"Gun?" Winnie said. "The big, bad guy can't say *gun?* What is this world coming to?"

Richard didn't have time to tell her because he was too preoccupied trying to find a parking space. Usually the street was clear in front of the convent, but today was a little different.

"Ah, Monsignor Grace came through," I said.

Four large trucks were parked at the curb. One from Providence Gas, one from Narragansett Electric Company, one from Ouillette Brothers Electric Contractors (*There's Good, and Then There's Magnifique!*), and the last from New England Telephone. Men in four different kinds of uniforms hauled wires and gizmos and gadgets onto the front stoop and right through the front door of the convent.

"You were wrong, Richard," I said. "There's your small army of men, and not one of them is hiding." We watched the hustle and bustle for a moment, for the first time as silent as dust. Finally, I sighed. "Amazing, isn't it, what a simple telephone call can do when it comes from the Chancery Office?"

Richard laughed. "What's so amazing about it? In Rhode Island there are three things that get instant attention. Newport big shots like your friend Mrs. Vandergelder."

"The snob mob," Winnie said.

"The leaders of the Italian community . . ."

"The real mob."

Richard wasn't going to be distracted. "The leaders of the Italian community. And, most of all, the Church." He waited, but there was no retort from Winnie on that one. "Hah! That's the God mob." He shook his head and grinned. "Here in Little Rhody, it's all about loyalty. And money. Money talks for the snob mob. Votes talk for the leaders of the Italian community."

"Real mob," Winnie muttered.

"And salvation talks for the Church."

"God mob."

Richard was chuckling by now. "I'll take salvation every time."

"Ah, but will salvation take you?"

We both caught it — the inflection in Winnie's voice. It brought happiness to my heart.

Richard countered with, "Was that a joke? Were you kidding with me?" He swiveled his head to see across the seat to Winnie. "You can't hide it. Your lips are on an upward curve. It's a grin. You're grinning." He sat back with a characteristic toss of his head. Men's vanity — got them every time. "Methinks she doth protest too much. I'm beginning to grow on her."

"Like fungus," Winnie said, but her chuckle ruined a great comeback. "Okay, you're not half-bad — especially with that analysis of our dear, beloved state."

"That's the best compliment I've had in years. *Grazie* to a not half-bad nun, your ladyship."

It wouldn't last. Winnie was too protective — and so was Richard. They just had different ways of showing it, so it was inevitable that they would clash again. But for now, this was unexpected and wonderful!

Richard scanned the lines of workers and his face brightened. "I can get a ringer in there."

"That's what they're doing, Richard. Taking out the gas and putting in electricity and a telephone. We're going to have more rings than we need."

"Not rings, Aggie. Ringer. Someone in disguise. Someone I can trust to protect you. Protect all you sisters. And he'll be able to go above stairs."

"That won't happen."

"They don't have women in these crews. So some of these men are going to have to work on all the floors, shutting off the gas lines, running wires, putting in plugs and switches. It's going to take weeks to do this job."

A noisy car pulled up behind us, and we knew without turning that it was the rusty bucket that Josiah used.

"Uh-oh. Here comes trouble. If they arrest me again, Aggie, call Vincent."

"I'll do better than that. I'll call Monsignor Grace."

When he got beside Richard's car, Josiah took a small notepad out of his breast pocket and a pencil out of his pants pocket, then tapped on the window. Richard cranked it down.

"We still don't have an identification on the dead girl, Aggie. But some old woman at the home said she was the dead woman's granddaughter."

"Yes. Bonnie."

"Bonnie? Bonnie Young?"

"Maybe. Did Mildred have sons or daughters, Winnie?"

"Both."

"You could try Bonnie Young," I told Josiah. *You were right, Lord. Cooperation is great. For Josiah.*

"Where was Mildred from?" he asked.

"Six blocks over, on Ralston. Green triple-decker with black shutters and trim. Two houses up from Watson. The neighbors should know about the family — if any of them still remember Bonnie or Mildred. But I wouldn't count on it. There have been lots of newcomers lately."

"Thanks." He tipped his hat and shut his notepad.

Before he left, I prodded, *"Quid pro quo,* Josiah. When you find out anything, bring it to me, okay?" From the grim line of his mouth, I knew he wanted to say no, but he had lots of family history behind him to know that he'd get nothing from me now, or ever, if he didn't share. He nodded and hurried back to the cop car. They turned in the middle of the block, apparently headed for Ralston.

"You're something, Aggie," Richard said.

"Yes. I'm late. We've got hours of things to do and with this lot running in and out of the convent, it's going to be damn . . .

177

darned hard to do them." *Heard You, Lord. Two hundred and sixteen decades of the rosary. I promise to whittle that down tonight.* "Most of all, Winnie and I have to identify that girl and figure out what she was doing to get herself killed."

"And you think you're going to do that all by yourself, stuck here in the convent with no phone?"

"No. I think we're going to need your help. And the help of your boss, Vincent Ricci. And Monsignor Grace."

"What are you planning now, Aggie?" Winnie asked.

"A meeting, I think."

"A meeting?" Richard put his head in his hands and shook with laughter. "Let me get this straight, in the same room you want to put two nuns, a Catholic monsignor, and two . . ."

"Mobsters," Winnie said.

". . . leaders of the Italian community."

I nodded. "Yes. And Mother Frances."

"This," Richard said, "is going to be good. Or very, very bad."

"Bad isn't the word I'd use," I said. "I'd say that combination — and everything that's been happening around here these days — is dangerous as sin."

CHAPTER FOURTEEN

After Richard left us at the curb, Winnie and I made our way through the maze of men and tools stationed in the front yard. What looked like white ceramic boxes were heaped in piles next to the porch steps. Saws and hammers, screwdrivers, and pry bars were propped against, and on, the porch railing.

The front door stood open. "Oh, golly," I said, thinking I should whisper, but having to speak above the hubbub around us. "St. Catherine's convent, open to the whole world. Mother Frances will never recover."

"She will once she gets that telephone and electricity. She loves the news, remember."

She did, and often sneaked over to the neighbors on Sunday evenings when President Roosevelt addressed the nation about the efforts to halt the Depression. I couldn't fault her on that. It was her only vice; but now it would be a normal, daily event. The world was changing. After the last two days' events, I wondered whether for good or for evil.

We made way for a weary worker who looked gaunt and pale, but was carrying a huge roll of wire on his back. He eased the roll to the ground and wiped his forehead with a rag. "Good day to you, Sisters. The Lord is smiling on us this day."

"He does that each day," Winnie said. "He loves us that much."

"Naw, this is different." He moved his arm in an arc, defining the mess in the yard. "This here's the first real work in near two years. Us, here, we're lucky to have a job. But mostly, we only gets two or three half-days a week. Kin hardly feed a family on that. But now we're to be here all day, six days a week, for three weeks. Then it's on to the rectory for another three weeks. The wages are more money than any of us has seen since Black Thursday. I kin finally take care of my family, and my parents, and my sister's family for maybe a whole year." He grasped my hand and wrung it. "God bless you all, Sisters."

Darn my socks! There were tears in his eyes to match mine, but a smile on his face as he hefted the roll onto his back, and walked with pride and dignity to the truck.

Winnie tucked her arm in mine. "You did that."

"Not me." I pointed to the heavens.

"Him through you. You. The nun with a gun. God works in mysterious ways."

We were both chuckling as we tried to maneuver our way into the convent.

"Step carefully, there, Sisters," a big, burly man said.

Lucky he warned us! The vestibule and the front hall were strewn with black, brown, and white wires, some as thick as my index finger. Already, the hall wainscoting had been pulled off and men with Providence Gas patches on their shoulder were turning large clamps against the pipes in the wall. I jumped when a pipe broke, and watched as they removed sections and capped the ends. We passed other men who were carefully extricating the lantern parts from the wall. The etched glass shades had already been piled on the hall tables. I hoped they would be used for the new electric lights, or for something, somewhere. They were too beautiful to throw away.

"Holy Mary, Mother of God!" Winnie clutched my arm and nodded toward Mother Frances' office.

Mother Frances' door was not closed.

Winnie and I looked at each other, and a

mixture of fear and astonishment crossed her features. We both made the sign of the cross. Out of fear, but also out of supplication. We were going to need all the help it could give.

Mother Frances' coyote eyesight was working overtime! She called, "Don't stand out there, Sisters! Come!"

She didn't say one word about the commotion. She didn't admonish us. She didn't question us. She only said, "Tell me what you discovered," with a finality that spoke of her capitulation. It was more frightening than the sight of Mildred under the water. Because this — this was our world, the convent, a community of women in a world of men; and she was our beacon, and beacons were supposed to remain fixed, unchanging, immoveable. This one, like the great, beautiful lighthouse on Block Island, was losing its bedrock. Little by little the sand was washing away, and some day the lighthouse would be gone. As for us, the world teetered as we related the events of the morning.

Mother Frances blanched when I described finding Mildred's body, but she brightened a tad at the possibility of identifying the girl.

"Bonnie Young. I don't recognize that

name; but I've only been here three years. She could have come to us before my time, then gone."

"Or she might not have been one of ours at all," I pointed out. "Her grandmother might have gotten that uniform blouse in the rummage sale, and given it to Bonnie. She probably wore it because it was all she had."

She shuffled some papers on her desk in an absentminded manner. So uncharacteristic! "I suppose she was going to visit her grandmother again."

"It's possible," I said.

"But you don't agree."

"If she were going to visit Mildred, why was she here? There's a streetcar stop right across from Mary McBride's. Our stop is six blocks away from her grandmother, so she must have gotten out here, and this must have been her destination."

"Perhaps she came in a car, and this was where they dropped her off."

"Then why hasn't anyone come looking for her?"

"Perhaps," Winnie said, "she hitched a ride. The young people are starting to do that, waiting on street corners until someone comes along, then sticking a thumb out. That's how the drivers know to stop."

"That looks good in the moving pictures and it always turns out okay for Claudette Colbert or Buster Keaton or Charlie Chaplin. But the real world is a dangerous place, and that would have been a very stupid thing for a young girl to do. Mildred Young wasn't a stupid person. I don't imagine her granddaughter was, either. I think Bonnie was murdered because she came here to find out something. Something the murderer didn't want her to know, or didn't want the world to know. In fact, I'm sure of it."

I then had to sketch in the contents of the note to Mother Frances, but didn't explain how I'd gotten it, or show it to her, although it was still in my pocket. I only hoped it had survived Mildred's bath water.

She looked up at me for several beats of my heart, and I fully expected to be packed off then and there to the wilds of Exeter.

Instead, she nodded and sighed. "You're very good at this, aren't you?"

Keeping things from her? "I beg your pardon?"

"Trying to make sense out of everything. Using logic. I think they call it detecting."

Mayetta Morgan, do not let your mouth drop open! Do not show astonishment. And if you cry, the police will record the first case of self-

strangulation. Oh, my God. My dear Lord. Now what are you going to do? She didn't send you away. And she just complimented you for thinking. So, think! And say something!

"Um, thank . . ."

"If you were male, you would have joined the police department and become a better detective than your cousin."

Back-handed compliment! Give with one sentence, take back with the other. Might as well have shouted it. YOU ARE NOT A REAL NUN. Big surprise!

"Thank you, Mother; but I chose the convent, and that is where I will stay. It gives me great satisfaction to teach young minds, and more satisfaction to worship God in a community of women."

"No one chooses the convent, Sister Agnes. God calls those He wants."

Whoops! Mother Frances' acerbic side was back. Darn. Too bad I couldn't have said what I was thinking: *He wants me! Even though I owe Him two hundred and sixteen decades of the rosary, He still talks to me. He wants me. He does.*

No, I couldn't have said that to her. Mostly because I wasn't sure He did want me. Also because I wasn't sure I was called. I chose to join the convent for my own reasons, for very, very good reasons, reasons that I had prayed about, reasons that I had lain at the feet of the Blessed Virgin. The reasons were as valid now as they were then. And regardless of what Mother Frances believed, I thought I was a good nun. My students liked me. Their parents liked me. Our parish priests hardly noticed me — a very good thing! All in all — regardless of the rules I broke, the times I fell asleep in chapel, the sloppiness of my sewing, the indigestible food I cooked — I wasn't doing too badly.

Yes, Lord, I know that was a pretty long list of infractions! But I'm striving to be tempered, to be built into that which You want me to be. I just haven't quite figured out what that is. But I'm working at it!

Hold on to that, Aggie! It's going to be a bumpy ride.

Especially when she found out about the meeting.

"You're a coward," Winnie said.

"Guilty as charged."

We were setting the table. Fork on left or right? I never could figure that out and had to sneak a peek at Winnie's perfectly laid places. Left! So silly, when most of us were right-handed.

"I'll tell her when I have all the answers to

186

any questions she might throw at me."

"Hell will freeze over."

We didn't have to wait that long. My reprieve came in a note delivered by hand by a young priest. Sister Claire carried it balanced in her palm as if it were a pure gold offering, and she looked at me with a little less fear, and a little more cunning.

"I'm thinking this is more of your doing," she said, then whisked herself away to Mother Frances' office.

"I'm thinking that young chit doesn't make friends easily," Winnie said.

"We best get this finished quickly before . . ."

"Sisters!"

"Too late."

She stood at the door, a tall, forbidding sentry. "We have been summoned. Tea. Tomorrow. Two o'clock. At the Chancery office. A car will pick us up at one-thirty. Be ready." She spun and was gone, but the frosty air lingered.

"As Richard would say, Holy Toledo! Have you ever been in the Chancery office?" Winnie asked.

"Has anyone in the Order?"

"I need something to do so I won't think about tomorrow."

"You have plenty to do, Winnie. Lunch.

Charity visits. Chores. Confession. Supper. Papers to grade. Undergarments to wash."

"And our weekly bath. Now, that, I look forward to. My sister sent me some lavender water to put in the bath. She says it soothes the nerves."

"Holy Toledo! Got enough for two?"

Lunch was a silent affair. The other sisters must have known what was happening because they peeked at us, but not one of them said a word. They dug into Sister Phillippe's vegetable casserole with soda biscuits — a most forgettable meal, yet still better than my slop. I was grateful when Mother Frances gave the closing prayer and we gathered our small offerings for the charity visits.

We had been making rounds every Saturday since Winnie and I got assigned to St. Catherine's. Each set of nuns visited four families in need. We brought donated items — anything we could beg from merchants, or whatever had been left in the poor boxes at the back of the church. Today, we had seven small bars of soap, two tubes of brilliantine for the men, eight handkerchiefs that Justina had lovingly sewn from remnants that Cranston Print Works donated, three small rolls of summer sausage, four pepperoni sausages, two packets of crackers, and three jars of peanut butter. It wasn't much, but it would help stretch the relief supplies our poorest parishioners received.

Our visits were brief, but productive. At our second stop we located one of our students who had dropped out of class two months ago.

"He's in New Bedford," his mother told us, as she balanced a baby boy on her hip. "Working on the docks whenever he can and living with his uncle."

"But he should be in school, Mrs. Clementi," Winnie said. "He was one of my best math students."

"Since my husband left four months ago — to try to find work, he said, but I haven't heard from him since — the only math we know here is what rent and lights and food add up to. He's where he needs to be, Sisters. Stephano's the man of the house, now."

"Please tell him I was asking after him," Winnie said.

"When or if I see him, I will do that."

"I wonder . . . could you help us?" I asked.

"Me help you? And how would I do that, Sister?"

"Winnie, show her the photo."

"If it's of that dead girl, don't bother. The

189

cops were here, sticking that picture in the door, but I didn't tell them anything."

"Was there something to tell?"

"Well, I didn't really take a good look at the picture. I was riled by their nerve in coming here, when they rousted my Genio for setting up an apple stand. They didn't like an Italian selling apples in their Irish neck of the woods, so they kicked it over and almost half the apples were bruised and no good to sell. We didn't make a dime on those apples and we still owe the company twelve dollars. That's when he left. So, I'd never let them in. Not for anything."

Winnie brought out the photograph. "Please take a look at this. It's very important. Does she look familiar? Perhaps your son knew her?"

She looked at the photo carefully, not reacting at all to the signs of death, then passed it back to Winnie.

"No, he didn't know her. But I saw her here in the neighborhood."

Hearts did soar. Or, at least expectations did. I almost stammered in my haste to discover something important. "Where? When?"

"In Adler's variety store. Yesterday. Early. About six or six-thirty. I went to get canned milk for the baby and that girl was in the aisle. She wasn't buying anything, just looking out the window, down the street. I turned to put the price of the milk in Mr. Adler's charge book, and the bell over the door went off. When I turned around, she was gone."

We thanked her and left, and I dragged Winnie back two blocks to the variety store.

"What in the world are we doing here? We have two more stops to make."

"I need to check something."

The bell tinkled as we entered and Mr. Adler waved to us as he stocked canned applesauce on the shelf. I pulled Winnie down the center aisle, up to the canned milk section. "Sweet Sacred Heart! I thought so."

"Thought what?"

I pointed out the one wide window. "If she stood here yesterday morning at six a.m., and looked there, down the street, what would she have seen?"

I knew the instant she realized the ramifications of my question. It slammed into her the same way it had slammed into me as Mrs. Clementi was describing it.

"The soup line. She was watching the soup line. But why?"

"I think that's obvious. She wanted to confirm what she thought she knew about the goings-on at St. Catherine's."

191

"But the soup line wouldn't tell her that."

"Maybe it would if we ask another question."

"From Mr. Adler?"

"No. The other question is one for us."

She scoffed. "We don't know anything."

"That's right. We don't know why she was watching the soup line. And the reason we don't know why she was watching the soup line is because we don't know who she was watching. If we can figure that out . . ."

"Then we'll know the murderer."

CHAPTER FIFTEEN

Winnie groaned. "That's an impossible task. There were three times as many souls in the line yesterday than we normally get. We were doling out stew so fast, I don't remember who was there and who wasn't. And all those new faces! They were a blur."

"Not quite. I remember some vividly. The mother with all those small children. The really tall, fat woman in a rummage sale dress who limped her way down the line. The teenaged boys with their nothing-can-hurt-me-air, when you just knew that they had already been hurt by this madness around them."

"Wait! I remember them. And I remember seeing them again . . . where was it?"

Come on, Winnie! It's simple. You can do it. Whoops! Maybe not. It's not math.

"I've got it! They were there last night."
Hallelujah!

"At the corner. Only one block from Mary

McBride's." She shuddered as if she had just realized that there might have been trouble brewing with them. "It could have been those lads that Bonnie was watching. They're about the same age."

"Yes, they are. But so were some of the mothers with babes. I think three of them went up the path towards Carmichael's Cleansers. They would have passed within two feet of the root cellar. And with that dense copse covering them, they would have been out of sight of everyone else. They — or at least one of them — could have veered off towards the root cellar."

"But that just makes more suspects!"

"And more questions to ask."

"More detecting to do, you mean. Your cousin should issue you a badge."

"Well, there's nothing more we can do here. But at least we know what Bonnie was doing before she was killed."

"I poured you some lemonade, Sisters," Mr. Adler called from his perch behind the counter. "Set a spell."

Winnie was absolutely addicted to lemonade — although she liked hers with a little shot of whiskey. She sped to the front, tucked her basket next to the canned soup display, and slid onto one of the stools. I laid my basket next to hers and dropped onto the smooth oak seat.

"Ah, my arches welcome this break, Mr. Adler," I said. "Thank you."

"My pleasure."

He turned down the radio — which was playing American popular songs — and took his tobacco pouch out of his shirt pocket and his fixings out of his pant pocket. We sipped our drinks as he rolled and lit his small brown cigaret. Winnie was eying the pot-bellied jar next to the straw container. Ginger snaps. We both favored them over other cookies. Their tart sweetness and their crispness allowed them to melt in the mouth for a very long time. I liked them best with milk. But Winnie was a slave to the flavor of ginger with lemon. She must have been salivating, but, schooled by several Mother Franceses, she said not a word. Thank goodness Mr. Adler saw her interest, leaned over, and pushed the jar her way. Another two seconds and she might have scooped them up. Pretty close to breaking the theft commandment, that would be. Exeter, here comes Winnie!

"Did you find out who that girl was?" Mr. Adler asked.

Winnie swallowed, and spoke with a mouthful of snaps! "Yyngh."

"She means *yes*. She was Mildred Young's

granddaughter."

"I should have known. Spitting image, she was."

"You saw her, then?"

"If it's the same one — blue skirt, white blouse, good-looker with bright green eyes?"

Not when I saw them. Then, they were dulled by death. I pulled out the photo and pushed it across the counter.

"Yep. Not so pretty there, though." He sighed. "What's the world coming to?"

"Was she here often?"

"Often enough for me to remember her. Guess she's been hanging around here off and on for a few days, maybe a week. Played with that gangster's kid sometimes. Had a few pennies in her pocket for sweets for the boy, but didn't eat anything herself, at least not from this store. Skinny. All the girls today are too skinny. Need some meat on their bones to keep from getting sickly." Belying his words, he pulled the ginger snap jar away from Winnie, who was on her fourth cookie. "You know, now that I think on it, I remember her from a couple of years back. She hung around with the Coletti boy, Steve."

Good grief! It was true. The hairs on the back of your neck did stand up. Okay, thanks to the convent's mortification process, we sisters had a close cut. Yes, I didn't have any hairs there, only stubble. But no hair or stubble, something was standing!

"You mean Clementi?" I asked Mr. Adler.

"Yep. That's the one."

At that shocker, Winnie dropped her last snap. Well, if she didn't want it . . . but she batted my hand away.

"Come to think of it," Mr. Adler continued, "I haven't seen Steve around here lately."

"New Bedford," Winnie said, nibbling. "Working on the docks."

"Sure. And I'm Herbert Hoover."

Winnie huffed. "His mother told us . . ."

"Sister, unless you're a fisherman with your own boat, there hasn't been work on the docks in New Bedford for two years. But if that's what he told her, then that's what he wants her to think."

"Damson plums! Heliotrope! Serpent's wings!"

Winnie pinched my elbow. "People are looking at you! What are you talking about?"

"I'm swearing. Or as close as I can come to it." I stopped abruptly and whirled to look back. "Mrs. Clementi lied to us!"

"Yep. She did." Winnie tugged me towards the next charity visit. "People have a habit of doing that, Aggie. They can't help it."

"Yes, they can. It's a commandment. Thou shalt not bear false witness."

"And I suppose you don't lie."

"Not since taking the cowl."

She snickered. "Mayetta Morgan, you lied to Mother Frances."

"I did not. I evaded the truth, but I did not directly lie to her. There is a difference."

"A very small difference."

Yeah. About as small as the Grand Canyon. It was called a sin of omission. "You're right."

"Glory be to God! I never thought I'd see the day . . ."

"Don't be smug. I admit that I use evasion almost like lying. It serves my purpose — to deflect someone from probing what I don't want them to probe."

"And that's what Mrs. Clementi did."

"You think so?"

Winnie nodded. "Why else did she think she needed to lie to us? I could understand her reluctance to tell the truth to the police. But she could have trusted us."

"Obviously, she didn't. I wonder why not?"

The question plagued me during our last two visits, and I hardly heard a word anyone said. Why? Why? Why? Why? Why? Damson

198

plum that word! It was like some devil in my ear, sneering at me, wanting to make me mad. Not angry. I was already angry. Mad. Like crazy. *As if Mother Frances doesn't already think you're crazy. Shut up!* At least Monsignor Grace didn't.

"I need a telephone!"

Felicia Leone — our final charity recipient — gasped. "Sister?"

"I'm sorry, but I just remem . . ." *Don't lie!* ". . . thought of something and I wonder if you have a telephone so I can check on it?"

"Why, of course. It's in the kitchen."

Yep. Another of those wall things. A pox on them! At least now I knew how to use it. I picked up the earpiece and began to crank it when I heard shrieks coming out of the cone. What in the world? "Hello?"

"Who is this," a voice asked.

"Sister Mary Agnes."

"Oh, Sister. Sorry. This is Dot Klein."

"But I didn't call you."

"No, of course you didn't."

Had the entire world gone mad?

"I'm talking to Mary McBride, now," Dot said.

"Hello, Sister Agnes," Mary said.

"Hello." What a wonderful instrument! You didn't even have to call someone. They were just there.

"We'll be off in a minute," Dot said.

"Should I wait?"

"Just hang up the earpiece, Sister."

I did what she asked and returned to the parlor.

"What's wrong, Sister Agnes?" Felicia asked.

"It's a puzzle. Maybe some kind of mistake? You ought to let the telephone people know. Dot Klein was already talking when I picked up the cone thing."

"Oh, that happens all the time. There are two other people besides Dot on our party line."

"What is a party line?"

"It's all most of us have these days. Four to six people share one telephone line. It's lots cheaper. We just signal each other when the line's available again." Two rings sounded and then silence. "That's Dot, letting you know she's finished. You can make a call now."

"Amazing."

I made my call — which was accompanied by cracklings, clicks, clunks, and whirs on the line — and we took leave of Felicia. The rest of the day went much as usual for a Saturday. Winnie and I graded papers for an hour. I noted that Dante had made four errors on his spelling test. Very unusual, that. And very confusing. Dante was the best speller in the class — perhaps in the entire school. Something must have been troubling him. I would have to speak to him on Monday.

"I have some sewing to do, but I think I'll do it in my room, Winnie."

"Leave the sewing basket," Mary Claire all but ordered.

Okay, Lord. That may not be quite true. Sister Claire didn't "all but." She definitely ordered, like queen of the May. Yes, chit was the right name for her, and that was NOT an exaggeration. Regardless, I overlooked her breach of etiquette — difficult for me, but I did it — and only took one of the small rolls of black thread, two needles, and one small pair of scissors up to my room. I wasn't looking forward to the next ten minutes.

Fifteen minutes later and "Damson plums" were flying through the stuffiness of my cell. Damson plums! Damson plums! Damson plums! *Lord, are there no skills You could have given me? It's bad enough that I can't cook. Or iron. Or make a bed. But not to be able to ply a needle! Why did You make me female at all?*

"Ouch!" I sucked the five thousandth needle prick and tried to mollify myself with the idea that exaggeration wasn't lying! *Okay, Lord, I heard You. It is. But, golly, gee, couldn't You help make this easier?*

My door opened and Winnie leaned casually against the jamb. *You always come through, Lord. Ask and ye shall receive.* Prayer. It's like a spiritual telephone call. Without the party line.

For one moment there, something niggled at my thoughts, but I couldn't quite pluck it out of the air. *Leave it for now. If it's important, it will come back.*

"Need help?" Winnie asked. She leaned forward to see what I was doing. "I thought I gave you enough time to get completely exasperated. There yet?"

I heard the unmistakable sound of brogans on the stairs and motioned Winnie inside. "Close the door." I pulled over the one straight-backed chair and held out my spare skirt. "I'm trying to concoct a hiding place. Something attached to the pocket, easy to get into, but away from anyone's casual glance. I especially don't want anything to fall out of it."

"Like a gun?"

"Shush! Someone has already searched this cell. With all the commotion in the halls right now, we have to be quiet."

"Let's see what you've done." She examined my attempts and, within a blink, she mashed her lips together, fighting hard not to laugh.

"Go ahead," I said. "Get it out."

She laughed without one sound for two minutes. I timed her. One hundred and thirty-six beats of my heart, but they sort of speeded up as I counted. That's how angry I was getting.

"That's enough. You got it out. Now help me," I said.

"Is this your cowl you cut up?"

"An old one, with a ton of moth holes."

"Putting worn-out things to good use. How unlike you." She tested the fabric, as if I hadn't! "Strong enough." She began pulling out stitches as I slipped out of the skirt I had on and into one of my cold weather skirts. "Oh, May. There has to be something you can do besides get into trouble." She smoothed out the pieces I had cut. "Well, maybe there is something you can do. This is a very good design. Too bad you can't sew it up without mooshing it all together."

"Moosh. That's a good word for it. Mooo! A nun with hooves for fingers."

"You just need practice. You avoid sewing, and therefore you can't do it well."

"Good. I can't do it good."

"You're right. This is pretty bad. But it

shouldn't take much time to straighten out the stitches."

"You do that. I'll do your chores."

"Okay. But I'll need buttons."

"In the bottom drawer. Cough drop box."

I bolted out of the room and hurried to the library to dust a zillion books for Winnie (*No more decades, please, Lord!*), then zipped into the kitchen to scrub down the counter and chopping block, and wash, dry, and put away all the glasses and crockery that had accumulated over the day. By the time I got back, Winnie had finished the two hiding places in both my skirts.

"This is perfect!"

"Thanks. Although I'm not sure I should have helped you with this."

"It will be okay."

"Sure it will."

The pockets were duplicated. The regular pockets were deep and capacious, and attached to them were smaller but certainly large enough pockets that were hidden by a placket. The twinned pockets stayed together by braided strips of thread that looped over the buttons. I pulled up my pillow and withdrew the case and note that I had tucked under it when I got back to my cell. I took the gun out of the case and dropped it on the bed. Winnie scooted away from it, eyeing it as if it would go off any minute. The case and note went into my spare skirt's new hidden pocket and I hung it on the clothes peg.

While I changed from my winter skirt into the one I wore each day, Winnie watched me carefully. When I picked up the gun, she shook her head and her gaze was both pleading and frightened.

"Sister Agnes, don't do it."

I looked at the tips of my brogans and then at the crucifix on the wall. He hung there, nails in His hands and feet. After the agony in the Garden, after bleeding from every pore, after asking His father to remove the burden from Him, He had walked into His betrayal, knowing what was about to happen. He was the son of God. I wasn't. But I was betting He would understand.

I looked at Winnie and tried without words to make her understand. She sighed and nodded.

I turned to look at the crucified Christ, then put the gun in my new hidden pocket, wondering if I was about to walk into my own betrayal.

If so, who would be my Judas?

Who, my Pontius Pilate?

CHAPTER SIXTEEN

Confession is good for the soul.

Depending on who was hearing that confession.

Usually, our Pastor, Father Lawton, heard confessions. Father Lawton was — the name said it all.

The weight of the Law, all ten of the Lord's and quite a few that the Vatican had thrown in over the years, was a fearsome thing in and of itself. Father Lawton, however, wasn't satisfied with heavenly or ecclesiastical rules. He had his own pet laws, which only he administered.

Like: *Thou shalt not chew gum.* He spent two entire Sunday sermons explaining how it stuck to everything and was hard as the devil to scrape off of beautiful wood and travertine marble — like the miles of it at St. Catherine's. Of course, he was right. I should know. We nuns had to try to get it off, and our fingernails attested to the impossibility of it. So, if he even suspected that someone had chewed gum, he'd levy a recitation of the entire rosary — usually, the sorrowful mysteries. I had chewed gum only once this week, and nowhere near the church. That wouldn't count with him. He'd ask if I had chewed. I'd be forced to answer. And I wouldn't be able to lie or prevaricate. Darn my socks! With 216 decades that I already owed God, I didn't need ten more exacted by Father Lawton for my penance.

Another Lawton Law: *Thou shalt not sneeze or cough during Mass.* According to the good Father, it destroyed the beauty of the liturgy. And if you believe that, there's this bridge in Brooklyn . . . I was convinced that the real reason he demanded that people leave the Mass and sneeze or cough off church grounds was because just about anything broke his concentration. During the flowering and haying seasons and the winter months, half the church emptied out! It's a wonder anyone heard the entire Mass.

Then there was the granddaddy of all Lawton's Laws: *Thou shalt not see or hear what thou wast not meant to see or hear.* Of course, it started because he wanted to protect the morals of his parishioners. But it went way beyond that. If he had had his way, none of us would have been allowed to read a newspaper or magazine, listen to the radio, or enter a moving picture house. Luckily, the mother house and the Chancery agreed that newspapers were essential, some radio programs were educational and entertaining, and some moving pictures were wholesome fun. On the whole, they discouraged reading magazines. That was okay. Books were better. The Chancery distributed an approved list of radio programs and movies. Since we didn't have radio — yet — we sisters were allowed only one day a month to view the latest Lawton-approved moving picture production. Under this law, if most moving pictures were bad to see, what would Father Lawton say about two murders? I'd probably get a month, maybe a year, of rosaries levied on me!

Lord, please don't shove me in his direction. I'll be on my knees at dawn, trying to pray my penance.

"Who's hearing confession?" I said to Winnie. Please let it be one of the substitute priests. They're young, hardly out of the seminary. They might not even know what had happened and my part in it.

DON'T COUNT ON IT!

Was that Your booming voice, Lord? Is it because of the lethal thing in my pocket? I promise I won't use it. Unless I must.

There was no lightning bolt, so I could breathe again. "So, who is it?" I asked Winnie.

"Father Lawton."

Groan.

"And Father Bryant."

"What?"

"It's the Saturday closest to the Ides of March, Aggie. And one of the four days all year that he hears confessions."

"If he doesn't turn off his hearing aid." Well, darn my socks! This could work to my advantage. "I'll take Father Bryant."

Winnie rolled her eyes. "Of course you will."

I decorously dashed to the confessional on the other side of the nave and checked the sliders next to the thick velvet drapes. The one on the left read Occupied, and I could hear deep-toned mumbles and drones and an angry rise in tone, which meant someone was in that box. Wonders of wonders, he was actually trying to confess, and Father Bryant didn't like what he was hearing. Good luck to the man behind the drape. Since I had the right side for myself, I slid over the panel, and slipped inside. If anyone else came for confession — and that was doubtful, since Father Bryant usually snored his way through the confession hours

— then they would know this side was also taken. I knelt and prayed for help in making a good confession. The mumblings stopped and I waited for Father Bryant to slide open the grate between his box and mine.

And waited.

And waited some more.

There were no snores, so what was going on? Should I try to find out?

No! No! No! No running in where angels feared. Not again. But the minutes droned on, and, darn my socks, someone had to find out what the problem was. I looked through the gloom of the box up to the heavens. *Why me, Lord? Isn't there some other way You can temper me? Must I always rush from the frying pan into the fire?*

Nix on the fire! I'm okay with a few problems. *If You want me to open the confessional door and roust Father Bryant, who am I to argue with You? Okay, don't shout! I'm not going to roust him. I'll just gently tap him on the shoulder and wake him up.*

If he wasn't sleeping the sleep of the dead, that is.

I sighed, resigned to my fate, rose from the kneeler, and left the box. Resigned, yes; but it was weird opening the priest's confessional box during confession hours. It should be locked from the inside while confessions were being heard. But I knew it wasn't since I helped clean it once a week, and had been there when the lock got broken. And, no, it wasn't me who broke it, but one of the novices. Sister Claire, Sister Angelica, Sister Paul? I couldn't remember.

"Father Bryant?" I tapped on the door and, when I got no answer, turned the knob. I eased the door open and got the shock of my life when a hand clamped itself on the back of my neck, tipping back my cowl. "Yipes!"

"What the heck are you doing?"

"Richard!" I settled my cowl, then smacked him. With my fist. Couldn't help it. That's what upper arms are for. "You took three years off my life. What are you doing here?"

"Does the word *confession* mean anything to you?"

There was a commotion of some sort close to the altar. Looked as if someone had fainted. Should never fast before confession, only before communion. But some of the older parishioners did it anyway. Soon, everyone who had been watching us was looking towards the front of the church.

"Help me wake up Father Bryant," I said to Richard. "I've been waiting twenty minutes in that box and he never slid over the grate."

"Woo, boy, you must be really afraid of Father Lawton."

"A whole rosary, that's what I'd get."

He chuckled and pulled open the door. "Nobody here."

I pushed him out of the way. "There must be. I heard voices and then silence. I didn't hear this door open or close. And he's supposed to be here. It's the Saturday closest to the . . ."

"Ides of March? Yeah, I know."

"So that's what you're doing on this side of the church. You didn't want to confess to Father Lawton, either. Pot calling the kettle black, Richard. And I wonder what that confession would have been like."

"You'll never know."

Winnie strode up and cocked an eyebrow. "Finished?"

"He's not here."

"What do you mean, he's not here?" I went through the whole thing again. She frowned and said, "But that's not possible. This is the Saturday closest . . ."

"I know! But he's still not here."

Richard entered the inner sanctum and felt around the walls. He had to be kidding. "Do you think there's a secret panel?"

"No, Aggie. But I didn't know what else to do."

"I do," Winnie said. "I'll get Father Lawton."

Both Richard and I got out the only word possible in this situation. "No!"

"Don't be silly. He's not going to bite." Suddenly, Winnie's eyes rounded and she pointed to the floor. "What's that?"

Richard knelt and touched a dark spot next to the left confessional box. He raised it and showed it to us. Dark and sticky.

"It looks like . . . Oh," I said, "not again."

Winnie blanched and sat with a thump in the nearest pew. She knelt to pray and I figured that was a good idea, but didn't have time. "Pray for all of us," I said.

She kept her head down, her eyes closed, and her hands peaked, but she nodded.

I turned to Richard. "Any other — uh — droplets?"

Richard checked the marble floor. Father Lawton was going to add one more law: *Thou shalt not spill blood in the church.*

Please, Lord, just let it be simple. Like a cut finger or something. I'd give a whole rosary for a cut finger.

"One more. Here by the drape." He pulled the velvet curtain back, and stiffened. "Found Father Bryant."

213

Richard bent to pick him up and a few drops of blood plopped onto his camel hair jacket.

"Cold water will get that out," I said.

We looked at each other, then he smiled slightly. "You're getting too used to this, Aggie."

My heart hurt. "I know."

Father Bryant had a huge gash over his right eye and a bump on the back of his head. He groaned, and it was obvious that he was in great pain. "Wish we had a telephone," I said. "He looks dreadful, but at least he's still alive." I went over to Winnie. "I never thought I'd say this, but go get Father Lawton."

She jumped up, crossed herself, and ran across the church to Father Lawton's side.

Richard gently laid the old priest on the pew Winnie had just vacated. He took off his camel hair jacket, balled it up, and put it under Father Bryant's head. That jacket probably cost twenty-five dollars — enough to feed a family for months — but Father Bryant needed it more than he did.

I knew what the next thirty minutes were going to be like. "I hate this. I wish . . ."

"Leave," Richard said. "Now. Before anyone gets here. I'll tell them I found Father Bryant. It won't be a lie. I did."

"Richard, you know I can't leave."

"Yeah. But you should."

"Why is this happening?"

He shrugged. "The world is a dangerous place."

"Oh, please," I scoffed. "This is a church. Someone chose to do this. Two days ago, they chose a convent. It might happen every day out there, but it is not supposed to happen in here!"

A small form appeared out of nowhere. Okay, from the milling people at the back of the church.

"Uncle Richard," Dante said, "when can we go home?"

"Oh, cripes, Dan, I forgot. I'm sorry."

Richard usually brought Dante to confession of a Saturday. I should have remembered. I ruffled Dante's hair and forced a smile for the boy's sake. "Back to work, I see," I said to Richard.

"Yep. The kid needs me."

And I believe you need him, too. "He called you uncle. Something I don't know about?"

"I was engaged to his oldest sister."

"Wow. And I thought we didn't have secrets."

"*Was* engaged, Aggie. She called it off."

Dante interrupted us when he took Richard's hand and peeked over the back of the

215

pew to see what Richard had been doing. "What happened to Father Bryant?"

"We don't know."

"Was it the same thing that happened to Bonnie?"

Oh, dear Lord! Now this young boy was getting used to things no one should have to get used to. "No, Dan. Father Bryant probably slipped and fell. He's getting old, you know."

"He *is* old."

"Yes, he is."

Father Lawton rushed across the church, his open surplice and his stole flapping behind him. With him was one of the seminarians who helped out with parish duties. Father Lawton pushed me aside and bent over the elderly priest.

"Father McCoy, run across to Adler's and ask to use the telephone. Call the police, tell them what's happened, and tell them to call Dr. Giordano and to send an ambulance." He turned to us, and didn't at all seem surprised to see me in the midst of this new mess. "What happened this time?"

"I have no idea. He wasn't in the confessional. I waited a long time. Richard came up and we, um, found him like this."

"Lying on the pew?"

"No, Father," Richard said. "He was in

the left box."

"The left box? What was he doing in there?"

"I have no idea," Richard said, and I could tell by the tightness of his lips that he was getting riled.

"Do you have any idea, Sister Agnes?"

"No, Father."

"Well, somebody must know something."

You can count on it. But probably not where you would look. Don't see what you shouldn't see. Unbelievable!

A crowd was gathering, but Father Lawton shooed them away, including Dante. I tried to keep my eye on him. Yesterday, I would have let him wander about the church on his own. Today, after this latest horror, I wanted to make sure he was okay and stayed that way.

I whispered to Richard, "Is Dan's bodyguard here?"

He nodded. "But I can't see him in this crowd."

"Father," I said, "may I be excused for just a moment? I need to . . . go."

One flick of his wrist and away I sped. Dante had headed towards the altar, so that's where I went. There was a small prayer corner set aside for statues of the Blessed Virgin and St. Catherine, and plenty of candles for the faithful to offer up prayers. Dante often visited there when we brought the class to the church. He once said he liked the lilies St. Catherine carried. I figured that was his destination.

I rounded the corner in time to see Dante being dragged across the floor by a tall figure in a dark green coat.

"Dante! You, there! Stop! In the name of God, let him go!"

CHAPTER SEVENTEEN

Oh, Lord! Now I sounded like some second-rate moving picture actor!

"Richard DelVecchio is right behind me! He has a gun." *And if he doesn't, I do.*

The tall figure hesitated just a bit and Dante kicked him. Hard.

Yelling in church was going to get me an audience with the Pope — and it wouldn't be pleasant. Regardless — "Kick him again!"

He did, and the man cursed roundly, then back-handed Dante.

With a quick look over his shoulder, the man who had taken Dante pushed him out of the way and rushed out of the church through the side door. Dante stumbled back, fell against the statue of St. Catherine, but stayed on his feet.

I flew to Dante's side. He flung his arms around my legs, nearly knocking me to the floor, but I righted myself, and forgetting how heavy he was, scooped him up into my arms, settling him on my hip so I could see his eyes, hoping that there wouldn't be fear in them. I was wrong. My heart hurt from the knowledge of just how frightened this young boy had been, and still was.

"Are you okay?" I asked.

He nodded and sucked in air three or four times, fighting back tears, trying to keep a brave face, trying to be a boy.

"It's okay to cry, Dante. Look, I'm crying, too."

"That's 'cause you're a girl."

"No. It's because nothing bad happened to you. Sometimes tears are God's way of showing how thankful we are for getting out of a bad situation."

"I guess I could. Maybe just one." But a few trickled down and I wiped them away with the edge of my cowl.

Richard rounded the corner, with Dante's bodyguard right behind. Some bodyguard! I was going to have a talk with his mother. Better yet, Winnie would. That should put the fear of God in him.

Richard quickly checked out all Dante's extremities, then, when he found only a red mark on the boy's face, but whole bones and no blood, chucked him under his chin. "You okay, sport?"

"Yep."

"He's shaking, Richard."

"Here, let me take him."

"No. You can put me down," Dante said, and wriggled out of my arms. He was trying to put a brave face on it, but he stood close to Richard. Close enough so their clothes touched. Comfort, for Dante, came in the form of a man. Richard. That was a good thing, because he had chosen the best man I knew in this church at this time.

I guess my shouts had carried. Mother Frances would love that! She had one more black mark to strike next to my name. Damson plums! Parishioners flocked to this third commotion, but Dante's bodyguard forcibly kept them back — until one tall, angry nun shoved him aside.

"I lived next to your parents when I was a kid, Paul Felice, and I've known you since you were a snot-nosed youth, so don't tell me to keep away. And what kind of a bodyguard are you, anyway? Letting this happen? Really!"

Trust Winnie! Yep, his mother was going to hear about this.

She got down on her knees and began to raise her hands and for one moment there, I thought she was going to throw up her hands and praise God. If she did, I was going to pop her one. Instead, her palms cupped Dante's cheeks and she looked him right in the eye and studied him as I had done, just on a different level. His.

When she was satisfied with what she found, she smiled. "So," she said to Dante, "you ready to tell us what happened?"

"He smelled funny."

"Who?" Richard asked.

"The guy who pulled my arm."

Richard prodded, "Did you see him?"

Dante had to think about that for a minute. "Not really. He wore a hat — a fedora, like Dad's, I think — pulled way down over his forehead. I think he had grayish hair. His face was covered on the bottom because he had his coat collar turned up."

Josiah materialized out of the crowd, notepad and pencil in hand. "What kind of coat, kid?"

"Green. Long. With big fancy buttons."

"What do you mean by fancy?" I asked.

"I don't know. Fancy. With designs on them. Like that lee flower you told us about when we studied France."

"The fleur de lis?"

"Yep."

"Shoes, kid?"

Dante got this devil-in-his-eyes look and I

knew Dante was going to be okay — and that Josiah had met his match.

"Yep," Dante said.

Josiah sighed. "Not was he wearing any. What kind were they?"

"Brown. Or black. I can't remember that good. But they were dark."

Josiah — who had absolutely no experience with children — silently appealed to me. I bent to look at Dan. "Were the shoes like Richard's or like Officer Morgan's or maybe Paul's?"

Dante took his time examining all the shoes, then he shook his head. "Nope. They were more like . . . like yours."

"Brogans? The man wore brogans?"

"Yep. And funny socks."

"How funny?" Winnie asked, as Josiah made notes.

"They weren't dark. Dad and Richard always wear dark socks. These were lighter colored. Like tan. And heavy. With lots of wrinkles."

Richard nudged Josiah. "You got enough? I'd like to get Dante home. This has been a shock."

"It's okay, Uncle Richard. I might forget if I don't tell them now."

Richard's surprise wasn't lost on me. He seemed pleased, and he smiled for the first time since we'd "lost" Dante. "Yeah, I guess you might, at that. Go ahead, sport. Tell them what you can remember."

"It will help them find the bad guy, right?"

"Right."

"So how come you didn't ask me why he smelled funny?"

Whoops! That was an error, and Richard knew it. He looked just a bit shame-faced. But he shook it off, and hunkered down to Dante's level, too.

"I was pretty scared, sport," he said. "I don't really know what I said or why. I was only paying attention to how you were feeling."

What a crew! Kneeling, squatting, hunkering down — because a boy we all loved had almost been . . . nope, I wasn't going to think that way. Dante wasn't.

"So," I said, "what way did he smell funny?"

Dante laughed; that devil-in-his-eyes look was back. "No, Sister Agnes. He didn't smell funny. He had a nose, didn't he?"

"I don't know, Dante. Did he?"

"Course he did. He could smell okay. But his clothes smelled. Like when Mom, um —" The devilish look was erased by deep hurt, and then he rushed to get the rest out. "Like when she used to take them out of the cedar chest." He took a deep breath, dug in his pocket, and pulled out two pennies. "Sister Winifred, would you light a candle for me before I forget? That's why I came here. To light a candle for my Mom. Her name was Catherine, you know. And she loved lilies, just like St. Catherine."

"Oh, my God," Winnie whispered. She took his two cents and ruffled his hair. "I'll say a 'Hail Mary,' too."

"Shoot," Josiah said. "We all will."

How do children do it — show adults the things that are truly important? Dante was alive. He was safe. He was missing his dead — possibly murdered — mother. First things first.

Winnie led us in a "Hail Mary" and Richard added a "Glory Be to the Father."

When it was finished, I said, "Mothballs."

"Yeah, that's it," Dante said. "How'd you know?"

"My Gran does it every year. Mothballs at the end of summer and the end of winter. When you take things out of storage, you have to hang everything on the line to take away the smell. Sometimes you have to spray them with lemon water."

Josiah made a note in his book. "So this guy . . ."

"Was wearing clothes that just came out

of mothballs," I said.

"What does that mean?" he said. "And where does it get us?"

"I don't know yet. But it's something to think about."

After a few more minor questions (eye color and other things that Dante couldn't remember, or hadn't seen) and a few more minutes, Richard took Dante home and Winnie and I went to check on Father Bryant. We learned that Dr. Giordano had accompanied him to the hospital in the ambulance, and they wouldn't know anything until he woke up. If he woke up. What a dreadful thought!

Father Lawton was finishing up the confessions while the police took photos and dusted the place with white and black powder, searching for fingerprints, they said.

"Probably take weeks before we have a match," Josiah said.

"If you get a match," I said. "I saw in one of the newsreels that there weren't many records yet."

"We're working on it."

"Work fast."

I studied the confessional booths, trying to make sense of what had happened.

"Why Father Bryant?" Winnie asked.

"What could he do to hurt anyone? What did he know?"

"I'm more inclined to think he stumbled into something and the attack on him was a mistake, or a spur of the moment thing," I said.

Josiah looked at me as if I had three heads. Lately, I've had a constant headache trying to keep everything straight, and to figure out this stupidity, this true evil. Things were mixed up, with too many suspects, too few clues, and no reason for all this to happen. But I thought I was right about Father Bryant.

"It must have been a mistake, Josiah. He isn't usually here. If you understand that, then you understand what happened tonight."

"You're talking in riddles."

"No. I'm not. It's only Platonic logic." I ticked off the things that had occurred to me over the last half hour. "One, this is the Saturday closest to the Ides of March. Two, Father Bryant only hears confession once every quarter. The Saturday closest to the Ides of March is one of those times. Three, I forgot he was going to be here."

Winnie jumped in, "So, if you forgot, then the bad guy might have, too!"

"Doesn't that make sense?" I said. "And

the rest of it makes sense too. Four, if the bad guy forgot Father Bryant was going to be here, he would have expected this confessional and this side of the church to be empty. Five, an empty confessional, or even just the corner near it, is a great place to meet someone you don't want to be seen with. Six, the bad guy was the one I heard arguing with someone. Seven, Father Bryant must have surprised them when he came to hear confessions. Maybe he heard something he shouldn't have heard, maybe he saw something he shouldn't have seen, so they had to silence him."

"Why hit him like that?" Winnie asked. "That was a huge bump, especially for an elderly priest. I think it showed hate."

"Perhaps. Or maybe they were scared. Or just plain mean. I don't know," I said. "I haven't figured out that part, yet."

"And you haven't figured out who the bad guy was talking to."

"A woman."

"You sure of that?" Josiah asked.

"I wasn't. But I am now. The first voice was definitely a low, gravelly voice. The sound of it carried pretty well, but not the words. The second voice was harder to hear. The only reason I can think of for that to happen is if it were higher-pitched but spoken softer."

"So," Josiah said, "a feminine voice. A dame and a gangster."

"Really? Not all crimes," I said, "are committed by gangsters."

"And very few by dames," he said. "But if you're right, this one has a dame smack, dab in the middle of it. And we haven't the foggiest notion who she is."

"We know one thing. She has plenty to do with St. Catherine's."

And maybe (There was the note and the search, after all; but, *oh, God, please don't let it be so!*) something to do with the convent.

CHAPTER EIGHTEEN

The night would never end. Winnie and I had laundry to do. Vespers to attend. Our weekly bath to take. Ah! The one thing I was really looking forward to — bathing and soaking in a relatively hot tub with a little of Winnie's lavender water tipped in.

But Mother Frances sent Sister Claire to fetch us.

Claire looked at us as if we were lice to be drowned in kerosene. "I didn't realize just how much trouble a nun could get herself into. When is your term of service here due to end?"

Chit? My bet is that Richard would have another word for this nun. "I don't know," I said as sweetly as I could without choking on it. "Perhaps we'll stay forever. But aren't you about to be transferred? Did I hear them say Exeter?"

Technically, not lies, only questions. But I hear You loud and clear, Lord. Two hundred eighteen decades, here I come!

Claire's anger was palpable. Her eyes wrinkled up in a defiant squint. Not an attractive expression, wrinkles coming fast! She searched our faces, but Winnie and I had been taught by the best of them. We could school our features so nothing showed. Except our own hardly noticeable wrinkles. Claire couldn't crack our façades, and fled with a swish of her skirts.

"That wasn't nice," Winnie said. "But satisfying."

Mother Frances received us standing up, so we didn't dare sit down, even though my legs and feet were screaming for a good soak and soothing sleep. We weren't the only ones affected by this. The Reverend Mother looked as if she had been hit by *two* Model Ts.

"When Sister Angelica came back from confession," Mother Frances said, "she told me about Father Bryant. He is old, frail. What was done to him was evil, and the person who did this — there has to be a special place in hell for that kind of blackness of soul." A deep breath in, a deep breath out, and our Mother was settled, as she tried to teach us to be. "I wanted to rush right over, but thought it best to stay here in the convent, calming down the other sisters. I would, however, like to know how Father Bryant is doing."

"We don't know," Winnie said. "Josiah — Sister Agnes's cousin — said he'd get word to us if there was any change."

"And the boy?"

"He's fine," I said. "Shaken up. Missing his mother. But Richard and his father will help him work through his fears."

"Thank you. I will pray for both of them."

In silence we walked over wires and edged around workmen's tools until we got to my cell, where we had privacy.

"Holy Toledo!" Winnie said.

"Yes. The world is changing right in front of our eyes and sometimes it isn't all bad."

We set about getting out our dirty laundry. And I had to transfer the gun from the habit I was going to launder to the one I wore until my habit was dry. The irony of what I'd just done forced a reaction I hadn't expected to voice. I was preparing for danger. Mother Frances was . . .

"Did you see the look in Mother's eyes?" I asked Winnie.

"Yes. Hot to cold in a blink."

"It was more than that. All that pain, even fear, then a deep breath, and . . . nothing. Neither bitterness nor anger. Just nothing. She washed it out of her, the way we will wash the dirt out of our habits. That easy. How does she do it? Is it her nun's cowl that makes her so unflappable? I don't have that ability."

"No, you react quickly, emotionally."

"Do you think the way she does it is good, Winnie? Should we all be like that?"

"Isn't that what we're striving for, what she's teaching us, what being tempered means?"

"I suppose. But for a brief moment back there, I wondered whether that much tempering is good, or an easy way out."

"Easy way out? Most of us have a very hard time doing it."

"I know; and I admire that you can. My problem is that I struggle daily because I don't want to push down what she pushed down. For one moment, there, she was feeling. For one moment the pain and fear were real. And then she 'tempered' herself and forced everything away." My hands trembled from the force of my emotions and I started to clench them to make them stop. But then I realized that stopping the trembling was giving in to tempering. "I can't do it. Winnie, I want to *feel* that pain. I want to know what it's like for everyone else. I don't want to *be* everyone else. I just don't think I can do them any good if I don't feel what they feel. If that makes me a bad nun, then so be it."

"You're not a bad nun, Mayetta Morgan. Just different."

"Yes. But therein lies a problem. How much difference can the Church take?"

"I think before this is all over, we're going to find out."

Once in the laundry room, we each knew our parts in the routine we'd established over the years. Hot water, washing tubs, Ivory Snow, newspapers, clothespins, clothesline. It was almost syncopated rhythm. After the clothes had soaked in the Ivory Snow for five minutes, I worked on our undergarments and the habits we had worn all week with good old yellow pumice soap. Smelled awful, but did the trick on the worst stains. I handed each garment to Winnie and she scrubbed them on the washboard. Twice. I rinsed. Thrice. While I was doing that, she unwound a clothesline and strung it across the room, hanging it from pegs on opposite walls, one more line in a succession of five others. It would have been better to hang all our clothes outside, but nuns did not show their undergarments. They would have to drip dry onto newspapers that were strewn double thick on the worn wooden floor. Winnie hung the habits outside. While she was gone, I was supposed to spread the newspapers.

Not the best job for a news-hungry nun!

I sneaked a peek at the headlines, for this was the first time I'd seen a paper in three days. *Bishop-Designate Keough Makes First Public Appearance. Vows to Strengthen Catholic Schools.* Photo of him. Handsome man. Monsignor Grace in the background. Since it was about the schools, I ripped the article out to read later. *DelVecchio Arrested, Bail Set at One Million.* Didn't need to read that one. He was out. Who cared what happened to him yesterday? *Upsurge in Wayward Youth Violence.* Nope. Had my fill of violence. *New Bedford Knitting Mills to Stay Closed until Further Notice.* Not enough capital or sales to open them, the first paragraph said. Sad. So many people out of work. I wondered if it would affect our parishioners, and put the article in my pocket. *Spring and Summer Fashions Hit Local Stores.* How ironic! Right next to each other. But there were some people who had money. The photo with the article showed a lovely spring coat and a fedora worn as a woman's hat, complete with a tiny feather in the ribbon trim. *Just Right for Chilly Nights.* Well, Winnie and I didn't have to worry about any fashions, but it did look stunning on the model. Sixty-five dollars? Were they kidding? Who besides the very rich had that kind of money these days?

Sister Joseph stuck her head in the door. "Are the tubs empty? I forgot to wash my stockings."

"Help yourself," I said, finishing up the front page and perusing the second and third. I read aloud, "*Sixteen Organists Vie for Job at Strand Theater.* Sixteen? I didn't know there were sixteen out-of-work moving picture organists in the state."

"There are probably more than that," Sister Joseph said. "Today, even churches are feeling the pinch. Not much money in the collection baskets, so they can't pay their organists."

"*What's Happening to Our Children?* Hah! What isn't happening? This is too long. I'll read it later." I ripped out half the page and stuck it in my pocket. "*Teen Found Murdered.*"

"That's us."

"Wonder if they discovered Bonnie's last name? Nope."

"Yesterday's paper."

"According to this article, no one even knew her first name. They do now, much good it will do her!" There was more emotionally charged trouble. Didn't they ever have good things to announce? *"Teenage Gangs Roam Providence Streets; Homes Vandalized, Residents Robbed."*

"Right around the corner, just four days ago."

Steve Clementi popped into my head. I wondered how far the teen violence extended. All the way to New Bedford? Another article for later. I ripped that out and pocketed it, pushing down the other articles, and feeling the weight of the gun on my hip. And the weight of the world — our world — on my shoulders.

The side door snapped closed. "Done," Winnie said. "What in the world? You haven't started hanging the undergarments! Honestly, Aggie, sometimes you vex me beyond endurance."

Sister Joseph laughed when Winnie plucked the newspaper out of my hands and dropped it under the clothesline. The two of them helped me layer the rest of the paper and hang our garments. Joseph made sure there was plenty of room between her stockings and our clothes.

"Don't want to get them mixed in with yours."

Not likely. Her stockings were as old as she was, and thick and stretchy, woven that way to hold in her swollen ankles and legs. Because we stood almost the entire day, and walked everywhere, I expected Winnie and I would both have to wear something like them as we aged. For now, problems with our legs could be solved with a soaking bath.

Too bad we couldn't have one every day!

Vespers was short and sweet, the only surprise was Mother Frances' inclusion of Dante's family in the prayers. I didn't know if I could take more surprises.

Bath time was always too short. Three tubs in the room (separated by heavy drapes strung on more clothesline, of course) and bathing dresses (after all, nuns were modest in all things, including their bathtub), gave us plenty of privacy, if not enough time to enjoy it. Get in, every two minutes try to keep the tent dress from floating, and soap up. We would be lucky to get five minutes to rinse and lie back to soak away our aches and pains. But, oh, those five minutes!

"I'll take some of that lavender water, now, Winnie." She edged it around the curtain and I poured a bit into the water. The smell was heady and my limbs seemed weightless. "I look forward to this all week. It must be sinful, it's so wonderful."

"Oh, no, not you two!"

"Well, if it isn't our favorite sister," I said

to Sister Claire. I peeked out of the cubicle and had to choke down a laugh. There she was, looking from right to left like a spectator at a tennis match in Newport. She began backing out of the bathing room, but the kettle was steaming and she was going to have to take a bath sometime, so she shrugged and took the far cubicle.

"I am not going to Exeter," she said in a strangled voice that announced she was struggling to get into her bathing dress. "Mother Frances assured me that I would finish out my preparation here, close to the mother house."

Oh, joy! Living out the rest of our time here with Claire and Mother Frances? *Lord, can't You do something? It's like never-ending doses of fingernails scraping on chalkboard.* Maybe settling wasn't so bad after all. Although I liked this kind of settling better. If I ever become a Mother Superior, soaking baths will be a daily routine! *Work on that, for all of us, would You, please, Lord?*

Winnie and I rose from the tubs and each of us headed for the privacy of one of the folding screens in the corner. I hated getting out of the cold, wet bathing dress, but finally managed it, toweled myself dry, and donned the nightdress and robe I had brought with me. Holding the wet dress out so I didn't get soaked, I hung it on the clothesline in the corner, then shook out the towel and hung it to dry on the rack. Winnie did the same and then sniffed the air.

"What is that you're using for your bath, Sister Claire?" she asked. "It smells heavenly."

"Something my fian . . . a gift from a friend."

"It's not lavender."

"No. Bath oil."

"And its name?"

"That shouldn't trouble you. You couldn't possibly afford it."

Winnie balled her fists and I had to pull her out of the room and down the hall lest she forget to temper herself.

"She will probably become a Mother Superior in her later years," I said.

"If someone doesn't kill her first."

CHAPTER NINETEEN

Spiders skittered up and down my arms and legs. Okay, it only felt that way. Anticipation of our visit to the Chancery. Even Mother Frances was not immune. She took more breaths, several at morning Mass, and the struggle to temper must have been incalculable, because she finally gave up and closeted herself in her office.

The other sisters found innumerable excuses to peek out the parlor windows, and Sisters Claire and Angelica were none too pleased to be assigned the Mary McBride visit. Winnie very pleasantly waved them farewell, a slightly pompous smile on her face — which she quickly schooled when Mother Frances re-entered the room and held out a stole she had been working on. It was beautifully wrought, with embroidered crosier and lilies, St. Catherine's flower.

"I thought we would bring a gift to the new Bishop."

"Wasn't that for Father Lawton?" I asked. "Sister!"

Whoops! Not starting out all that great.

She showed it to Justina. "I ran out of the green for the last few leaves. Do you have any?"

Justina plucked the stole out of her hands and rummaged in her large stitchery box. "I can finish for you, Mother. Won't take me but a minute or two."

It wouldn't. She could knit, sew, tat, and embroider with much delicacy and speed when she was wide awake. It was when she began to get sleepy that her stitches meandered every which way, as if they had a mind of their own — Van Gogh's.

Lord, keep her awake. I'd hate to have to flick her nose.

"I'll, um, help her," I said.

Did I hear Mother Frances say, "Lord save us"?

"Thank you for that offer, Sister Agnes," Mother said. "But I think we can safely leave this to Sister Justina. She's had four cups of coffee."

I jumped up. "I'll bring her more."

Mother Frances blinked her eyes in surprise. "That would be kind."

Less than ten minutes later, and the finished product was breathtaking. Thousands of tiny stitches on a blue field. A glorious addition to any priest's liturgical wardrobe. Mother Frances had been painstakingly working on it for two years, and every minute had been worthwhile. And Father Lawton would never receive it, now.

"It's beautiful, Mother Frances," I said. "Shall I help you wrap it?"

Like a cornered animal, her eyes darted here and there. And then she must have realized that the entire parlor audience was holding its collective breath. "Paper? Tissue, if you can find some, would be nice."

Wow! That must have been difficult for her. I wanted to pat her on the back and say, *That didn't hurt much, did it?* But knowing the answer, instead I said, "There's a small pile in the laundry room. I'll get it." I smoothed the tissue so most of the wrinkles wouldn't show, then pulled out some of the pretty green-and-white string that Richard had used to tie up his packages — we never threw away anything that might be made useful. Mother Frances and Winnie folded the stole — which must have been ten feet long — and laid it atop the pile. Prest-o, change-o! Mother Frances had a respectable gift for the new bishop. Once inside the large touring car that Monsignor Grace had sent, she cradled it in her arms like a fine china service all the way to the Chancery office.

Richard's spiffy, shining Cord roadster was at the curb, and when we were escorted to the visitors' parlor, he rose to greet us. "Great place, huh?"

It was, indeed. Floor-to-ceiling bookshelves on two walls, filled with books. Leather-bound copies of *Lives of the Saints* took up three shelves! There were dozens of sets of yearbooks from St. Xavier and La-Salle Academies. And art — glorious sacred art — adorned all the walls. Mother Frances set her precious bundle on a sturdy side table and took down one of the lives of the saints. Winnie and I went to study a life-sized painting of St. George slaying the dragon. I was especially interested in the fine musculature of St. George when Vincent Ricci and a "friend" of his strode in. Vincent nodded to Richard, bowed slightly to Mother Frances, and crossed the room to me and Winnie.

He cocked his head at the painting I had been perusing, winked, grasped my hand, and said with great emotion, "Thank you for last night. If there is anything I can do for you. Anything. Any time. It will be done." I knew what Winnie was thinking by the way she slightly reared back. She must have thought she had cleverly hidden it by tugging on her cowl, but Vincent chuckled and touched her arm. "Same goes for you, Sister."

"There is one tiny thing," I said.

Vincent's chuckle turned into a full-blown laugh. "I thought there might be more than one!"

"Actually, I just thought of another one. So, only two tiny things."

Even his friend grinned. But when I very privately told him what they were, Vincent feigned terror. "Next you'll want to fly over the Atlantic."

"No, that was Amelia Earhart. I'd want to do something quite different. Perhaps the Pacific?"

"When this is over, Sister, you can count on me."

"Thank you."

"Might it be over soon, Vincent?" Monsignor Grace asked, coming into the room. I was surprised to see Josiah with him.

"It might, Robert. If your friend, there, can work with and not against us."

First-name basis! This was getting good.

"Which is why I asked you all to come today," Monsignor Grace said. "So Holy Mother the Church, the police, and the . . ."

"The Italian business community?" Richard offered.

Monsignor Grace nodded, and pursed his lips as he tried to hide a smile. I liked this monsignor!

"Ah, yes. We will bind together with the Italian business community and these imaginative and intelligent sisters, working together to eradicate this evil that has been dumped on our doorstep." He settled himself in a large wingback chair and indicated seats for all of us. "Vincent, I believe you have been making inquiries."

"You believe correctly."

"Where?"

"Labor, community, social halls . . ."

"Snitches," Josiah offered.

Vincent gave an age-old gesture — waggling his right hand in front of his chin — which said *yes and no* to the Italian community. "Whatever's productive."

Monsignor prodded, "And you found?"

"That we had to go all the way to Massachusetts to find out who she was. Her name was Bonnie Greco."

"Ah, yes," Monsignor said. "That was one of the extended Young family that made my list."

"Her mother died two months ago," Vincent continued. "Complications from pneumonia, brought on when they couldn't afford to bring her to the hospital. Her father took off right after the funeral."

Josiah flipped open his notepad. "Greco? I've got a notation somewhere." He riffled through several front pages. "Bingo! Missing person report. Julia Greco reported that she hadn't seen her niece in six weeks, and feared foul play."

"Murder most foul," I said. *Hamlet? Macbeth?* "And the police did nothing?"

"Aggie, uh, Sister Agnes! Give us a break."

I suspected what kind of break Vincent and Richard would like to give him, and cringed inside that he was my cousin.

"We have reports like this every day," Josiah continued; but he would have to explain really hard to me to justify his lack of attention to this report. "Look, in this damnable Depression, kids take off. We can't chase down all of them. And ninety percent of the time, nothing's wrong. Maybe they're trying to earn a living. Maybe they're trying to help their mother. Maybe they're trying to keep their own body and soul alive. Or maybe they're trying to get away from a hellish family life."

"Or maybe they're trying to be the man of the house," I said.

Josiah nodded vigorously. "You got it!"

Thoughts began whirling. Reasons, suppositions — but all of them whisking in and out, mere shadows on the wall of my skull. I needed Plato's light to banish the dark and bring this horror out into the open.

"That poor child," Mother Frances said.

"All of them," I mumbled, and louder, "all of them are poor and need our help."

"Sister Agnes," Mother Frances said, "I believe that we should just listen."

"Not at all," the monsignor said. "I invited you sisters here today because the Church would like to hear what you, Mother, and Sisters Agnes and Winifred can contribute."

With the monsignor's blessing so loud and clear, I turned to my cousin. "Josiah, there must be a mortician's report by now."

"The coroner did a post-mortem."

"I stand corrected, Cousin."

"Well, you should know that she hadn't been, uh, interfered with. And she died from several stab wounds. Two very deep. One directly into the heart. DelVecchio's knife, but the handle was wiped clean."

I could have caught flies, my mouth hung open that long. "Oh, for crying out loud," I said. "Picture that. Richard stabbing someone. A young woman, nearly a child. Then wiping the knife handle clean. But leaving the knife there?! Winnie, does that, what do you call it in mathematics, equate?"

"No," she said, and louder, "no, it does not equate. It does not make sense. He would have to be an absolute idiot to do that." She examined Richard's slightly mocking expression. "There is one thing I've learned over the past couple of days. Richard DelVecchio is not an absolute idiot."

"Thank you, Sister Winifred," Richard said.

"So it was probably someone else who did this?" Mother Frances' surprise cracked through the air like a jockey's whip and in its wake, silence. Only her deep, deep breaths gave evidence of her struggle. "Mr. DelVecchio, I owe you an apology. I assumed if it were your knife, then . . ."

"It must be me?" Richard shook his head. "No, Mother."

Vincent cleared his throat. "Richard is my friend, and my son's driver. Most of all, he is my son's friend. And because of his daily contact with my son, he must be the kind of person I would wish Dante to emulate. That kind of person does not stab young ladies."

How many times had he had to defend Richard? How many times had I? Tears were difficult to push back once started, so I allowed a couple to make their way down my cheeks, but forced myself to swallow the others down. Hard.

Josiah, however, had a most stubborn expression on his face. *I do not believe,* it read. Noodle-brain!

"Yeah, well," he said. "The knife thing isn't important one way or the other. We'll get the evidence we need to solve this."

"That's it?" I said. "You arrest Richard because you find his knife, but you discredit the knife because you can't make sense of it? No, *we* can't make sense of it. *You* just figure everything is going to fall into place regardless of the sense it doesn't make. That's what you call evidence? And the postmortem — that's all it showed, that she was stabbed? But we already knew that!"

"The rest is medical stuff. Not important."

"Perhaps not," Monsignor agreed. "Or, perhaps it is very important. How will we know if you do not tell us?"

"It hasn't been released yet."

"All the more reason," Monsignor prodded, then just sat back and remained silent, staring fixedly at Josiah — a bug on a rug. Well, to be fair, a chair. The weight of the Church. I'd seen it wielded all my life. No time more important than right now, I hope. *But with a prayer directed to You, Lord, for good measure.*

Josiah was less than gracious when he gave

in, reciting just the bare facts. "Hands cracked and cut, with deep dye stains. Several different colors. Green, blue, and pink mostly. Cotton and wool fibers in the lungs. No food in the stomach. Bones brittle. Extreme case of malnutrition."

The shadows shifted just a bit and my thoughts began to coalesce. Dye. Lungs. Dust. Hungry. Dye-Lungs-Dust-Hungry. Dyelungsdusthungry.

Damson plums! I reached for something I had seen. Or heard.

And it was gone. Just like that. Poof!

Damson plums! Damson plums! Damson plums!

Two hundred nineteen decades, and rising, Lord. By the way — You could part the Red Sea. Why can't You part these shadows in my noodle-brain? If this keeps happening, all I'll need is meatballs and sauce and I'll have a meal. If someone else cooked it? Thou art very clever, or very cruel. The jury's out on that.

Richard hadn't taken his gaze off me since those two tears. "You have a glimmer, Aggie?"

"Not really. Just some shadows trying to break through the muck."

He leaned over to Winnie. "Plato, again. She's been enamored of his *Republic* since we were in grade school."

"The Allegory of the Cave?" Monsignor Grace asked. At my nod, he beamed. "My particular favorite, too. St. Thomas saw Christ in the light."

"Whatever the truth is, that is the light," I said.

"Ah! A free-thinker in service to her church and fellow beings. Well done, Sister Agnes."

"Your Eminence."

He rose to push a button on his desk. "I've arranged a small collation. Would you follow me?"

It must have been a conference room we entered, but it had been made comfortable with upholstered chairs. An embroidered linen cloth covered the large table, and a very tasteful spread of delicacies took up center stage.

And people outside these privileged walls were hungry. I wondered how many of these things I could sneak into my pockets? All three of them. Or would the filling ooze out and corrupt the gun?

Monsignor Grace must be able to read minds — or faces. He pushed a button on the wall and spoke into a phone-like thing. "You may transfer the boxes now," he said. He turned and smiled at me. "Not to worry,

Sister Agnes. Reverend Mother, I've had several dozen sandwiches made up for you to give out in your soup line tomorrow."

"Thank you, Monsignor," Mother Frances said.

"There's Irish coffee. Anyone?"

"I'll have one," Richard said.

"Sisters?"

Oh, why not? If the Church was plying good whiskey — and it was probably the best — then who was I to refuse? I raised my index finger.

"Good for you, Sister. Vincent? There's espresso."

"Grazie."

"And tea and regular coffee."

A quiet, very young priest materialized out of the corner of the room and began pouring the beverages. Monsignor Grace passed the first silver platter of sandwiches (cucumber and cress, cream cheese and green olive, ham salad).

"It's a regular English high tea," I said.

"You're familiar with the practice?"

"My great-uncle married a Brit. She often served us high tea. To teach us manners, she said."

"Well, she succeeded," Monsignor Grace complimented. "And perhaps injected a wee bit of British spunk?"

"No, that's the Irish," I said. "Willful and stubborn as all get-out."

"Which we are teaching her to temper," Mother said.

"Not too much tempering, Mother. The Church needs hot pokers every so often."

Holy mackerel, did You see that reaction to the Monsignor's words, Lord? She did great. Hardly choked on her tea!

"Yes, Your Eminence," she said.

The Irish coffee was delicious. Just enough whipped cream and only a tiny dollop of whiskey. But picked me right up. The cup was interesting, more glass than cup, although it matched the tea and coffee service that the others were using. Pretty little pattern, not at all the kind of thing I'd expect the priests to favor. When Mother Frances tipped her cup up, I tried to read the label on the bottom. *Havil* was all I got.

"Well, if we are finished, I have one more thing," Monsignor Grace said. He motioned to the priest in the corner, who brought over a large paper-wrapped bundle. "This was delivered by a very delightful lady who made particular reference to an afternoon tea she had had with two nuns from our parish. They suggested that this might find a home where it would be given supreme honor. I agreed, and assured her that we in the Church would always treasure her gift. She assured me she had found treasure enough for many lifetimes, but only a few good people who thought nothing of personal gain, but everything of personal worth." When the young priest cleared a place on the table, Monsignor Grace laid the package in front of Mother Frances. "This is why I particularly asked you to come here today. It's for your convent. When you see the contents, you will know why."

Mother Frances looked confused, but with the help of Monsignor Grace, she opened the package. And the St. Catherine I remembered from that day in Newport was revealed. Gorgeous oil paint highlighted the vigor in her face, the sweetness of her soul, the stubborn tilt of her head.

"Oh!" Mother turned her head to look at him. "But . . ."

He smiled. "She's beautiful, isn't she?"

"Yes."

"If you remember her history, you will recall that she — a mere sister in service to the Church — chastised the Pope and the Church about the errors of their ways, and instructed the hierarchy on what was God's will for His church. She was, I believe, what we would call today, the first free-thinker —

a great deal like someone close to us, don't you think?"

She didn't, it was obvious to me, but she was completely flummoxed by all that was happening, and made no protest.

"When they canonized St. Catherine of Siena," Monsignor Grace said, "they called her Doctor of the Faith. She is the patron saint of victims and virgins. And I believe that describes Bonnie Greco and her grandmother. I am convinced that St. Catherine will help us solve this case."

"I've seen other paintings like this," she said. "Of course they weren't originals, only copies. I've always been particularly fond of works by Bartolomeo. This looks like one of his."

"In his style, yes," the monsignor said, "and quite possibly from his school, but not necessarily the grand master. At least four hundred years old, Mrs. Vandergelder said it was. I believe her. It has been in her paternal family, she said, for several generations. Now, it is yours. Guard it well, Mother."

"I will."

"I would advise you to keep it hidden, even from your sisters, until I give the word to reveal it."

Mother's gaze flicked to me and Winnie.

"Don't worry about these two. They're the ones who found the painting. They're the ones who made a friend of Mrs. Vandergelder."

"Oh!"

No tempering in that statement!

"So, you will keep this hidden until we know what that message meant."

"Message?" Mother Frances asked.

"*There is something wrong at the convent,* wasn't that it, Vincent?" Monsignor Grace answered.

"Something like that," Vincent said.

"Too many somethings," I said. "Specifically, Bonnie's message was, *There is something wrong at St. Catherine's.*"

Oh, but there was substance in what he said! Maybe it was St. Catherine, speaking from the other world. Maybe it was finally a connection in my own brain. Monsignor Grace saw it as a problem at the convent. Bonnie Greco had been murdered at the convent. That had started it. No, the missing vegetables had started it. Then Bonnie. Then the search of my cell. So, had Monsignor Grace hit the nail on the head?

What if the note should have read, *There is something wrong at St. Catherine's convent?*

I looked at the portrait of our saint and

searched her visage. "She saw the errors of the Church and moved to correct them, all the way up to the Pope." I shook my head, angry at myself for my stupidity. "We have all been in error on this search. We have been searching for Bonnie. What we should have been searching for — what we should have been trying to find out — was why Bonnie thought there was something wrong at the convent." I now knew what we had to do. "Richard, I would like you to drive Winnie and me to New Bedford," I said.

"Sure. Why?"

"We are going to look for Steve Clementi."

"Another why!"

"Because New Bedford, where he is reported to be, and Fall River, where Bonnie was said to be living, are right next to each other. And if he's not working on the docks, then what is he doing? But most of all, was Bonnie doing it too, and did it get her killed?"

CHAPTER TWENTY

"I know it's important that this be done. But must it be done by you? It's almost four o'clock," Mother Frances said. "And the two of you have classes tomorrow. The police can handle this."

"Perhaps not," Josiah said, and for this I give him credit. "The Providence police cannot just waltz into New Bedford and search. We need sufficient reason to do something like that, and we have to have the cooperation of the authorities in New Bedford, including the courts. That isn't going to be easy to get. There's no reason that the Providence police can give them to let us in. We don't even know what my cousin is looking for, and it doesn't sound as if she does, either."

"Oh, now, Josiah! Steve Clementi is missing," I said.

"Someone reported him missing?"

"Well, no. But he is missing. At the very

least, he's a witness."

"To what? The murders were committed here and he's supposedly working in New Bedford. What did he witness? Do you know? No, obviously you don't. Yet you say it's important to find him. But is it important that the police find him? If it is, we have to have an official report that he's missing, or we have to have evidence that he's a material witness to either crime. We don't! And we sure don't have the manpower to do a search. If we had a missing person's report, it might be different."

"Oh, great, then you'd do a search the way the search for Bonnie got done," Richard said.

"Look, I understand your frustration," Josiah said. "We're all frustrated, too."

"Yeah, that you haven't been able to pin this on me. But we shouldn't worry. You'll keep on trying to do that. Meantime, the real bad guys get away with this."

Josiah raked his fingers through his hair and looked around the room at the attentive faces. The expressions were interesting. Richard's, sullen and accusatory. Vincent's, angry. Mother Frances, confused, but expectant. Winnie's, scoffing at best, fury just below the surface. Monsignor's, impatient.

I wondered which one meant the most to Josiah?

"The most the captain can ask is for the police in New Bedford to investigate," he said. "They'll likely agree. But let's be honest. Like DelVecchio said, they'll put this on the bottom of their list. It's not their problem, so it will get shuffled until someone has time to do it. By the time they get around to it, whatever Sister Agnes is looking for may be gone." He looked at Mother Frances. "I'm sorry, Mother, but the police are not the ones to handle something like this."

"Thank you for that assessment," she said. "Even so, it's impossible for Sisters Agnes and Winifred to be relieved of their duties at this time. They are in service to the Church as teachers. They can hardly be expected to fulfill the duties of a police unit. It just isn't done."

"Until now," Monsignor Grace said. "The good sisters are, I think, perfectly suited to find this young man if he's needed to help discover the truth. After all, who can blend into the community more easily than two nuns? They are visible presences in our lives. We see them on the streets all the time. They come and go with no difficulty. They can walk into any establishment and be accorded good will." He smiled at her, but it was a steely smile. "The Bishop Designate wishes this to be cleared up quickly. He's left it up to me to get it done, and I believe these nuns can help. So, Mother, I will contact your superiors to send a replacement." I cleared my throat and waggled my finger between me and Winnie, and he smiled his agreement. "Two replacements. From what I have seen over the past few days, it's no doubt that these two nuns work better together. Formidable. Truly formidable."

I could hear the wheels turning in Mother Frances' head. If she had planned to banish me to Exeter, she would now have Monsignor Grace to answer to. If she couldn't banish me, she might be stuck with me and Winnie for as long as it pleased the Chancery. What had she done to deserve this?

Before we took leave, Mother Frances presented her gift for Bishop Keough to Monsignor Grace.

"May I open it?" he asked.

"Of course."

When the stole was revealed, he traced the intricate stitches with his finger, then held the sacred garment up. "It seems we are exchanging one beautiful artwork for another. This, I am sure, will be treasured, also. I will have it rewrapped and ready for his ordination."

Vincent waited for us at the curb. "Richard will be at your service for however long you need him. Anytime."

"Thank you."

He took me aside and scrutinized me carefully. "I've seen that look before, in my father's eyes when he was trying to solve a complicated problem. You have it figured out."

"Not completely, but it's coming together."

"Let me know when you have it all, and I'll take it from there."

"I can't do that."

"He tried to take Dante! He back-handed him!"

"And Father Bryant was brutally attacked and Bonnie and her grandmother were murdered. There will be an entire neighborhood wanting vengeance before this ends. But the Lord said *vengeance is mine*. Are you He whom we await?"

"Ah, Sister, you fight dirty."

"Ah, Vincent, that's not true. And I trust that it isn't true for you, either." At the ironic expression that passed over his face, I patted his hand and smiled. "I'm not a fool, Vincent. I only hope that you don't fight dirty in this case. We must see justice done for these good people who paid the highest price. Don't forget, it was Bonnie Greco who tried to warn you. She wanted to keep Dante safe, and she died because she tried to do that."

"Like I said, you don't play fair. Appealing to my heart. If word gets around that that works, my standing in — What did Richard call it? Ah, yes — my standing in the Italian business community will be shot to hell. Sorry, heck. Not quite the same force, is it? Heck?" He took my hand in both of his. "I like you, Sister Agnes. You know who you are. You know what's right. And you don't back down when you're fighting for what's right. I've known plenty of nuns in my life, but you are the best nun I have ever known."

I whooped with laughter. "That's a most generous and exaggerated description. Thank you. But there's not many who would agree with you."

"Then they're idiots." He tipped his hat and got into his car. It glided away, purring its power — a symbol of the man inside.

It was perplexing. Until this horror had been dumped on our doorstep, I thought I knew the world and the people in it. There were nice, safe boxes. The clergy who served

God in one box. The innocent children in another. The good parishioners in a third box. The evil in another. But I had seen an evil man who loved his son and his friend, a nun who seemed to love nothing except perhaps some smelly stuff she put in her bath and her standing with the Reverend Mother, innocent children thrown into the evil in this world, and people who seemed to be not what they seemed.

I know, Lord, convoluted thinking on that last part. But when all is said and done, only You know what is in anyone's heart. Please, I beg You — keep Vincent Ricci's heart pure for us for just a little bit longer, or I shall be forced to cook up a collation of my own, and the world as we in the parish know it might come to an end. What's that, Thou sayest? Bribery wilt get me nowhere? Oh, I don't know. Look where it got me with the Monsignor!

Ah, He had a sense of humor. I was still standing at the curb, in this world. On the way to New Bedford and Steve Clementi.

But first, Winnie and I had Mother Frances to face.

"Oh, boy, the silence in this car is heavy as lead," Richard said. "I've got four brothers and my mother always says that we need to get things out in the open or we'll burst. Want to try it? No? Too scared, or too

265

angry? Which?"

"Neither, Mr. DelVecchio," Mother Frances said from her seat next to Richard. "We nuns are not expected to show either of those emotions."

"Pardon me, Mother Frances, but what the heck are you talking about? You're human. This is a hard time. It's normal to be scared. Or mad. You just got your best nuns pulled out from under you. Of course, it's only for a day."

"That day leaves me in a quandary because I have charge of our parishioners' children. What if the replacements are not good enough, or do not meet our standards? I'm already having problems with one of our novices, who can't seem to read as well as her students. And when will their records come to us? I have to answer to the state, too, you know. I can't just toss anyone into those classrooms. I have to be certain they have the proper credentials. And the mother house is not known for getting records to the convents on time! They're supposed to send them with the nuns, but I've waited three weeks for some records to arrive." She turned to look over the seat at me. "This can't wait until Saturday?"

Damson plums! "Things have been moving very fast, Mother. I'm afraid if we wait until Saturday the murderers may make a run for it."

She reared back, closer to the door. "Murderers? There's more than one?"

"I'm not sure, but I think so."

"How? Why do you think that?"

"Remember, there was a man in the church who attacked Father Bryant. Can you see Mildred Young allowing him to walk in on her while she was in the bath? Just like that? No screams? No warnings? No fear?" Her torso began to tremble and I put both my hands on her left arm to try to offer her some comfort. Remarkably, she didn't jerk away. "I think Mildred's murderer was a woman. It's the only thing that makes sense. But we know there's a man involved, too. So, did the woman kill Bonnie? Or was it the man?"

"You'll get yourselves killed," she whispered.

Were those tears? Good grief, did she care? Was she angry because she couldn't show her feelings?

"Where will that leave the children?"

Well, that answered those questions.

When we got back, Winnie and I threw our clothes into a valise — and I packed everything I didn't want anyone to see, including the gun case and Bonnie's note

— just in case someone tried a second round of snooping. Mother Frances met us in the front hall and gave us an envelope.

"St. Philomena's is the best place to stay the night. I have written Mother Charles to request cooperation. I hope you find what you're looking for."

"Thank you, Mother," I said.

"Come back safely."

"Yes, Mother," I said, but inside I was praying really hard that I didn't get myself or Winnie killed. What was I saying? We had Richard, and God, and a loaded gun. As St. Catherine had shown in her dealings with the hierarchy of the Church, and President Roosevelt had said just after he was inaugurated, with right on our side, all we had to fear was fear itself.

CHAPTER
TWENTY-ONE

Richard's Cord roadster flew down the highway at fifty miles an hour! We were over the bridge into Fall River in twenty-five minutes and another twenty into New Bedford. But Winnie — who was safely ensconced in the back seat — didn't see any of it. As soon as the car's speed climbed over twenty miles an hour, she closed her eyes and pulled up the king-sized rosary that each of us wear in our belt. Her lips moved in pious supplication.

And, since it had worked so well with Monsignor Grace, I tried to make another bargain with God.

Half of Winnie's decades taken off my total, okay, Lord? At the rate she's going, we could have the 219 whittled down to a comfortable 200 by the time we reach New Bedford. Okay, okay, You don't have to shout! I'll do them myself. Well, at least I was thinking of You. Okay, I was thinking of myself. But at least I tried. Click. Click. Click. *Hail Mary, full of grace, the Lord is with thee.* Click. Click. Click. *Let's hope You're with us, Lord. Whoops! Starting that one over.* Click. Click. Click.

"Sounds like bullets being loaded into guns," Richard said.

"The only kind of bullets the Lord wants," I said.

Darn my socks! Starting that one over, too. Click. Click. Click.

Ten "Hail Marys" and one "Glory Be to the Father" later, and I had one decade complete. Down to 218. "You could pray along, you know," I said to Richard. Maybe the Lord would count his towards my total, since I would be the one talking Richard into it. *No?* I sighed. *You're a hard man to please.*

"You want me to pray along? Oh, absolutely. If I could only grow another set of hands to hold the wheel while I ply the beads."

"You don't need to be so sarcastic. And you don't need beads. You only need a clear conscience and a contrite heart."

"Great. Then could you tell her ladyship back there to stop clicking?!"

A weak voice piped up from the back, "Her ladyship can hear you, and I don't mean me." Click. Click. Click.

The great steel bridge over the Taunton River whizzed under the Cord's wheels, its Tinker Toy struts only a blur. The Cord took the hills of Fall River easily, with Richard doing all kinds of things to the stick on the floor.

I finished up one more decade — down to 217! — then let the rosary settle onto the seat. "What is that thing you keep moving around?"

"Shift."

I moved a little bit to the right. He bellowed so loud, I slapped my hands over my ears. "What's so funny?"

"Women." He pointed to the stick with the knob on top. "This is called a shift."

"Well, how was I supposed to know that? The only shift I've ever seen is the kind women wear under their dress."

"That's a slip."

"That's not what my Gran called it."

His turn to sigh. "This is a shift because it shifts gears."

"Ah-hah."

"Now *you* don't have to be so sarcastic."

"It's not sarcasm. I have no idea what a gear is."

"I thought you taught science."

"No, that's me," Winnie said.

"I take the literature and history part of our classes, she takes the science and math." I turned and leaned over the back. "God wants you to start that prayer over."

"Who are you? St. Catherine? You have a pipeline to God, now?"

"Don't you?"

"What?"

"Doesn't He talk to you?"

"Mayetta Morgan," Winnie said, "one of these days somebody is going to lock you up if you say that."

"I'm not kidding, Winnie. Doesn't He?"

"No. I talk to Him. Sometimes I feel what He wants me to do. But He does not speak directly to me."

"Oh! It never occurred to me . . . I thought everyone could hear Him." I appealed to Richard.

"Sorry, Aggie, not me either." He patted my knee. "Don't fret. You're not crazy, and I'll never let anybody lock you up."

"Thank you."

"What's He saying, now?" I slammed my closed fist into his arm. "Yeouch! Not talking, huh?"

"As a matter of fact, He said you were a horse's . . ."

"Mayetta Morgan!"

"Say your beads, Winnie. I'm okay."

Just a tad mad, but okay, right, Lord? About as mad as Jean d'Arc and St. Catherine, You say? I'm no saint, but You already knew that. It's nice, though, that I'm not alone. I smiled and finished another decade by the time we pulled into New Bedford.

Richard slowed down to a respectable twenty miles an hour. "It's okay, your ladyship," he said to Winnie. "You can open your eyes, now."

"You're not going to speed up again?" she asked.

"Nope. Too much traffic on these narrow streets."

"Of course they're narrow," I said. "They haven't changed much since the Revolution."

Richard tugged on the shift thing and the car slowed down even more as we crested a hill and went over it.

"Which revolution?" he asked. "The one with the guns, or the one with the industrial things?"

"Guns."

"Ah, which reminds me. Where's the toy I gave you?" I patted my pocket. "You've been carrying it with you all this time?"

"It's only been two days," Winnie reminded him. "And where do you expect her to put it? We only have three drawers in our

273

cells and the doors are always open. And now, with all these men running here and there in the convent, there's no safe hiding place."

"I was just asking!" He came to an intersection and stopped to look both ways. "We've still got plenty of light to look around. You want to start tonight or early tomorrow?"

"I'd like to get an idea what the city is like. I haven't been here in more than fifteen years."

"Eighteen years, to be exact. You were nine. I was twelve."

"That's right! You were with us. My father rented a sailboat."

"Which he didn't have the foggiest notion how to captain."

"But you did."

"Yeah. I used to love working the lines and tacking. Those sails filling up with wind — it's one of the best things to see and feel in this life."

"You still sail?"

"Don't have much time. Now, it's motoring in Vincent's power boat."

"Not the same, huh?"

"No."

He looked away and I knew him well enough to know not to prod any longer. He was a good friend, but a private man. He'd made lots of compromises in his life. Not all of them had worked out. But he kept going, and he was loyal and kind. *Not much more we can ask of our friends, right, Lord? And You should know. You had the Apostles. Well, there were those three times with Peter. Okay, okay, I'll shut up, now.*

We went down the hill towards the piers and the docks.

"This used to be the whaling capital of the world at one time," I said, breaking my promise to God almost immediately. Damson plums! I'd have to tack on another decade. *No? Thanks.* "Then it was the shirt-waist capital. Now the mills and warehouses have all closed."

"Not all of them," Richard said. "They still make darned good men's wear. Vincent gets his suits made by Donatelli Brothers, who have a small establishment and factory near Front Street. We should see it pretty soon."

The words were hardly out of his mouth when we saw the building housing Donatelli Brothers. It was the most prosperous of the factories and shops along Hamilton, on the corner of Front Street.

"Holy Toledo," I said.

This building was limestone and brick.

The front door was double-width oak slabs, with Donatelli Brothers painted on it in gold and black letters. Its huge windows sparkled in the fading light. They were draped with what looked like rich woolen fabric, which highlighted the suits and men's accessories prominently displayed in all five windows. This factory and showroom stood in stark contrast to the dozens of others that we had passed as we headed for the docks. Those had busted-out or boarded-up windows and huge locks on the doors.

"No wonder Mr. Ricci comes here," Winnie said. "Those suits are beautiful. And expensive."

"Well, he can afford it."

"Oh, no, not again," I said. "You two are not going to start nit-picking at each . . ." I couldn't get the rest out. I choked on it.

"Aggie?"

"May?" Winnie pushed on Richard's shoulder. "Is she okay?"

"I don't know! Let me pull over."

"No! It's okay," I said. "I just realized . . ." I grabbed Richard's arm. "Yes, pull over. Somewhere where there's plenty of light."

"There's a coffee shop right there, down the street, about a block away. Do you want me to pull in there?"

"Yes. I need light to read."

"Read? Read what?"

I dug into my pockets as Richard maneuvered the Cord close to the curb and shut off the engine. I pulled out the newspaper articles that I had tucked in there and never gotten around to reading. Holding them up to the fading light, I scanned them quickly to figure out if what I was remembering was real, was true, was damning.

It was, and I couldn't keep myself from trembling.

Richard must have seen it. Who couldn't? My entire frame was rattling. He grasped my shoulders and shook gently.

"Aggie? Are you okay?"

"No. I won't be okay until this is all over. But I'm getting there." I turned around to smile at Winnie, who had a fearful expression on her face. "Don't worry, Winnie. Everything is going to be okay. We're getting really close to the finish of all this madness. I'm finally beginning to realize the *why*."

CHAPTER
TWENTY-TWO

"You know," Richard said to Winnie, "I love her like she was my own sister, but sometimes, she scares me."

"She scares you and you gave her a gun." She shook her head and got out of the car. "I'm in a world of crazy people. Maybe this is only a nightmare, and when I wake up everything will be back to normal."

"I wish that were so," I said. "But it isn't. And it's going to get worse."

I left them speechless, stopped dead on the sidewalk, staring at me. I turned to take a few steps backwards, waving them on. "Don't just stand there. This is a coffee shop. Let's get some coffee."

Do all doors have bells on the top that ring when you enter the store? This one sounded like the one my aunt's goat wore. Baaaa!

The man behind the counter said, "Good evening, Sisters," as I slid onto one of his polished red-upholstered stools. "Oh, you don't want to sit there, Sister. Donatelli's got a big order from some la-de-dah store in Texas and has been working overtime and Sundays to get it filled. The late shift is just letting out for dinner and ten or more shift workers will be here any minute. There's a quiet booth in the back."

"Thank you," I said, and twirled twice on the rotating stool. "I've always wanted to do that," I told him, before hopping down and heading for the booth in the back. I sat where I'd get a good view of the door and the workers from Donatelli's. Who knew, maybe Steve Clementi would be one of them.

Then why would he lie to his mother? *Good point, Lord. He'd have a good, steady job at Donatelli's, one he could be proud of.* No, there would be no need for lies.

Winnie slid into the booth opposite me and Richard sat next to her.

"You're taking up the whole booth, May," Winnie said.

"And you two are too close together. Leave some room between you."

Richard and Winnie stared at me, looked at each other, then at the foot or so space that separated them, then back at me.

I sighed. "You're both too tall, and Richard is too wide. I need to see between you."

Winnie cocked her head and pursed her mouth. "You need to see what?"

I pointed towards the door. "Them."

Richard and Winnie didn't have to turn; the noise of the late shift coming in was enough. They each inched over a bit, but sufficiently for me to get a bird's eye view.

"So," the counterman said, coming up to the booth with menus in hand, "coffee to start?"

"Black for me," Winnie said.

"Plenty of cream and two sugars," Richard said.

"Ditto," I said.

I grabbed the menu and held it up so I could peek over the top and still look as if I were reading.

None of them were young; but I hadn't thought they would be, or my suppositions would be wrong. There were six men, the rest, women. I had only seen photographs of knitting mills and shirt factories, but could readily see these women bent over sewing machines, stitching the same thing every day, three or four days a week, since the seven-day workweek had been abolished. Some would sew collars, others shirt cuffs. Some would put on pockets, others attach the shiny lining. Still others would do nothing but iron the finished product. The men — what did they do? One of them had a pair of long scissors attached to his belt. Did he cut the fabric? Maybe others did, too. But Donatelli's also did custom work for people like Vincent. So one or two of these men must be tailors who would precision-fit assembly-line suits to the correct measurements.

Satisfied with what I'd seen, I quickly scanned the menu. "I'm really hungry, Richard. Can you afford to buy us a sandwich?"

"Are you kidding?"

"Nuns rarely carry much money. We're not paid, like priests. Most of us get pocket money from our families." I dug into my pocket, retrieved a change purse, and counted out fourteen cents — a dime and four pennies. "Enough for toast," I said.

"Put that away," Richard said. "Vincent said to get you anything you needed. But this is on me. Order whatever you want."

"But we can get a meal at the convent," Winnie said.

"Unless Mother Frances got to a telephone and called ahead, they won't be expecting us," I pointed out. "Whatever we get will be left-over and cold." I sniffed the delicious smells coming from the plates be-

281

ing plunked down on the counter. "Hamburgers? Is that hamburgers?"

"The menu says meatloaf," Winnie said.

"All the better." I read from the menu. "Sunday special: Meatloaf, brown gravy, mashed potatoes, carrots and peas." Suddenly, my throat closed up. I stroked it with my fingers, trying to swallow.

"Something wrong, Aggie?"

"Can't swallow, Richard."

"You haven't got anything to swallow yet."

"I can't reach across the table, but that deserved a punch." Winnie obliged. "Thanks! I was only remembering the carrots. They were the last things I saw in the root cellar before I found . . ."

"Bonnie," Richard said. He reached across the table and took the menu out of my hands. "I'll order. Be right back."

"He didn't even ask what I wanted," Winnie said.

"You're getting meatloaf."

"Good. That's what I wanted. But how did he know?"

"Richard always orders the daily special. He says he's never had a bad special."

Richard came back with our coffees and slid into the booth. "Three minutes, he said."

"I wonder if there are, uh, facilities?"

"Sign over your head says restrooms, Aggie."

"You need to wash your hands, Winnie?"

"Don't mind if I do."

Richard slid out again and let Winnie pass, then slid into the booth. "Why do women always have to go together?"

As Winnie went on ahead of me, I leaned down so others wouldn't hear. "Do you really want to wait as we go one by one into the restroom? Even Noah wasn't that stupid."

"Ouch! You got me."

I straightened up, and that's when I saw him. "Damson plums!" I slipped down until my head was barely above the table.

"What the hell is wrong with you?"

"Shhhh! I don't want him to see me."

"Who?"

"Don't look! Richard, for crying out loud, I told you not to look."

Winnie poked her head around the corner and I tried to shoo her away. She saw me almost sitting on the floor, rolled her eyes, but, thank goodness, slipped back into the gloom.

"I'll be right back," I said. "But don't look!"

"I wouldn't think of it. Women!"

As soon as I got into the restroom, Winnie

opened her mouth, but I shook my head. "Not now. Just hurry."

She was washing her hands when I came out and stood next to her. "Have I ever asked you to do something weird?" I asked.

"You're joking."

"Okay, in the past week have I asked you to do something weird?"

"Guns. Gangsters. Dead people. Car racing."

"Okay! But do you trust me?"

"With my life."

"Then take off your cowl."

"Mayetta Morgan, you have gone mad."

"He may recognize us if he sees the habit."

"Who?"

"I don't know who. But I think it's the man who attacked Father Bryant, and he might have seen both of us. At least, he saw me. We have to follow him, but he would definitely be suspicious of two nuns following him."

"Not according to Monsignor Grace."

"These nuns he would."

"We can't take off our cowls. Our hair!"

"We'll just take off the wimple and tie the cowl behind our head like the Italian grandmothers do." She looked dubious, but began taking the straight pins out of her cowl and wimple. "We need to take off our aprons, fold them, and put them in our pockets. And our rosaries can go inside, too. We'll look slightly like those folk in Pennsylvania. The Amish? We just can't look like nuns until we get back to the car. Then we can change."

When we returned to the booth, Richard nearly had a heart attack. "What the hell?"

"Hush! I can explain."

I quickly told him what I thought, and he turned livid.

"The guy who might be responsible for all this is back there?"

"The *might* is the most important word in that sentence. I don't know for sure."

"Look again. Be sure."

I did, and as I did the counter man brought over our meatloaf specials. He did a double-take like I'd seen in the movies. "We're in disguise," I said. "A little joke on a friend." *As You know, that wasn't exactly a lie, Lord. But if You want me to add another decade, I will. No? Thanks.*

"So you're not really nuns."

"Not right now," I said, and winked at him.

He laughed and put the check on the table.

"Eat fast!" I said. "We have to follow that guy when he leaves."

Richard's hand clamped on my wrist. "Is it him?"

"Uh . . . yeah, it's him."

He started to slide out of the booth. "Be right back."

I kicked him hard under the table and connected with his shin. "Slide back where you were!"

"I don't think I can."

"Richard!" He eased along the booth and rubbed his leg. "I'm sorry, but you're not going to muck this up with some hero stuff." I was chewing and talking, but noticed that the meatloaf was darned good. At least it had real meat in it. Score one for Richard. But he was two behind if he didn't react properly. "Vincent said he would cooperate. You, too!" Such a stubborn look he had. "Here's what I suspect. One, he's a hireling, not the boss. Two, we need to find Steve Clementi, who was a friend of Bonnie's and who disappeared just about the time she did. See the connection? Three, we need to get enough evidence so we can get the boss and throw the book at him. Or her. Four, none of that matters if we don't have more evidence that will connect everything together. Then we can call Josiah and get the wheels turning."

"Back up," Richard said.

"How far?"

"To the part where you said *her.*"

"But there's always been a *her.* The woman who killed Mildred."

"You said she might be the boss."

"Yes, I did. And, yes, she might be."

"Of all this, whatever it is?"

"What, are women incapable of doing something like this? Are they too stupid? Consider Madame Curie. Too sweet? Ever hear of Lizzie Borden? Too delicate? Would you really want to come up against the Amazons? Too —"

"Never mind. I get the picture."

"Good. Eat fast. He's on his dessert. Brownie with vanilla ice cream. Could we take some brownies with us? Never know where he's going to take us, and I might get hungry."

"That's not a might," Winnie said. "That's a definite."

She dragged out her own change purse and came up with a dollar. I stared at it. "You're rich! I never have that much."

"I save."

She waited until Richard had taken his final bite, then held the dollar out to him. He shook his head, picked up the check, and went to pay it. The counter man wrapped six brownies and tucked them into

287

a paper bag.

"They better have brownies in heaven or I'm not going," I said.

"Who said they'd let you in?" Winnie asked.

"They'll let me in. I just have to keep listening to God and do what He wants me to do."

"And what about this . . ." she waved her arm in the air, "this lunacy?"

"He's smiling."

"We're doomed. Now she can see Him."

"Okay! Let's go! He's leaving. And Richard's right behind him."

At the car, we changed quickly back to our real selves and finished just as Richard came up and got in, starting the engine. "He's got a car parked around back." He pointed to a grey touring car that looked like Vincent's. "That one."

"Expensive," Winnie said.

"Four years old," Richard said. "Probably stole it."

"I don't think they steal cars, Richard," I said. "I'm pretty sure they do make really good money, though."

"It got dark while we were in there," Richard said. "I'll have to use my head-lamps."

"Fine," I said. "Just don't let him know

he's being followed."

"Where the heck do you expect him to take us?"

"I thought that was obvious. To Steve Clementi, of course."

CHAPTER
TWENTY-THREE

"I had him alone back there," Richard said. "In the back of the coffee shop, just him and me. I could have taken him out right there."

"Have you ever taken out anyone in your whole life?" I asked. "And I'm assuming that doesn't mean beating them up, because I already know you can, and have, done that."

"You're not my confessor, Aggie."

"No, I'm just your lifelong friend."

"A woman, may I remind you, whom God talks to," Winnie said. She leaned over the front seat. "He's probably already told her the answer and she's just testing you to see if you'll lie to her."

"Jesus Christ!"

Winnie and I said together, "Exactly."

I could tell that he was doing what he'd taught me to do when faced with horror. "That's it," I said. "Breathe, Richard. In.

Hold. Out. In. Hold. Out. Yep, you've got it. Calm now?"

"Don't talk to me."

"You didn't answer my question; but that's okay. I already know the answer."

"Because God told you?"

"Because I know you."

"Aggie . . ."

"It is really all right. We're in this together. And remember, I'm the better shot."

"In more ways than one," he said. "In more ways than one."

"Not to interrupt you two while you're mutually liking each other," Winnie said, "but that bad guy's making an awful lot of turns, isn't he?"

"You saw *Scarface* with me," I said. "That's what the bad guys did when they didn't want anyone to know where they were going."

She mumbled, "In this dark, I don't even think *he* knows where he's going. Have you noticed there are no street lamps and no lights on in any of the buildings?"

"These are the buildings we passed coming into town that were all boarded up," Richard said. "They've probably been empty since the labor strike in the twenties. Whole blocks of factories closed down and moved South."

"Then why would they need electricity?" I asked.

"Probably just left it up when they moved out," Richard said.

"I don't think so. Remember, they're tearing up the convent to put in electricity. I've been watching them when I have a few minutes, and listening to them talk while I am doing my chores. So now I can tell the difference between new electric wires and old ones. The old ones are coated in rubber mixed with a lot of red and black fabric so they can bend easily. The guys working at the convent say that over time, because of the weather, the rubber gets brittle, the fabric breaks down, and the wires get frayed easily. They don't like taking them down; but they have to because old wires are dangerous to leave up.

"The new ones are coated in several layers. They use stronger rubber with only a little fabric, and you can't even see the fabric at all because it's under the rubber. I heard them talking about how long they would hold up. A long time they said, which makes them safer."

"What's your point, Aggie?" Richard asked.

"My point is that on one of the blocks we passed this afternoon I thought I saw new wires on the poles, going into one, maybe two of the boarded-up buildings. So, if nobody's using those places, why would they need new wires?"

"I have absolutely no idea. You got any, Winnie?" Richard asked.

"Not a clue."

"But it is a clue," I said. "It's a clue to the reason for all this murder and mayhem. I got that phrase from *Scarface,* too."

"They should never have let you see that movie," Richard said.

"It's been very instructive. It taught me to observe everything very carefully. Oh, Damson plums!"

He looked at me as if I'd just grown three heads. "Damson plums?"

"We can't swear," Winnie said, "so she uses words that come close without going over the line."

"That makes as much sense as anything else has tonight," Richard said.

"Try forever with her."

"You're not funny, Winnie," I said.

"Wasn't trying to be. But what did you almost swear about?"

"I completely forgot to read everything I wanted to read when I asked Richard to stop at the coffee shop. I skimmed the articles, that's all."

"We can't pull over now," Richard said.

"Do you have a flashlight?"

"In the gear box right there in front of you. Just push in that little knob."

I did, and the door fell down. "Oh, how clever." I rummaged inside and found a large brass flashlight with buttons on both ends. "Which one of these do I push?"

"Either one," he said. "It's a double-header."

"I thought that was a baseball phrase," I said.

"English is confusing, isn't it?"

"Life is confusing."

I pushed one of the buttons and a yellowish light came on. Not much, but good enough. The newspaper articles had been mashed all the way to the bottom of my pockets, and when I pulled them out a couple ripped. I wasn't sure which piece went with what, and had to turn pieces over to see how to fit everything together. Then I had to tuck the flashlight under my chin so the light shone on the page and didn't wiggle.

"You don't have much time on those batteries, because they're old," Richard said. "So read fast."

I zeroed in on the articles that interested me the most and looked at other parts of the newspaper, just in case I forgot anything. When I turned over one of the pieces and saw the ad for Providence's foremost jewelers, Tilden-Thurber's, some things began to coalesce. By combining it with the contents of one of the articles, it was as if a Fourth of July rocket zoomed through my brain and burst open.

Awestruck, all I could manage was, "Plato's light works again." I snapped off the flashlight and laid my hand on Richard's arm. "Don't lose him. We have to find where he's going, and what he's doing, and then we have to find a telephone to call Josiah." I turned to Winnie. "I think we should drop you off at the convent, Win."

"Not on your life. You won't be able to follow him."

"But you'll be safe."

"Where you go, I go. Besides, this bad guy hasn't used a gun yet. But Richard's got a gun . . . doesn't he?"

"You bet, your ladyship," he said.

"And you've got a gun, Aggie, and you're a better shot than Richard. You can protect all of us."

"He's pulling in down there," Richard said. "In case he's seen us, I'm going to go right past and then circle back around the block."

"You saw *Scarface,* too, huh?"

"Aggie, sometimes you're a real pain in the as . . ."

"Richard!"

"Aspidistra."

When we came around the block again, Richard shut the lights and engine off before anyone could see or hear us and glided silently and darkly into the curb.

"I don't see him, Richard!"

"Take it easy, Aggie. Let your eyes adjust to the dark."

He must have coyote eyes like Mother Frances, because he pointed to a small door tucked into an alcove on the left side of the building and said, "There he is!"

"Oh, darn my socks! He's knocking on the door, which means someone else is in there. Yes, I can see him against the light from inside. Someone else did let him in."

Suddenly, someone knocked on the glass next to Richard.

"Damn," he said, "cops." He wound down the window. "What can I do for you, Officer? Ah, hell."

"I've been following you since Providence," Josiah said. "Lost you several times when you speeded up; but since I knew where you were going, and since you drive this fancy car, it wasn't hard to pick up your trail. Don't you ever look behind you?"

"You alone?"

"Yes, Aggie, I'm alone. I couldn't get anyone else to come with me. What's going on? Who's that guy you've been following?"

So I had to go through it again, quickly.

"You sure about this, Aggie?" Josiah asked. I glared at him. Noodle-brain! "Josiah . . ."

"Had to ask." He looked around the deserted streets. "You'll need help. I could go get help, call the cops, something."

"Or you could stay here and go inside with us," I offered.

"You just said someone let him in. What are you going to do, walk up and knock on the door, and just merrily waltz in there?"

"I didn't think that would work, Josiah," I said, "but now that you describe it so well, maybe it will. They will hardly be expecting us. And you could bop the guy on the head or something."

"Bop?" Josiah winked at Richard. "You into bopping, DelVecchio?"

"She's a little crazy tonight, but she's right about them not expecting us. We just might be able to get the drop on the guy at the door."

"If I could put a word in," Winnie said, "that's a reasonable plan, considering you're all carrying weapons."

"All? I figured on DelVecchio," Josiah said. "Who else?"

"Me," I said. "Just a little one."

"Good Lord! Did you know she's a crack shot, DelVecchio?"

"Yep."

"And I suppose you gave it to her?"

For the first time in my life, I actually harrumphed. "It's not important who gave it to me! Let's get going! I'll knock on the door. You knock out the guy who opens it. Simple." I sighed. "I know, it's about as simple as taming a rattlesnake, but what else can we do? As you said, Josiah, we have no proof, and sitting here arguing isn't getting us any. The only way is to go in and get that proof. Let's go, Winnie. We're two little nuns who have lost our way."

She linked her arm with mine. "Baa, baa, baa."

I was trying to keep a stiff upper lip for Winnie's sake, but my knees were knocking together and I could feel my heart's blood whooshing through my veins. So I did what any scared, self-respecting nun did and made sure I had my little toy gun in my hand when I knocked on the door. I wasn't looking forward to ka-powing off a shot, but I would if I had to. Just to scare them. Better them than me.

We should have been generals planning the action at Verdun. The door opened to our knock. The guy looked puzzled but let us in when I begged to use a telephone. And Josiah cracked him over the head. All in less than three minutes!

When we got inside, we realized why we'd been able to get away with this little ploy. There was so much noise overhead, someone could have let off a zillion firecrackers and no one would have heard them.

Richard found some rope and tied the doorkeeper to a post in the corner of the room, making sure his arms were bound tightly behind him and his legs were hogtied so he couldn't move.

I looked around the huge open space the door had let into. Crates and packing cases stood ready to go, others were half packed. I pulled out one of the contents — a pretty blue woolen sweater with pink, yellow, and green embroidery at the neck. Winnie found several boxes of cotton dresses. The labels on the boxes were for fancy stores all around New England and New York.

"That explains the post-mortem's cotton and wool fibers," I said to Josiah. He looked startled, and rightly so. "Yes, Bonnie Greco. She must have known about this place."

"What's so important about this place that

someone killed her?" Josiah asked.

"So she couldn't tell," I answered.

"About what?"

"The answer to that, I'm guessing, is upstairs where all that noise is coming from."

CHAPTER
TWENTY-FOUR

At first I thought Winnie and I should take off our steel-tipped brogans because of the noise they made on wooden stairs, but with all that racket coming from overhead, no one was going to hear anything. God works in mysterious ways.

And then the noise stopped.

Thanks a lot!

"Three minutes," a voice bellowed, "then back to work."

It was bedlam upstairs. Something clanged, other things dragged across the floor.

But there were no voices.

I knew someone could hear me if I talked in a normal voice, so I whispered to Richard, "Why aren't they talking?"

"Damned if I know."

I raised my foot to go up one more stair and realized the steel-tipped brogans were going to echo loudly. I whispered to Winnie, "Off with your shoes."

She slipped them off, as I did, and followed Richard and Josiah very cautiously up the staircase. Halfway up, Richard pulled out his shiny silver gun and Josiah reached into his holster and pulled out a bigger black one. Holy Hannah! I didn't trust my cousin with croquet mallets, and here he was with deadly fire in his hand. Yet, he seemed comfortable with it. In fact, he seemed to become taller, larger. Maybe it was self-confidence. He was a cop, carrying himself as a cop. It was good for him.

At the top of the stairs there were three doors. If we chose the wrong one, we were in trouble.

"In *Scarface* . . ."

Richard held up his hand, and hissed, "Enough about that damned movie, Aggie."

I got it all out quiet and fast. "They knew that the cops were coming when they saw the shadows under the door." Both Josiah and Richard turned to look at me. I shrugged. "Hey, it worked in the moving picture."

And it worked now. Richard lowered himself to scan the space beneath each door, then pointed to the door closest to us. "That one."

"Now, what?" Winnie asked.

"What's sauce for the goose . . ." I pushed past a surprised Richard and knocked on the door. When it was jerked open, I smiled at the big, bad guy and said, "Hello. Your friend downstairs said you would have a telephone I could use." I'm sure he recognized me because his eyes widened and his mouth dropped open and his lips flapped up and down, but no words came out. Me? I merely edged right past him, Josiah and Richard at my back with their guns drawn.

No bullets. No blood. Just . . .

"Oh, my God!"

I should have expected something like this. A short section in the article about the mills had gotten me thinking about what was going on with Bonnie and Steve. It told about how hard it was to enforce child labor laws and how some manufacturers were getting away with hiring under-aged workers — and both Bonnie and Steve would qualify for that, because they both needed money desperately in order to survive.

But the article didn't mention anything that resembled the hell inside that building.

The hell these children were enduring to feed themselves and their families.

Boys and girls were jammed together in one room that reeked of urine and feces and decaying food and one other horrific odor that I'd smelled at my grandfather's farm. I set that thought aside to study the children. They were filthy, with scabs on their arms and faces and matted hair so corrupted that I couldn't distinguish blond from brunette.

Worse — they were chained like slaves, with shackles on their ankles and chains — long, awful steel chains — attached to bolts in the floor. They had enough slack in the chains for them to get to waste receptacles in each corner, but no privacy.

"Who would do something like this?" Winnie asked me, as she swept past me to take a sobbing girl into her arms. Others gathered around her and she tumbled to the floor under their exuberant hugs.

"Someone evil," I said to myself, the anger boiling inside me. "Very evil. And that man helped." I marched up to the big guy, slipping in the debris strewn everywhere, and back-handed his face as Dante's had been. The kids cheered as I spit words at him.

"You have no soul and will pay for this one day. Soon, and later. Now, give me the key to those chains."

He laughed. Richard reared back and punched his lights out.

"Go, Richard!" Winnie shouted.

And the kids surrounding her roared with laughter and joy, chorusing, *Go Richard! Go*

Richard! Go Richard!

He smiled sheepishly and I let him and Josiah pat down the big guy for the key while I searched for the one face I was eager to find. One young man stepped forward, and I went up to him. "Steve Clementi, right?"

"Yes, Sister Agnes."

"Are you okay?"

"We are now." He threw his arms around my neck and, even at his age, tears flowed freely. "Thank you."

I hugged him tightly. "You're welcome."

Between his sobs and giggles, he managed to ask, "Did Bonnie send you?"

"In a way, yes, she did."

He doesn't need to hear it all now, Lord. But when the time comes and he asks, I will be the one to tell him. That will close the circle and perhaps bring him some peace. True peace, he will find only in You.

"Any of you kids know where there's a telephone?" Josiah asked.

"Call Monsignor Grace," I said.

"If I can find a telephone, I'm calling the whole damned world," Josiah said. "Except reporters. This has to stay out of the papers until we round up every damned one of these creeps."

"Office is downstairs," Steve said. The

tears had left tracks on his dirty face, but he paid them no mind because he was the first kid let loose by Richard. He rubbed his ankles, which oozed with blood. There might be scars — on his body and his mind — but he would have the support of the Church and the community to help him heal.

"Winnie," I called, "we have to get these children cleaned up."

"Not yet," Richard said. The kids let out some boos and a few cries, and Richard looked stricken. "I'm sorry, kids. But the cops will want to record all of this, including your condition. It will help put these bad guys in jail, maybe forever."

The kids cheered. But I didn't. I did understand what Richard said, but it infuriated me that I couldn't put everything right for them.

"Damson plums! I hate waiting!"

Steve giggled, but it got choked off so fast that I wondered how long it had been since he'd had a good laugh.

"You helped Bonnie get away, didn't you?" I asked him.

"Yeah. She was throwing up all the time and I knew she wouldn't last too long. So when they let us out to walk around one day, I showed her a little hole I'd discovered in the wall. I couldn't get through, but she was so skinny, she could." He shrugged. "One of us had to try."

"Yes, one of you did." I ruffled his dirty hair, but he hunched his shoulders and shied away. Good. He was beginning to get his independent nature back, the one that would make him a man. "How long have you been here?"

"Too damn long."

I didn't even chastise him, just said, "Go help Mr. DelVecchio, the one who unlocked your chains."

He scurried away just as Josiah came back upstairs. He motioned me from the doorway, and I followed him into the hall. "Look what I found in the office."

I read the two bills of lading he gave me. They were instructive, and set my mind whirling and my anger climbing. But what made it reach the boiling point was a receipt from Tilden-Thurber's. Service for twelve, plus coffee set-up. Haviland Clover Leaf pattern.

"Oh, my God! This costs more than I've ever seen!"

Josiah pointed to the next item. "Think that's costly? Look at the Gorham's silver service."

My heart ached. "Is this worth two innocent lives and the destruction of those children?"

"Looks like it."

The angry wet mongoose came roaring back. "How long before we can get back to Providence, Josiah?"

"You're thinking they might run?"

"Yes. But I'm more interested in catching them. Now. Before I explode."

"Calm down, Aggie. I asked the captain to post lookouts, just in case that happened." He leaned down and whispered, "See? I'm not such a noodle-brain after all."

"No, you're not; and I'm sorry I ever thought so."

"What the hell," he said, shrugging, "I was a noodle-brain about DelVecchio." He winked. "This time."

It felt good to laugh, but I cut it short when Josiah said, "As soon as the cops get here, we can leave. The captain is sending more Providence cops to help clear up this mess. He said I should see this through back there and be in at the end."

"There'll be a promotion in this for you."

"Yeah, but not the one I expected. I would have gotten one for getting DelVecchio convicted, and I would have been wrong. So now I don't think I deserve one for this. This is really your promotion, Cousin."

"Not at all. You came here when all your training told you I was nuts."

"You're family. I couldn't abandon you to big, bad DelVecchio."

We grinned at each other, cousins in truth.

"You just graduated from noodle-braindom," I said. "Welcome to the other world."

Police swarmed into the building — local and state — and even one very tired police photographer who began taking shots of the room and the kids, paying particular attention to the chains. While they were doing their preliminary work, I rummaged through a half dozen boxes and found enough clothing to dress the kids. They had probably never worn garments this expensive; but it was fitting. They had sewed their blood, sweat, and tears into them.

Josiah put Steve Clementi in his car, promising to sound the siren at least once, and I gave him the bag of brownies, which Steve began devouring. I wondered if he chewed at all.

"I promised the New Bedford cops that I'd be responsible for delivering him for depositions and the trials. See you at his house."

Winnie promised the children that we would come visit each and every one of them. I only hoped their families would be as happy to see them as the kids would be to see their families. But I doubted it. There might be a few "missing" children here, but I was betting that most of the families — like Steve's — knew exactly where their kids were and exactly what they were doing. That's how desperate, or corrupted, they had become.

On the way back, Richard kept the car at a respectable thirty-five miles an hour, so Josiah wouldn't fall too far behind. Winnie took a little nap in the back, but Richard and I kept our sights on the target — the lights of Providence.

When we bounced over the state line, Richard let out a sigh of relief. "Are we almost through, Aggie?"

"Almost. We know what Bonnie knew. We know she was going to tell, and that was part of the reason she was killed."

"Part of the reason?"

"Uh-huh. The other part of the reason has to do with the murderer and the secret about her that she thought Bonnie knew."

"And was also going to tell."

"Yes, but only if what Bonnie thought she knew was true. That's why she was at Adler's Variety Store. To find out if her suspicions were correct, and obviously they were and she died because they were."

"You going to tell me what those suspicions were?"

"Sure, why not? But let me wake up Winnie first, so I don't have to tell this too many times."

"I'm awake. Who can sleep with you two blabbering?" She sat forward and leaned on the front seat rests. "Spill it, doll face."

At my indrawn breath, she laughed. *"Scarface!"*

She wasn't laughing when I finished telling the two of them who had killed Bonnie. There was shock when I told them who had killed Mildred. And there was downright fury when I told them who was the mastermind behind it all.

"I can't believe it," Winnie said. "You have to be mistaken, May."

"No mistake. The signatures at the bottom of the bills of lading were specific and the Tilden-Thurber's receipt told the final chapter. They all killed for different reasons, but behind it all was only one reason."

"Money," Richard said.

"Yes."

We pulled up to the curb at Steve's house and waited for Josiah to park behind us. Solemnly, we knocked on the door. When Mrs. Clementi opened it, she saw Steve,

311

front and center, and anger was the first emotion that skewed her features. Then she saw us, and she swept Steve into her arms and babbled on about missing him and how glad she was to have him home after all these months on the docks.

I didn't believe a word of it.

Josiah leaned closer to me and said, "Take Steve to his room and pack some clothes, enough for a few nights."

We were in the hall when Steve looked up at me and shook his head. "I heard what the cop said. She always was a bad actress. Even Dad said so. What's going to happen to her?"

"I think she's going to be arrested. I'm sorry, Steve."

"I don't think I am. If she knew where I was and what I was doing and didn't come to get me out, then the hell with her. Now I can go find my dad."

"But what about your brother and sister?"

"We'll be okay. Anything is better than knowing your mother doesn't give a damn about you." A high-pitched shriek went up in the front parlor. "Guess we better pack enough for the kids, too."

CHAPTER
TWENTY-FIVE

Josiah surprised everyone by offering to take Steve and the little ones home with him.

"I could call the children's home," he explained. "But that's no place for Steve to be after all this. Besides, Ma is missing Pete, and there's plenty of bed space in his old room for the three of them. She'd love to get her hands on Steve. The kid is starving, and you know how she stuffs us with food, Aggie."

"Yeah, I know. My stomach always ached after a holiday at your house."

"And I'm responsible for him, anyway. So this will work out great. And keeping his old lady in jail will stop her from giving a shout out to the rest of the bunch."

"Oh, *these* people are a bunch. *My* people are gangsters," Richard said, but his tone mocked his words. "Put her in my old cell, Josiah. The stones ooze cold sweat, and that's appropriate because she is one cold lady."

"She's no lady," Josiah said, and scooped up the sleepy middle child while Steve carried his sleeping baby brother. Richard helped them tote the bundles to Josiah's car.

It was so late when we left Steve's house, no one was on the porch to see what was happening, nor did a curtain next door or across the street fall into place to give mute evidence that anyone was watching. A few lights down the street illuminated rooms, but they were far enough away that our actions might not get noticed.

You going to help out, here, Lord? We need to catch all of them unaware, and we can only do it with Your help. Or are You sleeping, like Winnie and I should be? Wow, You have a big voice. And twenty-four hour service, apparently. By the way, thanks. And p.s. — We really have to talk about all those decades. I think some of this detecting stuff could be counted against my sins of omission, don't You? You do? Yahoo! So, can we start at one hundred? How about one hundred and fifty? Will You settle for one hundred and fifty-one? Okay, one hundred and fifty-six, it is!

He knocked fifty decades off my total. Amazing.

Amazing, too, was our success in getting

314

into the convent. One of the workmen must have left the window in the parlor open. It only took Richard's boosting to get us up and over the sill.

"You really have to lay off those rolls, Aggie," he said. "Life would be so much easier if you were a tad lighter."

"Richard, I will get you for that."

"No doubt."

Winnie flopped over the sill and brushed herself off. "Good night, Richard," she said.

" 'Night ladies. You both did good work. I'm proud of you."

Winnie and I threw our arms around each other and had a little cry. Just a little one. Then we pulled ourselves together and hefted our satchels to creep up the stairs without disturbing the entire household.

"Wait," I said, and bolted back to the window to pull the lock tight.

"You know, Winnie, I thought for a moment there that we were going to have to sleep in the root cellar." I stopped abruptly and she plowed into my right shoulder. "Holy Toledo! Now I know about the carrots. But where did she take them?"

"I'm too tired to try to figure that one out. 'Night, Aggie."

" 'Night, Win."

Something sounded like a cat scratching

to get in. I looked back into the parlor. There, silhouetted against the parlor window we had just come through was a familiar face peering in.

Winnie implored, "Let her sleep on the porch."

"Oh, no. I'd rather have something to hold over her." I went to unbolt the window and raised it a few inches. "Did you want something special, Sister Claire? And at this hour, too! Tsk, tsk, tsk. Not exactly nun-like behavior, sneaking in, in the middle of the night. Care to tell us where you've been? No? Well, let me hazard a guess. You've been with your fian . . . or was it your mother who gave you that expensive bath stuff?" I finally helped her into the parlor. "You never know when you'll need a friend, Claire, and never know whom you've made an enemy. Don't make us your enemies. You won't win."

"I've already won," she said rebelliously.

A light beam split the darkness around us. "No, my dear, you haven't," Mother Frances said, dispirited yet steeled. "Get to bed, now. I will deal with this in the morning. Sister Agnes, you stay. Come with me to my office."

"Yes, Mother."

Sister Claire's smirk saddened me, for I

knew how lonely it could be without true companions in this woman's domain. And she had no true companions.

"Close the door, please."

"Yes, Mother."

She sighed. "I don't know what to do with her. I've tried very hard to mold her into the nun she needs to be, but she defies me, and in the process, she defies God. I may have to suggest that she go home."

"A true nun could be destroyed by that decision, Mother. But I think Claire would welcome it. It's an awesome decision. Were I in your place, I would . . ."

"Send her home? Yes, I'm sure you would."

"No. Sister Claire needs to be here."

She seemed taken aback by that. "Why?"

"Because she lacks discipline to survive unscathed in the outside world. She is, right now, the kind of woman who could be corrupted. Send her out there, and she may well succumb. Keep her in here, and she may hate it at first, but she will be altered — for the good, I think."

"There appears to be more depth to you than you care to show."

"Or less."

She laughed. "Why are you back?"

"I have to sit down for this."

"Please do."

Carefully, leaving nothing out, not even the horror, I told her of the night's activities and my suspicions. With each word, her head lowered to her upraised hands until she sat with her face completely covered, her body a quivering mass. For several minutes after I finished, she was unable to articulate a thought.

Finally, she whispered, "Oh, God, You who love children, help them."

"Perhaps," I said, "you could help them in His stead."

She raised her head. "Anything."

"In the morning, have Sister Claire go up to the variety store and make calls to Federal Hill's butchers. Have her ask if anyone donated large numbers of carrots to feed the rabbits. And when she's finished with that, have her call all the stables. And after that, the pig farms. I think Bonnie was making sure some of what we had went to the animals she loved."

"Bless her, but what about the meat that was stolen? The coroner said she was malnourished."

"I'm guessing that ended up on the tables of whoever broke the lock."

"Well, if they needed it, they needed it. Vincent will send more."

"Mother Frances! You have more facets than a kaleidoscope!"

She smiled. "What I don't understand, though, is how getting Sister Claire to do this will help the children?"

"It will keep her out of our hair until we can finish this and put everyone involved behind bars."

"Ah. A wise move. But there must be something more I can do."

"Yes." There were a few minor, but important, things I asked her to do, then ended with, "And then you can find out which one of the novitiates is not who she seems."

Monday. Another day to set up the soup line. This time, I was in the kitchen only four hours after I got to sleep. It was Rhode Island clam chowder this morning, and I knew how to make that. Sister Phillippe had shucked and ground the quahogs the night before, as she always did. Sisters Joseph and Paul had cut up the vegetables and fried the salt pork and onions last night, too. And they had put all the ingredients in big containers in the icebox to meld overnight, because all Rhode Islanders knew that chowder was best the second day. What was my contribution? I heated the water in two kettles on the day we were to serve the chowder. When we knew how many people were going to be on the line, I poured in enough water for all of them and I helped get the large pots out to the sidewalk. Yep, I was a good chowder-maker.

Okay, I hear You, Lord! It was just a slight exaggeration. Correction coming up, so don't tack on any more decades. I was a good water-boiler and pot-carrier.

Mother Frances had Sister Gabriel bring Monsignor Grace's sandwiches out to the wall. Gabriel and Joseph made certain that each one on the soup line received at least one of the gourmet sandwiches. Through everything, Mother Frances walked up and down the line, giving encouragement, greeting regulars. When the line dwindled down, she called over Sisters Angelica and Paul. "Mary McBride's for you two," she said. "And bring her the stale bread."

"But . . . done it. Last three times," Sister Angelica said. "Sister Gabriel. This time?"

"You're younger and faster. Rush over there, now, and hurry right back for school."

The two novices left, grumbling from Sister Angelica wafting our way loud and clear. I leaned over to Mother Frances and whispered, "You did great. Just one more to go."

A few minutes later, Mother Frances

called Sister Gabriel to her side. "Where was my head this morning? I completely forgot to send the rest of these sandwiches over to Mary McBride's. The old folks depend on them. I'm going to let you go alone, this once, since two of our sisters are already there with the soup and bread."

"Yes, Mother."

Three blocks away from the convent, Richard, Josiah, Winnie, and I watched as Sister Gabriel dumped Monsignor Grace's sandwiches in a can behind Adler's variety store. Josiah blew a whistle and several police surrounded her. We approached, and Josiah said, "Helen DeRosier?"

She screamed and whirled around, only to be closed in by the police while a half dozen of Vincent's bodyguards brought up the second rank.

Josiah jerked her arm back and snapped steel cuffs on her hands. "Helen DeRosier, you are under arrest for the murder of Bonnie Greco."

She spit, and then saw me. "You bitch!"

For the first time in my life I said nothing. It wasn't a time to gloat, nor to mourn. We would do that at Bonnie's and Mildred's funeral. Right now, we had one more stop to make.

CHAPTER
TWENTY-SIX

Josiah made certain the fake nun was completely restrained in the back of the police van, then came back to us. "The guy we caught last night is Howard Brennerman. He's saying he didn't kill Mildred Young or attack Father Bryant."

"I know," I said. "He didn't."

"You know who did?" Josiah asked.

"Oh, yes."

"You gonna tell me?"

"Absolutely. As soon as our little errand is finished."

He walked to his car, but snapped his fingers and rushed back. "Forgot to tell you. Monsignor Grace called me this morning. He wishes us God's blessing and said there will be many things changed at the mother house."

"Good."

Richard came up and put his hand on my shoulder. He watched me for a couple of moments, studying, deciding, then asked, "You sure you're ready for this?"

"Yes. Each of us must stand tall for justice, Richard. That's what our Lord would want. And that's what Plato espoused for his perfect state. It has always been that way, since the beginning of time. We're just a small part of it. But for Father Bryant, Bonnie, Mildred, and those children, we're the most important part of all."

"No jokes this morning, I see."

"No jokes, Richard. All of this is too tragic for jokes."

We pulled up in front of the triple-decker, Richard's Cord roadster behind Josiah's rundown police vehicle. And down the street, Vincent's sleek touring car. If force was needed, we had it aplenty.

"Well, and what a pleasant surprise 'tis," Mary McBride said when she opened the door to our knock. "Yer two young sisters, they just now left."

Josiah made a gesture with his arm and five officers peeled out of line and took off down the street.

Mary looked at me, and I wondered what was going on behind those blue eyes. "Dot an' Josie are here, havin' coffee," she said. "Mayn't I offer you some? You take yers with plenty a cream an' two sugars, right

Sister Agnes?"

"Right," I said. "Thank you for the offer."

"Come on inta the dining room and set," she said. "I'll jest put t'other pot on ta boil. If you could bring in some straight chairs from the front room, please, Richard?"

"There's no need. Most of us will be standing," Josiah said.

Mary paused for a moment, but recovered her equilibrium, squared her shoulders, and went through the archway into the kitchen. Winnie and I followed her. She turned to face us and her gaze darted from us to the window to the doorways. Outside, we could see the police ringing her backyard.

"I'm supposin' that Vincent Ricci is in front with his men?" she asked.

"Yes," I said.

"So that's why I couldna get through to New Bedford this mornin'."

I nodded. "We picked up your associates last night. We found the children and enough evidence to convict you, Mary. You're going to go away for a long, long time. The only question is whether you will face the death penalty in Massachusetts or life in prison here in Rhode Island."

"I didna kill anyone."

"Technically, that may be true," I said. "But you sent others out to do it, and that

324

makes you just as guilty."

Winnie had tears in her eyes. "How could you do this? How could you keep children chained like slaves? How could you starve them? Humiliate them?"

Mary crossed her arms and hugged them against her chest. "I don't have ta tell you lot anything."

"No, you don't," I said. "But you're going to listen as I tell you what you did and why you did it."

"Ya don't know Jack 'bout what I did an why I did it."

I walked over to the glass-fronted cupboard and yanked it open. "This is one of the reasons you did it. Haviland china. Gorham silver. I saw the Tilden-Thurber's ad. This china set costs enough to feed an entire family in this neighborhood for five years. The cost of this silver would feed the entire parish!" I marched over to the wall telephone and picked the earpiece off the hook. "Oh, my gosh! No one's talking. No party line. How much did that cost?" I pointed to her bosom. "And what's that you keep hiding from the world behind crossed arms? A pure gold necklace?" Now, I crossed my arms. "Why you did it? You did it for money. You did it for the love of making more money."

"The love of money is the root of all evil," Winnie said. "You, Mary McBride, are evil."

"Such a touching speech n' all, Sister. But ya live a pretty sheltered life behind those convent walls. Yev never been left with nothin'. Nothin'! Himself died and left me nothin'. I refuse ta be poor."

"So you plotted and schemed to corrupt others," I said. "And you took in these frail old women as a cover for your real work — to use slave labor to make you rich. You exploited those who were poor, desperately poor, so poor that they would sell you their children for a steady income. They'll be arrested soon and they will tell us how you approached and perhaps bribed them. So you will be tried for that, too."

"And then there was the convent," Winnie said. "You even used us!"

" 'Twas easy, that," Mary said.

"For you, yes," I said. "Because you were always at the convent, or always at the church, you listened closely and discovered the weakness in our mother house's assignment plan. Records coming in with the sisters, or records coming weeks later than the sisters arrive. It gave you a perfect refuge for your — well, we can't call them associates. They were more like your gang, Mary. So you found out that we were expecting new sisters, two novices and one third-grade teacher. Sister Angelique, Sister Paul, Sister Gabriel. Where are the real ones, Mary? Buried in your factory?" I was shaking by now, but she wasn't. My voice rose several notches, but I didn't try once to temper myself. "And let's take a good look at that factory. The New Bedford police are combing it from top to bottom, digging up any area that looks like it could be a grave. The smell alone will tell them where the bodies are. I recognized that stench last night. It's so much like the pits my uncle buries his pig carcasses in."

Richard came into the kitchen and put his hand on my shoulder. "Need some help?"

"No. I have to finish this."

"Okay. But I'm staying here."

I nodded and leaned against the wall. "I don't know what you did, Mary. I may not know it all, but I know enough. Your fake nuns settled in the convent so they could scour the school records to find the kids whose families were the most desperate, or the most corruptible. And then those good nuns swooped down during our charity visits with such a generous offer. Keeping families eating! You sacrificed a child — several children — and you did it without a second thought. But to be successful, you had to keep open one of your husband's deserted buildings. You contacted some of his customers, who, like you, were greedy enough not to ask too many questions as long as they could get their goods at the greatly reduced prices you offered. To keep it secret, you used your nieces and nephews to help you. They've been caught, by the way. Even Helen has been caught."

"No!"

"Yes. And she shall be tried for Bonnie's murder. She will be convicted. She will spend the rest of her life behind bars. That is what you have done by your greed, Mary. You condemned your own daughter."

I dropped my head to my chest and did that breathing in and out thing that Richard had taught me, then I straightened up. "And then you attacked a good, old priest."

Winnie sucked in her breath and even Richard shifted into fight mode. "At first," I said, "we thought it was your nephew, Brennerman. But that's what you wanted us to think. You're not a short woman, Mary. With the right clothes, you could look like a man. Just like Brennerman looked like a woman in the soup line. All you had to do was dress up a little. Your mistake was in wearing the new green coat and fedora hat you had bought at Shepherd's — a coat and hat that were advertised in the newspaper. I saw the ad. But it triggered something only a woman would know. No man's coat has those kinds of buttons. And no man wears flesh-colored lisle stockings that wrinkle almost as soon as they're put on — the kind of stockings that some of our sisters also wear to correct swelling in their legs. Your problem is that you were clever and very stupid. The stupidity comes because you think we are all stupid. And we are not."

I reached for Winnie's hand and she squeezed it. It gave me strength, but also told me that I had done all I could. "I'm finished. There's more, but it will unfold over the next few days while you're in prison awaiting trial. And all the money you've accumulated over the past couple of years won't get you out."

She laughed. "That lot next ta ya got out. I kin make bail, too."

"And because of what you did to his son, Vincent Gaetano Ricci is hoping you and all your family do exactly that," Richard said.

For the first time, she faltered. Her color swept away, her shoulders sagged. I was pretty sure she'd get back to her normal self — whatever that was, for I didn't think she was truly human. More animal than woman.

More demon than human. Ah, but for now, she was shaken to the core by the thought of Vincent's wrath.

"Josiah!" I called.

He and two of his men came to handcuff and shackle Mary. The officers had to practically carry her over the sill to get her out of her house. But the shackles were a fitting symbol, after what she had done to the children.

"Breathe deeply, Aggie," Richard said. "Almost finished."

Josiah asked, "You want me to end it?"

"No." I shook off the pain that lodged in my heart. "I found both Bonnie and Mildred. I have to be the one. Thank you — all of you — for your support."

"Okay. Then let's do it," Josiah said.

We left the kitchen and went back into the dining room. Josie was in tears, sobbing into her apron. Doris was white as the tablecloth. Pure Irish linen, if I had a guess.

"Doris?"

"Yes, Sister Agnes?"

"You'll have to go with Officer Morgan, too."

Josie hiccupped and raised her head. "Why?" she asked.

Josiah came up beside her. "Doris Klein, you are under arrest for the murder of

Mildred Young. Come quietly, please."

Josie stared at me. "Doris? But she was right here when Mildred was killed."

"No. She wasn't," I said. "She was supposed to be in the kitchen with Mary, helping to cut Richard's cake. Mary was cutting it. But Doris was upstairs, pushing Mildred's head under the water."

"How did you find out?" Doris asked.

It had only been a guess on my part. I just couldn't picture Mary doing more than manipulating the people around her. She was, when all was said and done, a coward. But Doris was a fool, and too eager to please someone with money, especially if she might get some.

"How did I know?" I leaned into her face. "You just told me."

Later that night, Josiah came to the grieving convent to report the discovery of our sisters' bodies. They were, indeed, buried under the cellar floor at the factory in Fall River.

"Massachusetts wants to try Mary McBride and her gang for multiple murders," he said. "They have the death penalty in Massachusetts."

"I don't think they were killed in Massachusetts, Josiah," I said.

331

He nodded. "Probably not. But the two states are out for blood, and I wouldn't be surprised if Rhode Island's attorney general agrees."

"That would be vengeance, not justice, Josiah."

"Here, maybe. But in Massachusetts, it's justice." He leaned over and kissed my forehead. "You did good, Mayetta Morgan. Accept it and go on. You have so much to give this world. Give it in joy. Bonnie would."

"Ah, Josiah, you're just like Richard. You don't play fair."

"I'm just like DelVecchio? Bite your tongue!"

Winnie and Josiah craned their necks to see up to the front of the cathedral. I settled back, too short to see over the crowd. It didn't matter. We were here, at the ordination of Bishop Keough. *We* were Richard, Winnie, Mother Frances, Vincent, Dante, Josiah, his mother, and their new family, which now legally included three additions. Oh, yes — and a couple of Vincent's bodyguards.

I tugged on Winnie's skirt. "Can you see him?"

"Not yet," Winnie said.

One of the caped and feather-hatted Knights of Columbus stopped at our pew. "Mother Frances?"

She looked up. "Yes?"

"Would you come with me?"

She put her hand to her heart and edged out of the pew. "What in the world . . ." she said.

"Well, it can't be anything bad," I said. "This is a great day!"

After she left, I tugged on Winnie's skirt again. "Do you see him yet?"

"Will you stop doing that? I'll tell you when I see him."

Dante wriggled and began blowing spit bubbles.

"Son," Vincent said, "just calm down. They'll start soon."

"Why don't you let him stand up on the seat for a while?" I said.

"Hey, yeah!" Dante said.

Vincent sighed. "Okay, but when the ceremony starts, you're sitting down."

"Aw, rats!"

"On my shoulders."

"Nifty!"

Dante hopped up and began scanning the crowd. "Hey, there's Piggy Williams. He's sitting on his dad's shoulders already, but way in the back. Not like us, huh, Dad? We're in the w.i.p. section."

"V.I.P.," Vincent said.

"What's that mean?"

"Very Important Person," Richard said.

"Hey! I'm a very important person. How'd I get to be that?"

"Because you're one of the best kids in the world," Vincent said. He mouthed *thank you* at me, but I shook my head and used my index finger to indicate everyone in the pew. He shook his head back and pointed at me.

Richard watched the byplay and, when it was finished, leaned over and whispered, "One thing I've never understood. Why did they want to take Dante?"

"Because," I whispered back, "he saw Helen when she killed Bonnie."

"He was in the root cellar?"

"No. He was in his hidey-hole in the supply closet. When they took him, I wondered if he'd been there, and, of course, I found him there right after the murder. He was playing knights in battle then and the stepladder was leaning on the wall right under that little window. I asked him. He saw her walking up the cinder path and into the school. She must have been coming back from the root cellar. Unfortunately, she also saw him, but Josiah and I were only seconds behind her and she couldn't do anything about it then."

"But he didn't really see anything! If he had, he would have told us. Look what he did in the church when Father Bryant was attacked."

"It didn't matter to them if he saw the actual killing. They weren't sure about him.

He might have seen her going into the root cellar or coming out. And if he had, he might let it slip some day. They were just trying to tie up loose ends."

"They might have killed him," Richard said.

"No," I said. "They *would* have killed him."

He looked at the little boy who meant plenty to him. "Then it's a good thing Massachusetts gets the first crack at them."

"Not all of them," I said.

"Enough."

"I see him," Winnie said. "He's fourth from the front." She sat back. "They're lining up. Things must be ready."

Vincent tapped my shoulder and I knew what was coming. Neither of those little things I'd asked him to do had yet been done. I figured he was about to worm his way out of his offer.

"If you're using this ceremony to tell me you won't keep your promise," I said, "I'll bop you. Here and now. In front of the people and God."

He laughed. "Well, for the first time in a long time, you are completely wrong, Sister Agnes."

"I am?"

"You are. The police are helping out.

They've started a youth group, whose first task will be to clear out the empty lots and build some playgrounds for the neighborhood."

"And you're supplying what?"

"I'm not supplying anything," he said with a wink. "It will all be donated by benevolent merchants."

"Sure it will. I couldn't have asked for a better birthday present. Thank you."

Richard and Vincent made a great chorus when they said in unison, "It's your birthday?"

"Yup. And isn't this a wonderful way to spend it?"

"We'll have to do something special just for you," Vincent said. "And I have just the thing. Although, it's been hard to get that second request done. But be ready right after school. Richard is going to pick you up."

My head snapped around, and I found Richard grinning. "You're going to teach me to drive?"

"Who better?" Vincent said.

I slumped in my seat. "You don't understand, Vincent. Ordinarily, this would be a great present. But Richard couldn't teach me to swim. I almost drowned. My Da had to apply pressure to get the water out of my lungs. Richard tried to teach me to cook and the first time I started up the stove, I almost burned down the house. His attempts at teaching me to garden had every last tomato dead on the vine in three days."

Vincent looked at Richard. "Remind me to call my insurance agent in the morning."

"I already called him, for both of us."

They laughed like men do at the follies of women. But it wasn't me. Richard didn't know how to teach.

Honestly, Lord. That had to be the reason, right? Not entirely? I need to be more teachable? How in the heck do I do that? You'll be there to guide me, right? Belinda? Who's Belinda? Guardian angels have names? That's amazing!

Mother Frances, escorted back to her seat by two Knights of Columbus, slid back into the pew.

"Oh, my goodness," she said, fanning herself with the program.

"What happened?" Winnie said.

"I met the Bishop," Mother Frances said. "He thanked me for the stole I made. He said it was beautiful and he wanted to wear it today, but there was special liturgical garb that was required for this ceremony. But then he said that the stole was so beautiful that all the world should see it. So he asked

338

me if Monsignor Grace could wear the stole during the ordination."

"What did you say?" Winnie asked, with a wink at me.

"Why, I said *yes,* of course. My stole is going to be there, on the altar, through the whole thing. Oh, my goodness."

Where was her tempering now, I wondered?

The music started. The choir's voices pierced the cathedral. We all stood as the priests and altar boys began the procession to welcome the new Bishop. And there, among the altar boys, in the fourth position from the front, was Steve Clementi, soon to be Morgan.

It was more than a great day. It was glorious!

I raised my eyes to the heavens. *Through You all things are possible. Thanks.*

RICHARD DELVECCHIO'S SINFULLY SUMPTUOUS STEW

2 lbs well-marbled chuck steak, cut in 1-inch cubes

6–8 medium sized potatoes, peeled (or well scrubbed) and cut into large chunks

6–8 large carrots, washed and scrubbed, and cut into large chunks

6–8 small whole onions, peeled and sliced into large wedges

1 green and 1 red pepper, seeds removed and cut into strips

2 cups sliced Portobello mushrooms

1 quart beef stock, made from boiling meaty beef bones (or canned stock)

1 large can crushed tomatoes

1/4 cup fresh parsley, chopped

5 cloves garlic, peeled

1 tablespoon Worcestershire sauce

1/4 cup balsamic vinegar

2 large bay leaves

1/2 teaspoon dried thyme

1/2 teaspoon dried nutmeg

1 teaspoon rosemary
1 teaspoon dried mustard
1 teaspoon black ground pepper
Salt to taste
Olive oil, preferably from Lucca, Italy
1–2 cups flour
Sour cream (optional)

Place flour in medium sized plastic or clean paper bag. Add thyme, nutmeg, rosemary, mustard, and ground pepper. Add chuck steak cubes and shake until cubes are well coated with flour mixture. Remove meat from flour and set flour aside.

In large Dutch oven, cover bottom with olive oil and heat for three to four minutes, or until hot enough to brown meat. Add floured meat and sear over medium heat, turning as the sides are browned. Remove meat from pan when well browned. Add onion chunks and carrots and brown slightly. Remove from pan. Add mushrooms and cook until caramel-colored. Remove from pan. Add red and green peppers and fry until browned, but not softened. Remove from pan. Add garlic cloves and brown slightly. Remove from pan.

Add 1/4 cup olive oil to pan. Add seasoned flour mixture to pan. Brown slightly. Meanwhile, combine beef stock and crushed tomatoes and heat in microwave oven. Add to browned flour a little at a time, stirring constantly with wire whisk to prevent lumps. Adjust gravy with water if too thick.

Put potatoes into pan. Add beef and bay leaves. Cook, covered, for 1/2 hour over low heat, keeping the gravy at slow simmer. Add browned vegetables and cook, covered, until carrots are cooked, but still slightly crunchy.

Add parsley, balsamic vinegar, and Worcestershire sauce and mix well. Check that the gravy is not too thick. Add water if needed. Cook, covered, an additional 20 minutes over low heat. Add salt, if needed, just before serving.

Serve with crusty, warm Italian bread or French baguettes and plenty of salted butter. Pass sour cream for a unique taste. Serves 6–8.

RICHARD DELVECCHIO'S GET OUT OF JAIL ON BAIL MILLION-DOLLAR CHOCOLATE CAKE

3 cups sugar
1 1/4 cups butter
3 cups flour
3/4 cup cocoa powder
3/4 teaspoon salt
3 teaspoons baking soda
3 eggs
2 teaspoons vanilla extract
Boiling water
Chopped walnuts, dusted with flour (optional)
10X confectioner's sugar or your favorite frosting

Preheat oven to 350 degrees.

Butter sides and bottom of extra large Pyrex dish; dust with a little flour. Set aside.

In very large mixing bowl, place sugar and butter. Add 2 1/4 cups boiling water. Allow butter to melt and stir gently.

Sift in the flour, cocoa powder, salt, and

baking soda. Mix well and add eggs and vanilla (mixture will be very loose). Add floured walnuts, if desired.

Put Pyrex pan on middle shelf of oven. Pour mixture into pan very carefully. The pan will be very full.

Bake at 350 degrees for 50 minutes.

Test cake by inserting knife into middle. It is done when knife comes out clean.

Top with confectioner's sugar, or frost. But this is best eaten without a topping, and with French vanilla ice cream.

Serves 12 generous slices.

NO CREAM, NO MILK, NO TOMATOES! IT TASTES BEST THE NEXT DAY RHODE ISLAND CLAM CHOWDER

Salt pork! (about 4 oz.)
3–4 large yellow onions, cut in half and sliced
6–8 large thin-skinned potatoes (red-skinned potatoes are good), cut into cubes
2–3 stalks celery, sliced
3–4 cups chopped quahog meat
2–4 cups quahog liquor
Boiling water
Salt and pepper to taste

Cut salt pork into bite-sized cubes. Fry carefully in chowder pot on medium-low heat, turning often to crisp the salt pork. When done, remove the pork and drain on a paper towel. Set aside. Do NOT remove pork fat from chowder pot.

Put onion, potatoes, and celery into chowder pot. Stir vegetables often and cook under low heat in hot pork fat until onion is golden — about 10 minutes. Add quahog meat and quahog liquor. Estimate how much water you need to make enough chowder to feed the crowd that will gather as soon as they smell this, and add to chowder pot.

Cover chowder pot and simmer gently on medium-low heat for 40–50 minutes, or until potatoes are done. Taste, and add salt and pepper if necessary.

Let sit on very low heat for about 30 minutes more, then serve piping hot with clam cakes on the side.

Serves 6 Rhode Islanders or 8–10 other kinds of Americans.

Note: By adding real cream to the pot just before serving, you can turn this into Boston-style clam chowder. But, as Richard would say, "Why would you?"

And, horror of horrors, Manhattan-style clam chowder is made by adding a small can of diced or crushed tomatoes to the pot about halfway through the cooking time.

Historically — and it is true today — at large family gatherings (especially for Fourth of July celebrations) Rhode Islanders cook chowder in the same white-speckled blue-enameled pan often used to cook lobsters.

THE BEST DANGED CLAM CAKES THIS SIDE OF BOSTON

2 pints quahog meat, chopped into small pieces
4 cups flour
5 teaspoons baking powder
1 cup quahog liquor (saved from shucking quahogs)
2/3 cup whole milk (NOT low-fat)
4 eggs, separated
1/4 teaspoon salt
1 teaspoon pepper

Prepare deep fat fryer with corn oil. Heat to deep fry stage (375 degrees). Or use very large soup kettle half filled with corn oil, and heat on medium-low.

Beat egg whites using high speed until very stiff.

Mix dry ingredients in large bowl. Add quahog liquor, milk, egg YOLKS, and clams. Stir until smooth.

Carefully fold in stiff-beaten egg whites.

Drop mixture by spoonful (teaspoon) into hot fat. Cook for 3–4 minutes until golden brown. You may have to turn them over once. Drain on paper towels.

Serves 16–20 people who don't live in Rhode Island. In Rhode Island this recipe serves 8.

The recipe may be halved for a small family, but use 3 teaspoons baking powder.

Note: Quahogs are NOT long-necked soft-shelled clams. They are large, hard-shelled clams, dug out of the shore at low tide, usually by using your own feet to locate them and a small, specially designed quahog rake to dig them out. However, out-of-state cooks may substitute canned, chopped clams — but it won't taste the way it does when you've done all the work yourself.

Historically, Rhode Islanders use the state's famous Rumford baking powder in their baked goods.

ABOUT THE AUTHOR

Barbara Cummings is an award-winning author of thirteen novels (comedy, mystery, romance, and young adult), three short stories, and seven poems.

In 1993, her mystery novel set in Victorian London (*Dead As Dead Can Be*) was voted one of the top ten best-selling original paperbacks by Mid-Atlantic Independent Mystery Booksellers. In 1994, she received the *Romantic Times* Reviewers' Choice Award for *Prime Time*. She is also a recipient of the Washington Romance Writers' Outstanding Achievement Award. She is a member of Phi Kappa Phi Honor Society, Romance Writers of America, Mystery Writers of America, Novelists, Inc., and Washington Romance Writers.

Ms. Cummings received an MA in English from the University of Rhode Island, studied for her doctorate, and currently teaches English at Shepherd University in Shepherdstown, West Virginia. She lives nearby with her husband of forty-five years. Ms. Cummings can be reached at www.thecummingsstudios.com.